Praise for

I0663092

McKingley

Risky Pleasures is a good read and McKenna Jeffries and Aliyah Burke presented very likeable characters, with just the right amount of heat.
~ *Long and Short Reviews*

McKINGLEY
Volume Two

Risky Pleasures

Pure Harmony

McKENNA JEFFRIES and
ALIYAH BURKE

McKingley Volume Two
ISBN # 978-1-78184-649-0
©Copyright McKenna Jeffries and Aliyah Burke 2013
Cover Art by Oliver Bennett ©Copyright 2013
Interior text design by Claire Siemaszkiewicz
Totally Bound Publishing

RISKY
PLEASURES

Dedication

To my big sis your strength and grace makes you my hero. With you by my side I know anything is possible.
—McKenna Jeffries

To all the unsung heroes, thank you, for all that you do. To my husband and friends who always have the encouragement when I need it most.
—Aliyah Burke

Chapter One

Delicia Wright kept her breathing even as she pounded along the trail. The early spring air helped her stay cool and, given the low humidity in New Mexico, the sweat dried almost immediately. A swift glance to the watch on her right wrist told her she was on pace with her self-imposed time.

Seven more miles to go. *Come on, we can do this,* she gave herself the usual pep talk. The upbeat music of The Black Eyed Peas played in her ears as she continued the remainder of her fifteen mile run. She could feel her body begin to tremble with exhaustion.

Suck it up, Delicia. If you wanted easy, we wouldn't be training for a triathlon.

She lost herself in the rhythmic feel of her feet stomping along the hard-packed dirt trail. Tired, hot and sweating, she checked her time when she reached the end of her run. Hands on her hips, she walked herself around to cool her body down. This was her year to do better. She'd trained harder than ever before, going farther than the actual triathlon would be.

It was three months away. *And I'm ready.* A satisfied smile turned up her lips as she moved to her bike. She entered the combination before unfastening the cable from where it secured her bike to the tree then stowed it before slowly straddling the bicycle. Delicia fastened her helmet and sighed. She pulled her water bottle from the back of her jersey, drank some then placed the container on the bike.

"Time to get home for a shower. And some food."

She removed one ear bud to hear traffic. Foot on the pedal, she pressed on it and looked up when a large truck drove by, then backed up to turn in the entrance to the pull off for the trailhead. She stared at the vehicle when it pulled before her. A white quad cab Dodge Dually. *Shit!*

The passenger window lowered and she found herself staring at a man who'd always made her feel like a babbling idiot. Archer Bennett. Country music poured from the cab and she fought off a shiver when he dipped his head to the side, exposing those damnable indigo eyes of his from behind his dark brown hair. Not black like a lot of people thought—it was just very dark brown.

Delicia hadn't any clue why he affected her this way. It was just how it was.

"Mornin', Delicia," he said, in that unhurried way of his which never failed to make her toes curl and skin tingle.

Dah-lish-a was how it sounded—damn near X-rated coming from his mouth. Almost everyone else called her Lis. Not him. The rare times they ran into each other and he would speak to her, it was Delicia.

"Archer," she replied.

He remained silent while his gaze travelled over her sweaty body. Before she knew what had happened, he

8

stood before her. Six feet tall, hard muscular body, dark brown hair and those blue eyes. His torn jeans moulded to his legs and he wore a white shirt, which only amplified his tanned skin and the strength of his upper body.

"Come on," he uttered.

She stared at his hand. Long, strong fingers, short, square nails. Swallowing, she looked back up at him.

"What?"

"You look like you're about to fall over. I'm giving you a ride home. Now either get off the bike or I'll remove you from it."

A thousand things ran through her mind to say. She should protest. She should stay on the bike just to have him put his hands upon her. But she didn't. With a nod, she got off the bicycle and removed her helmet. Archer stepped forward, effortlessly lifted it and carefully placed it in the bed of his truck. Then he took the helmet and dropped it in there as well.

"Get in," he said, without looking back at her.

Delicia didn't move, just stared at the way he filled out his jeans. Her core temperature skyrocketed. Heart pounding even faster than before, she licked her lips and barely stopped herself from stepping closer and touching him—just to see if he was truly as hard as he looked.

He looked over his shoulder at her and in the depths of his eyes she saw a sparkle. *It's like he knows I was checking him out.* Archer turned completely and leaned against the side of his truck, crossing his arms. A move which highlighted the strength in them.

"Something on your mind, Delicia?"

Hell yeah. A lot. Like you n' me doing the horizontal mambo right here. Or even in the back of your truck.

She shrugged and shook her head. "Nope." Swallowing her fear she asked, "Should there be?"

A flame flickered in his eyes before he sent her a slow, sensual grin. "Could be. Come on, I have to get to work."

A sharp retort was on the tip of her tongue, but she swallowed it back. She truly was exhausted and appreciated the ride. He held the front door for her and she walked towards him.

"Thank you," she said, slipping past him and onto the leather seat.

"My pleasure." His murmured reply followed her in.

Archer closed the door and was soon positioned behind the wheel. She buckled herself in while he did the same and smoothly shifted into gear to get them back on the road towards McKingley.

A few miles passed in silence and Delicia spent the time wishing she weren't damp with sweat, and that she had the ability to talk to him without sounding like a total moron. It didn't make sense—she never seemed to have this issue with any other man. Richer men than Archer. Men in top of the line suits. Cover model types, it didn't matter. But along came Archer in his torn jeans, grease-smeared shirt, hiking boots and baseball cap, and suddenly she couldn't say more than four words without sounding like an idiot.

Archer Bennett was the owner of the largest towing company in McKingley—Bennett's Towing. It was also an auto shop. He had been working there since forever and had been driving a tow truck since he was sixteen. When he turned twenty-four—four years ago—his father had retired and he'd taken over. She couldn't help but be impressed by the way he'd worked so damn hard for what he'd accomplished.

Archer Bennett was a frequent visitor to her dreams, but Delicia hadn't ever told anyone. She was three years younger than him and he'd been someone she'd admired from afar. When she'd gone to school functions, he hadn't been able to attend because he'd gone home to work. She took a deep breath and fought the urge to squirm as the scent of Archer filled her nose.

"Delicia?" Archer's warm, silvery voice broke into her wandering thoughts.

"Huh?" *Yep. Did I say I sound like an idiot around this man?*

"I asked if you were going to your house or wanted me to drop you off somewhere else."

"Umm. Let's go home." Heat flared up her cheeks. "The house. I mean, take me to my house."

"Your house it is," he uttered.

Delicia looked out of the window and prayed her embarrassment would fade. *What is it about him?* After a few more miles with only the music as a buffer against the quiet between them, she glanced at him. Her heart pounded harder and she felt a bit short of breath.

His left hand was on the wheel, his arm against the door. His right hand rested upon his leg while his bow-shaped lips moved as he sang quietly along with the music. Brown hair hung around his chiselled features giving him a rakish look. He had long curled lashes, then there were his eyes. Indigo. A vibrant, deep indigo.

"Hmm," he said turning so their eyes met. "You're staring again. Trying to make me self-conscious?"

She dropped her gaze. "No. I'm sorry."

"Nothing to apologise for."

Out of the corner of her eye, she saw him reach for the gearshift and curve those long fingers about the red flame on black knob. *What would his hands feel like on me?* Lifting her head, she noticed he was pulling into her driveway. *Wait, how does he know where I live?* Capturing her lower lip in her teeth, she unbuckled her belt and slipped from the interior, seconds after he put it in neutral and set the brake. She heard the door close as he got out of the truck.

"Let me get it," he muttered from behind her.

She held her breath when he brushed up against her. Synapses fired out of control and she fought to keep from sinking to the ground. With apparent ease, he lifted the bike out from the back and placed it on the ground beside her. Then he hung her helmet over the handlebar.

Delicia took a deep breath and looked at him. His intense eyes were focused on her face. *Invite him in!* Opening her mouth to do just that, another voice interfered.

"Lis! You okay?"

Archer's gaze shuttered and around the truck came her cousin, Justin.

"You?" Justin demanded. "What are you doing here?"

"Dropping her off." Archer's voice had about as much warmth in it as Justin's did.

I didn't know they knew each other. Waiting for Archer's gaze, she gave him a slight smile. "Can I offer you a drink?"

His eyes softened slightly before becoming distant. "No, thank you. I have to get to work. Perhaps a rain check?"

"I'd like that." *I'd like a whole lot of things when it comes to you, Archer Bennett.* She licked her lips. "Thanks again for the lift back."

"Anytime."

He nodded once, glared at Justin then walked to the driver's side and got in. She didn't move until his diesel truck backed out of her drive and he'd disappeared down the road.

"What were you doing with him?" Justin drilled her as she pushed her bike to the open garage.

"Don't talk to me like I'm a child, Justin. He gave me a ride home. I'm kind of exhausted, you know. It's not a flippin' cake walk training for this triathlon."

He waved away her tirade. "You need to stay away from him."

Leaning her bike against the wall, she turned to face her cousin, bristling in defence of the man who'd been in her thoughts for longer than she cared to remember. "You need to not tell me what to do. Besides, Archer is perfectly nice."

"He's not right for you, Lis."

Hands on hips, she glared. "So because you think that, I should have turned down the offer of the ride and biked my ass home? What's your problem with him anyway?"

Justin narrowed his eyes. "I have to go. I only stopped by to drop something off for you, it's on the kitchen table. Don't forget what I said. Keep away from him."

Jaw clenched, she watched him climb into his Ferrari and drive away. "Jackass," she muttered before heading inside the house, closing the garage on the way. She was normally very even keeled, and it took a lot for people to upset her, but Delicia was not pleased with her cousin's highhanded attempt to tell her who she could and couldn't be around. Especially with the way derision had dripped from his tone when he'd talked about—and to—Archer.

"Not like I'm good at talking to the man, but hell, if I could conquer that fear I'd be all over him."

Archer Bennett was on her mind as she took a long hot shower and got dressed for work.

* * * *

Archer 'Risk' Bennett watched Delicia in his rear-view mirror until he could no longer see her. She faced his direction as he drove away. Her toffee skin gleamed in the morning light, her white and purple bike jersey highlighted the mouth-watering curves of her body. He groaned and shifted on the seat. All he'd wanted to do was take her honey-hued, bone straight hair down from the ponytail it was in and let it run all over his skin as he made long, slow love to her.

Seeing her this morning at one of the trailheads, he'd had to stop. Delicia Wright was the only woman in town who could get under his skin. Not that she would know it—they rarely ran into each other.

Her family's name was pretty much synonymous with founding the town in conjunction with the McKingley family, for whom the town was named. He wasn't even close to her social circle. Not that that stopped his fantasies of her. And as a whole, the majority of the Wright's all seemed to be in professions dedicated to helping people. But on the rare occasion, he ran into one like Justin Wright— couldn't stand the man for more than a few reasons. Shaking off the ugly feelings Justin brought to his mind, Archer thought about Delicia again. She remained in his thoughts until he pulled into the large lot his business was on. He groaned when he spotted his father's truck there.

"Crap. What's he doing here?"

Parking his truck, he got out and headed for the door, putting on his ball cap as he walked. He pushed through the door and entered the building, his nose assaulted by the scent of strong coffee and his ears by the sounds of Marty Robbins.

"Mornin', Pa."

"Archer." His father lifted the mug in his hand by way of greeting.

"What are you doing here?" He poured himself a cup of java. "Thought the purpose of retiring was so you weren't here."

"Am I not allowed to come in and see my business?"

Facing his father, Archer said, "It's mine, Pa, and that doesn't answer my question of what you're doing here."

The salt-and-pepper haired man shifted in the seat he occupied and Archer narrowed his eyes and waited for the bomb to drop. It wasn't long in coming.

"Your mom called this morning. She wants to see you."

"And she called you why?"

"You don't return her calls."

Archer sipped some hot coffee and shrugged without remorse. "She abandoned us. Why should I bother with her?"

"Well, she's coming to visit and wants to see you. Apparently she's bringing her new boyfriend along as well."

Staring at his father, Archer waited to see if there was any lingering pain when discussing his ex-wife. There was nothing. Apparently he was the one holding a grudge, not his dad. He'd always admired his father for doing what he had to and not becoming a bitter old man. But for him personally, his mother had ceased to exist—no cards, calls, nothing until he took over the business. Since then, Victoria Cross had done nothing but try to reconnect with him.

"When does she claim she is coming?"

She'd been leaving him messages for over two years saying she was coming for a visit. Even given dates of when she would arrive on a few of them. She had yet to actually show up. He briefly wondered if her calling his father actually meant she was going to come. Not that it mattered. He didn't want anything to do with her, and if he had to, he would tell her to her face.

"Next week. And she said she was bringing along someone else as well. It's a surprise or something like that."

Great. Her and a surprise. "Uh-huh. Why doesn't that make me feel any better?"

"I don't know. But, that's not the only reason I stopped by. Joe is down with the flu today, so I'll drive for him. That way you don't have to stop working in the garage to cover for him."

Sitting down on the edge of the desk, Archer studied him. "You sure? You don't have something else you'd rather do?"

Todd Bennett pushed to his feet and strode to stand before him. One large hand settled upon his shoulder. "I know it's now your business, son, but I'm here to help. I've got the towing end covered unless we really get backed up. You go ahead on and work in the shop, I know you've got a few things waiting for your attention."

"Thanks, Pa. Dani will be in soon to handle dispatch."

"Dani? Is she still single?"

Archer groaned and got to his feet, coffee in hand. "I believe she is and no, before you ask, I don't want to date her. There's nothing wrong with her, she's just not the one for me."

"You'll be my age at the rate you're going before you have kids. What the hell are you looking for in a woman anyway that you've not found yet?"

Who says I haven't found it? "Now's not the time for this, Pa."

"It never is with you," his dad groused.

Another barely muffled groan left him as he departed the office area and entered the garage. Turning on some music, he pulled on the blue service shirt he worked in and had the first car up on the lift within moments. It wasn't too long before everyone had come in and they were all working. The trucks were out on calls and the workers left at the garage were busy on the vehicles they had there.

Time passed and, close to closing, Archer was by his truck when a tingle ran up his spine. Lifting his head, he watched as a green Jeep pulled in. The stiffening in his pants told him all he needed to know — it never failed, his body always knew when Delicia was around. He watched her climb out and look around.

Damn, she made that look good. She wore her uniform, a short sleeved light blue shirt and reflective EMS trousers. Her hair was back in a French braid and he longed to release it. Licking his lips, he shut his truck door and ambled over to where she stood talking to Mark, another one of his mechanics — a trainee actually, but he was a quick learner.

"Delicia," he said upon his approach.

Her amazing brown eyes, reminding him of chocolate mousse, flicked up and widened slightly. "Mr Bennett," she responded.

He disliked her calling him Mr Bennett but let it go for the moment. It was her thing, what she did when others were near. "Something I can help you with?"

Mark took the hint and walked away, leaving them alone. She looked just about everywhere else, except at him. And Archer realised she was nervous around him.

"Delicia?" he asked, stepping closer and inhaling the scent of tangerines that surrounded her.

"Hi...umm...I'm sorry to stop by without a...um...appointment, but I needed my oil changed, if possible."

"Of course. I'll do it for you right now."

Her gaze flew up to meet his and he sent her what he hoped was a disarming smile. His cock stirred when her tongue sneaked out and wet her lips.

"If you're sure. I don't want to make anyone stay late."

He held her stare. "It's fine. Keys in the ignition?"

"Yes."

"Go on in to the waiting room and have a seat. I'll be done in no time."

Reaching out, he turned her and gave her a gentle nudge towards the main door. The urge to draw her closer and kiss her swarmed him. He clenched his hands into fists and repressed the desire. Instead he just watched her walk towards the door and with one look back at him, she slipped inside.

Archer walked to her Jeep and paused right before getting behind the wheel. A throat clearing behind him pulled his attention from the vehicle. He turned to find Mark there.

"Want me to get this one, Risk?"

"No, it's okay, Mark. I got it."

A knowing smile curved up Mark's lips and he narrowed his gaze in response. "Sure thing, boss. I'll go clear a bay for you." Hand outstretched, he offered the plastic seat cover then walked off.

"Do that," he muttered, protecting the seat then getting behind the wheel.

Delicia had a six-speed Wrangler and he could tell she did a lot of outdoors stuff—her vehicle was decked out for it. There was nothing girly about this Jeep. And he liked it. Before long, he was draining the oil and checking air pressure on her tyres. Out of the corner of his eyes, he could see his employees watching him closely.

"What?" he asked Mark who continued to hover around.

"Nothing."

With a grunt, Archer looked at Mark. A seventeen year old boy who had been working here since he was fourteen. The kid was a whiz with cars and loved nothing more than working on them, despite only having been actually working on cars for a year—before that he'd cleaned up around the shop.

"You sure seem to be interested in what I'm doing for a man who's claiming nothing. You got nothing else to do?"

"Well, it's just that...how well do you know Lis?"

Biting back his growl at the familiar way Mark spoke about Delicia, he swallowed. "What are you looking to know?"

"I...I..." A flush moved up the boy's dark cheeks and he figured it out.

"She's older than you, you know." Archer poured in the oil.

"I know, but…"

"She's got a man, too, Mark. I'm sorry." He capped it and wiped his hands off on a rag from his pocket.

"She does?" He sighed. "Who?"

Waiting until the young man looked at him, Archer then said, "Me."

He stepped from the hood and slammed it shut. Going to the driver's side, he got in and drove through and around to the front. Once in the waiting room, he walked up to where Delicia sat thumbing through a magazine and said, "You're all set."

Chapter Two

Delicia looked up at the sound of Archer's deep timbre. The moisture in her mouth vanished as she stared at him. *This man is just too damn fine.* With what she hoped was a normal smile, she pushed to her feet and stood before him.

"Wow. That was fast. Thank you. For taking me." Okay, *that* was not supposed to be said. She squeezed her eyes shut and wished she were anywhere but where she was. "I mean, for taking care of my car."

His gaze burnt hot when she met it again and there was this hint of knowing within the depths of his eyes. "No problem. Anytime, Delicia."

Pulses of electricity moved along her skin at his tone and words. "I...I should get going so I don't hold you up any more."

She slid past him and moved towards to the counter where she paid. Archer was there when she finished and paced her to the door. "I'll walk you out," he murmured.

Delicia didn't comment, she figured everyone was already watching them, so why open her mouth and say something else stupid to increase gossip. Silence was between them until she stood beside her Jeep.

"Have dinner with me," he said, placing a hand on her arm.

Turning to face him, she blinked a few times, unsure if she'd been hearing things or not. The sincerity in his eyes told her that she hadn't made any mistake on that front.

"What?" *Jesus, there I go again. Why can't I just sound intelligent around him?*

He stepped closer and lowered his head. "You heard me, Delicia. Have dinner with me."

She found it incredibly difficult to concentrate when he stood so close, surrounding her with his heat and the mixed scents of cocoa beans and slightly smoky wood, with warm, flinty accents. The urge to touch and explore his muscled physique ran roughshod over her.

"I'm sorry, I'm working tonight. I'm on my way back in." *But I would much rather be with you.*

His eyes darkened. "When are you done?"

"Five-thirty in the morning."

"Breakfast, then? The old family diner out near where I picked you up today? The Enchanted."

Take a leap. Delicia answered, "Okay, breakfast. Six sound okay?"

His gaze honed in on her lips before going back to her eyes. "Yes." He reached into his pocket and withdrew a card, then pressed it into her hand. "My cell is on the back, call me if you have to work late."

Leaning over into the back of her vehicle, she dug into her bag and pulled out her own card. His fingertips brushed hers when he took it from her, sending tremors throughout her entire being. "Same here. Or if…you get a better offer for the night and can't make it."

Archer never blinked. "I'll be there."

She shifted beneath his burning stare. "I'll see you then."

"I'm looking forward to it. Be safe tonight." He dragged his knuckles down the side of her face, setting up a flutter deep within her.

With a nod she climbed into her Jeep and started the engine. "Good night, Archer."

"Night, Delicia," he purred before stepping back.

Driving away, she stole glances at his strong body standing there in the parking lot of his business. She wanted him—that was no secret, well not to her. She had for a long, long time now.

"What the hell did I just do?" she whimpered. "I can hardly speak coherently around him, why did I just agree to breakfast?"

She pulled into the fire station and climbed out. With her bag tossed over her shoulder, she hurried to the ambulance where her partner Thomas Christian worked on the pre-check. Kind of a moot point, given they were doing another shift and knew what was in their vehicle.

"Hey, Thom."

"Lis." He looked up and smiled at her, his white teeth gleaming against his bronzed skin. "Wondered where you were. Was getting ready to give you a ring."

"Sorry. Got the oil changed on my Jeep." She tossed her bag in and stowed it out of the way. *And I got a date for tomorrow morning.*

"No prob. I know you'd call if something came up. I'm just not used to you not being here before me, even if we only have a few hours to chill."

"I'm going to grab some drinks. Want me to get you some?"

"Please," he said from where he sat on the stretcher taking inventory.

Rubbing her eyes, she walked off. "Be right back." When she returned she helped Thom take inventory until they had to start their shift.

In less than half an hour, she and Thom were beginning their shift. She sat behind the wheel and Thom told her about his younger sister, Erica, and her state volleyball competition. It was a pretty mundane night. There wasn't many calls as the night progressed. They stopped for a bite to eat around midnight.

"Hey, you two," the waitress said when they walked in.

"Candy," Delicia spoke with a smile.

"Your usuals?"

"Please," they said at the same time.

In a booth, Delicia stretched out her legs and rested her head against the window.

"How you doing?" Thom asked.

Turning her head to stare at her partner, she took in his good looks. Bronze skin, black wavy hair, firm body, chiselled features. He was a man who garnered lots of reactions from the ladies.

"You know. I'm hanging in there."

"When's your triathlon?"

"About three months away. I did training before coming on shift. Part of the reason I was dragging."

"I admire your dedication to it. I couldn't do what you do."

She grinned and reached for the coffee. "Well, we just expend our energy in different ways. I do triathlons, you...you do...other extracurricular activities."

Thom laughed. "When you say it like that, you make it sound so dirty."

"I don't know how else to say it."

"Ahh, come on, Lis. I'm just waiting for the right woman to come along."

"Hey, I'm not your mom. No need to explain yourself to me."

He winked at her when Candy set down their food and she just shook her head. Female companionship was something he never lacked. It had been an issue when she'd met a few of his women, for they tended to see her as a threat. Now for the most part, it was very well known that she and Thom were partners and friends. Nothing more than a platonic relationship between them.

She dug into her pancakes, eggs and bacon with gusto, and was almost done when the radio at her side crackled. "Multiple car crash near Devil's Corner. All units available respond."

Delicia and Thom jumped to their feet. Tossing some money down on the table, they headed for the ambulance at a run. Seconds later they were speeding down the road, lights and sirens going.

"Devil's Corner. Shit, this isn't gonna be pretty," she said as she wove in and out of traffic before hitting the outskirts of town and really opening up the engine.

Slowing as they approached, she turned off the sirens and pulled up to the crash. The cop cars and fire trucks that had been following her did the same. Hopping out, Delicia and Thom got to work. The firemen were cutting through the door of one car while they checked out some of the other kids.

"Lis!" a shout reached her.

She hurried to where they were removing the top of the vehicle. Thom had the stretcher waiting. Climbing in, Delicia put a neck brace around the woman in the passenger side. Once it was secure, they worked together to get her out and lifted her onto the stretcher.

Shit! The woman was pregnant and non-responsive. Thom bagged her and they started to move her towards the ambulance. Delicia glanced back at the crushed car and her heart sank when a fireman covered a body with a sheet. The woman stared up at her as they hurried, panic overflowing in her gaze.

"Stay with me," Delicia said. "We're getting you to the hospital."

"One, two, three," Thom counted it off and they lifted her into the back.

She closed the door behind them and hustled to the driver's seat. Hitting the siren, she waited for the two pounds on the back door then pulled out carefully, turned around and the moment she was clear, pushed the pedal down. As the ambulance raced down the road, Delicia called it in to the emergency room she was headed for.

There were people waiting for them when she drove up. Throwing the vehicle into park, she then hopped out and helped lower the gurney. They rushed through the sliding glass doors and she heard Thom rattling off the stats he knew.

"We got it from here," a woman said with authority.

Delicia looked up and her mouth fell open. "Arissa?"

Light brown eyes met hers and softened briefly. A curvaceous woman with a reddish-gold pixie cut stared back at her. "Lis?"

"What are — ?"

"We're ready, doc," a nurse interrupted.

"I gotta go, Lis. Tomorrow, we'll catch up. Great to see you," she said as they hurried away. "You look great!"

Thom nudged her with his shoulder. "Who's that?"

A dry chuckle left her. "That's my sister, Arissa. Who last I knew was in Chicago." She ran a hand over her eyes. "What is she doing back here?"

"Think on the way. Let's go see if they need more help back there." Thom tugged on her arm.

She drove while he cleaned up the back. Delicia was saddened. Teens had been racing and had misjudged the corner, spinning out of control and hitting the oncoming car. A man driving his wife to the hospital. He'd died immediately and the wife was on her way to surgery.

Her heart sped up however, when her gaze landed upon a large flatbed and the man beside it. Archer. He stood talking to one of the cops. Two of the vehicles sat upon the truck. Parking behind one of the fire trucks, they got out to offer assistance. There were mostly superficial wounds to take care of now and she got to it, doing her best to ignore the handsome man who was extremely good at sucking her attention.

Archer only half listened to Dave as he talked to him. His gaze and focus had basically been upon Delicia from the moment he'd seen her step out of the ambulance. She looked tired, beautiful and sad. He wanted to hold her to him and offer his strength. When she headed around to the back of the ambulance, he pushed away from his truck and said to Dave, "Excuse me for a minute."

He walked to where he could see her. Her head was down as she looked through a bag for something.

Moving up behind her, he inhaled and was again hit by the scent of tangerines that flowed about her.

"Hello, Delicia," he muttered softly.

She stiffened before turning towards him. Her eyes roved up and down his body before she responded. "Hello, Archer."

Damn, I want to kiss her. "You hanging in there okay?"

There was some tightness around the corners of her mouth, yet she nodded. "Yes. I'll be glad when the night's over, though."

Archer heard her name being called and he asked, "We still on for breakfast? Or did you want to cancel?"

"Did you have a better offer?"

I can think of one for you. Breakfast in bed. My bed. "Nope. You just look really exhausted."

"I was looking forward to eating…having breakfast with you."

He smiled. "I'll see you in a few hours then."

"Yes." She stared at him a moment longer then slipped by him, bag in hand, and vanished.

Archer sighed and followed her back around. He could feel the gazes of some of the people there upon him. Those were ignored—he got back to work and soon had the totalled cars back at his place. Then he went back out for the other two.

* * * *

He was exhausted when he pulled into the parking lot of The Enchanted and parked his truck. Glancing around, he noticed Delicia's vehicle wasn't there. What if she'd changed her mind? He grabbed his cell and checked for any missed calls. There weren't any.

With a deep breath, he climbed out and headed for the door.

Music caught his attention and he turned his head in time to see a dirty green Jeep whip into a spot near his truck. Delicia. He bit his lower lip briefly when she jumped out and gave him a small smile accompanied by a slight wave. Warmth flowed through him and he faced her fully, waiting for her to reach his side.

"Sorry I'm late," she said by way of greeting.

"Right on time."

Archer dragged his eyes up and down her form—the woman had a body to die for. He could stare at her for hours and never grow bored. She had changed from her uniform to a pair of white shorts that made him long to drop to his knees and thank God, and a baggy navy blue shirt that had a black EMT symbol across her left breast.

"Perfect," she whispered.

As she strode past him, he chuckled at the image on the back, a stick figure in a mug with a kettle releasing a drop of water onto its head. The phrase surrounding it read, 'Instant EMT, just add hot water'. Archer stepped up to her side and held the door for her.

They got seated at a booth and he stared at her over the rim of his coffee mug. "Tell me about you, Delicia," he said, after they'd placed their order.

Her eyes flew up to meet his and he watched as her full lips moved a few times before anything came out. "What do you want to know?"

Everything. "What do you wish to share?"

"You get what you see with me. I'm a simple girl, love the outdoors and love my work."

"Do you know if the woman from last night is okay?"

Delicia took a deep breath and shook her head. "No, but I'll find out today. Apparently my sister is back in town and was one of the doctors on call last night. In fact, she was the one who treated the woman."

He cocked his head to the side. "Arissa? She's back?" It had been a long time since he'd seen her.

Her eyes narrowed slightly. "Yes. Not sure when she arrived, but she was there last night."

Archer sensed that was a sensitive path to go down, so he opted to change the subject. "What were you doing yesterday morning that had you so exhausted looking when I ran into you?"

A flush ran up her toffee skin, but a smile followed. "I was finishing my training."

"Training?" He smiled at the waitress when she delivered their food and again left them alone.

"I am currently training to run in the half Ironman in Taos in three months."

He whistled low. "Damn. I'm very impressed. How long are the distances for that?"

She sipped some coffee. "The swim is one-point-nine. The ride is ninety, and the run is twenty-one-point-one."

"Is that miles?"

"No, kilometres."

He did some quick math in his head and shook his head. "Wow. You are a very impressive lady, Delicia Wright."

Her blush intensified. "Thank you."

"Okay, you ask me one. Surely there's something you'd like to know about me."

"Would you sleep with me?"

He dropped his fork. He zoomed in on her face. Her beautiful eyes grew wide and her face paled as realisation set in.

"Oh...oh...oh my God. I...I..." Delicia slid towards the edge of the booth.

Archer knew she was about to bolt. He was there before she could escape, his arms pinning her in and his face level with hers. "Delicia," he said in a low tone.

Shaking her head, she pushed against him. "Let me go. I can't believe I said that. Please, get out of my way so I can go."

He didn't. Instead he slid onto the bench seat, crowding her. With one hand he lifted her chin. Her eyes scrunched shut. He ran his thumb along her lips, loving the soft satiny feel to them.

"Look at me, Delicia."

Slowly her lashes rose, exposing her big eyes to him. He could see her embarrassment but didn't comment on it. Instead, he kissed her. Delicia stiffened, parting her lips beneath his.

His body hardened instantly. So soft were her lush lips. He trailed his tongue along the seam before dipping into her mouth. Her taste hit him fast and hard, infusing his taste buds and imprinting onto his soul. With a low growl, he grabbed the back of her neck and thrust his tongue throughout the warm recess of her mouth. She placed a hand against his chest and raked her nails lightly down. Somehow he managed to end the kiss and stared down at her.

Her eyes were smoky with passion as she watched him, her full lips slightly swollen and open. Archer had never wanted a woman more than he did at that moment. Sliding his hand from the back of her neck to her cheek, he brushed his thumb from his other hand along her lower lip.

"The answer to your question is yes, Delicia. Anytime. Anywhere."

He kissed her quickly once more then returned to his side of the booth and picked up his fork. Her gaze dropped to her plate and she began to eat again. Out of the corner of his eye, he could see Rose leaning on the counter watching them, her expression amused.

Well, that is going to be around town before too long. Rose can't keep her mouth shut. Not to mention the other people in the diner. He'd already seen the looks when he and Delicia had entered together.

"Can I ask you something, Archer?"

Immediately he placed all his attention back on Delicia. "You can ask me anything."

"What's with you and Justin?"

He took a deep breath. "He and I have never gotten along. It started back in high school when our school played his in football. Since then, it's seemed to intensify."

Delicia leant forward, elbows on the table. The look on her face told him she wasn't buying it. "That's it?"

"Does it really matter?"

"Yes. After you left he told me you weren't right for me. I want to know why he thinks that."

Rage grew in his belly, but he kept it contained. "You should ask him." Archer reached across the table and briefly touched her hand. "I happen to think I am just perfect for you, Delicia Wright. And I have for a long time."

She pursed her lips and drank some coffee. "Could be risky."

One side of his mouth lifted into a grin. "Risky pleasures are usually the best kind."

Her brown eyes sparkled. "Isn't your nickname Risk?"

He leaned in. "Yes."

"And you got that how?"

"Football."

Her cell rang and he frowned when she answered it. He listened to her gentle, dulcet tone as she spoke. When she snapped the phone shut he waited. She didn't say a word.

"Everything okay?"

"Yes. That was my sister. She's waiting for me at the house."

"Do you need to go?"

"After breakfast. She can wait. I've got you now...and forget it. I can't talk."

Archer smiled with pleasure. It may have been years in the making, but this breakfast was the beginning of something special for the two of them. He just knew it.

Chapter Three

Delicia pushed open the front door and walked inside. She could almost feel Archer's lips pressed upon hers. A satisfied smile lifted the corners of her mouth. They had stood outside the diner and kissed for about five minutes before she'd finally left. Not that she'd wanted to. She longed to go with him and do things she'd been dreaming about for years.

"Well, you look all kinds of satisfied. Who is he?" Her sister's voice snapped her from the daydream.

After dropping her bag on the floor, she hurried to Arissa's side and pulled her in close for a hug. "Why didn't you say you were coming? How long are you here for?"

Her sister returned the hug and said, "I'm back for good."

She frowned and drew back. Staring into her sister's light brown eyes, she asked, "You're home for good and didn't tell us? How long have you been back? Where are you staying?" There was something going on with Arissa. And she let it go, knowing her sister would speak on it when she was ready.

"I didn't tell *everyone* I was coming back. I did send an email to the direct family—which includes you—along with a few people. If you would pay more attention to my emails you would have known. Been back for a few months. I'm staying at Deyon's for now. I'm surprised you haven't heard through the gossipers about my return and a few other things." Arissa smiled ruefully.

"Sorry. For the last few months between work and training I haven't been able to keep up with things. Figured for anything urgent I would get a call from someone." Delicia shrugged then continued. "What few things?"

"It's nothing. Enough about me. Tell me about you. Or do you need to sleep?"

Exhaustion had taken a back seat the moment she'd seen Archer this morning and she had two days off. "I'm okay. I'm good."

"You look good. When's the triathlon?"

"Three months."

"I'm so proud of you, Delicia. Now, tell me who this man is who put the sparkle in your eyes."

She hesitated slightly. Her family had a tendency to try and run her life at times, luckily she'd been so busy they'd left her alone. And having them interfere before she could even say there was something there didn't sit well with her. Plus, there was the way Archer had talked about her sister.

"Lis?"

"Archer."

Arissa frowned slightly. "Archer...Archer Bennett?" Her frown turned upside down and a huge grin filled her face. "You and Archer? Well, hell, it's about damn time."

"What do you mean it's about damn time?"

"Please, Lis. I've known you had a crush on him since you were in middle school. He was the only man I ever saw your eyes light up for." Arissa tugged her to sit on the couch. "Now, tell me all about him and you two."

"There isn't an *us* yet. I just had breakfast with him for the first time this morning. Jeez, Arissa. I can't even be around him without saying something stupid. I asked him this morning if he'd sleep with me."

"Nothing like getting to the point."

"It's not funny. He said he hadn't seen you in a while. When'd you see him?"

All the humour drained from Arissa's face. "I saw him in Chicago."

She furrowed her brow. "What was he doing there?"

Arissa shook her head. "I don't think it's my place to tell you. I was working when I saw him but, Lis, if you want to know more, you're going to have to hear it from him."

"Did something happen to him?"

"Not physically, no." Arissa reached out and squeezed her hand. "I'm happy for you, Lis. Give him a shot and don't let people tell you otherwise. Now, go get some sleep. We can catch up more later, have dinner, I want you to meet someone."

Delicia opened her mouth, but Arissa cut her off. "You're too tired and I rather you meet this person than tell you. I'll call you to set it up."

After hugging her sister one more time, she headed for her bedroom and was asleep moments later. The house was silent when she woke and with a groan, she rolled to her feet and padded to the kitchen to take care of her growling belly. With that crisis averted, she sat down on her couch and closed her eyes.

Ding dong.

Sitting up, Delicia realised she'd dozed off. She pushed to her feet, walked to the door then opened it. Christie Parker, a child from next door, stood there. "Hi, Christie. What can I do for you?"

"Sorry to bother you, Miss Delicia. But we're supposed to have a game today and the man, Mister Mike, who was gonna be our doctor there, got called away. Are you free?"

Stifling her yawn, she nodded. "I sure am, Christie. Give me a few moments to grab my stuff. You can come in if you want, or I can come to your house when I'm ready."

She grinned. "I should go home and tell Daddy you said okay. I'll be over there." Christie turned then faced back to her again. "Thanks so much, Miss Delicia." After a hug the child left, blonde ponytail bouncing with every step she took.

Rubbing her hands over her eyes, Delicia closed the door and went to her bedroom where she made her way to the adjoining master bath and took a quick shower and dressed. Bag in hand, she walked out to her Jeep and tossed it in the back. Then she jogged to Christie's house and rang her doorbell. Her father, Chad, answered.

"Thank you for doing this, Lis," he said with a smile. "I know you probably had things planned."

"I'm happy to do it. The kids have been looking forward to this game for a while. I'll meet you there."

"Thanks again."

"My pleasure," she said, heading back to her Jeep and climbing in.

She drove to the field and not too long after, she sat on the bleachers, watching the girls play soccer with her EMS medical bag at her feet. By the end of the game, she'd treated a few cuts and scrapes but thankfully nothing serious.

Christie hugged her again and stared up at her with brilliant blue eyes. "Thanks, Miss Delicia."

Looking down at the child, she smiled. "Glad to help. Congrats on the win."

"We've got the championships next month. Will you come watch and cheer for me with my parents?"

"If I can make it, I would love to. But I have my triathlon I'm training for as well as work, so if I don't make it, just know I'm cheering for you."

"Love you, Miss Delicia."

"Love you too, Christie. I think your team is waiting for you. Probably have a victory party to go to."

"Yes. Thanks again."

The young girl ran off. Chad looked back at her and smiled his thanks. She waved then zipped up her bag. Grabbing the handles, she walked slowly to her Jeep and stowed the bag.

"What's this I hear about you kissing Archer Bennett?" Justin demanded, incensed.

Grinding her jaw and rolling her eyes, she prayed for patience before turning to face her cousin. "Hello, Justin. I'm fine thanks. How are you doing?"

"Cut the crap, Lis. Answer me."

"One, I'm not in diapers, so who I kiss isn't any of your business. Two, you're not my parent, so again, it's not any of your business."

Justin stepped close, his face ugly in his anger. "Listen to me, little cousin. That man is not right for you. Stay away from him."

Lifting her chin, she held his gaze. "What is your problem with him? What did he do to you?"

"He'll hurt you, Lis. That man is violent. That's why he's divorced." He leant down. "Stay. Away. From. Him." Justin turned and walked away.

She couldn't believe what she'd heard. *I didn't even know he'd been married. But violent? I don't see Archer as being a violent man.* Unsettled, she slid behind the wheel and began to drive. Her mind raced with the news. Instead of going home, she drove by Bennett's Towing. She kept going when she didn't see his truck there.

Delicia knew where he lived but stopped short of driving there. Instead, she headed out of town. She stopped at an area she was familiar with from rockhounding and got out. Sitting on the tailgate, she swung her legs in the slight breeze and wished she could forget about Justin's words.

Everything else faded to the back when she heard the call for an ambulance come across her cb radio. After jumping into the seat, she started the motor and sped away as the location and further explanation came. Dust flew out from behind her Jeep as she careened from the dirt road onto the paved highway.

Flipping some switches and lowering her visor, she shifted and gunned the engine. The flashing head and taillights, along with the lights upon the visor, would hopefully get people to move out of her way.

At the scene, Delicia left her lights on and hopped out, grabbing her bag as she hurried to offer her assistance. She stayed until well after the ambulance arrived and left. Part of her had hoped it would be Archer who came to get the disabled vehicle but it wasn't.

"Hey, what are you doing here?" Thom asked materialising beside her.

"I heard the call. Was a first responder. What about you?"

"Saw your Jeep and pulled off behind you. Shouldn't you be sleeping or something like that?" he asked, draping an arm around her shoulders.

"Something like that. I slept some."

"Yeah, I also hear you did the game since Mike couldn't make it."

"What can I say, I live to serve."

He squeezed her. "Get some sleep will you? I don't want to lose my partner."

She rested her head on his shoulder. "I promise. I'm good. In fact, I'm on my way home now. I'm gonna rest before I go biking."

He pointed to the sky. "We're going to get some storms."

"Stationary bike today. I won't leave the house."

Thom dropped his arm and they walked to their vehicles. Behind hers, she saw the lights flashing on his as well. "Make sure you don't. I'll see you in two days."

"Bye, Thom." She tossed her bag in the back, climbed in and shut off the lights, then waited for a clearing to merge onto the highway so she could head home. An hour after she got home, she rode her stationary bike as a rainstorm dropped a deluge on McKingley.

* * * *

Archer couldn't explain his anger when he saw Delicia alongside the road with Thom's arm around her. He knew she didn't even see him, but he sure saw her. Grinding his back teeth, he took a deep breath and went home. A few hours later, he picked up his phone and called her.

"Hello?" Delicia's voice wound around him like a warm blanket.

"Hello, Delicia," he responded.

"Archer. How are you?"

"Fine. I saw you at the accident. How are you?"

"I'm fine, thanks."

"Are you free for dinner tonight, Delicia?"

"Well, it's in the oven as we speak, but you are more than welcome to come by if you'd like."

"I'll be right over."

He hung up and was on his way to her place in no time. His heart clenched when she drew open the door to admit him to her house. Her hair was unconfined and she stared up at him from beneath her thick black lashes.

"Hi," he murmured.

"Hey, yourself. Come on in."

She stepped back and he followed, entering her home for the first time. He cast a quick glance around then put his attention back on her face. Leaning in close, he kissed her lightly. "You have a beautiful home."

"Thank you. We can eat in about fifteen minutes. I hope you like shepherd's pie."

"Anything is fine."

She worried her lower lip and asked, "Can I get you anything to drink?"

"Whatever you have." He followed her into the kitchen and smiled at the grape motif throughout. She handed him a glass of Coke with ice. "Thank you."

"No problem."

He sat at the table and looked at her. "Is there anything going on with you and Thom?"

It was obvious his question had shocked her, for her eyes grew wide. "No, nothing. Why do you ask?"

"I saw him with his arm around you today."

She nodded. "Oh, okay. No. I'm not involved with anyone."

"Would you like to be?"

Her pupils dilated and her nose flared. "As in an exclusive kind of thing?"

"I don't share well." Something rose in her gaze that made him tilt his head to the side. "Is something wrong, Delicia?"

"I need to ask you something."

He grinned as he recalled her last question at the diner. "Ask away."

"What were you doing in the hospital in Chicago?"

He sighed and his chest tightened. "Arissa told you she saw me, but not why I was there?"

"She said it wasn't her place to tell me. Can you? Will you?"

He'd always liked Arissa, and her handling of that situation only made his appreciation grow. With a deep breath, he leant forward, resting his elbows on the table. "The night I was in the hospital there, I had just lost my son."

"Your son?"

He rubbed his hands together and pressed on. "Yes. When I was twenty-two I went to Vegas with some friends. I was stupid and drunk when I married Lacy. I tried to make it work with her but after a while, I realised it never would. So we got divorced about a year after we'd wed. She never told me she was pregnant, not until later." Bitterness rose swift and sharp. "Years later."

He stared at his drink briefly then closed his eyes. When he opened them, Delicia was waiting for him, compassion and sorrow overflowing in her gaze. "She contacted me because she wanted money for him. I took the money in person, wanting to meet my son. But I was too late. Lacy had been driving while intoxicated and had gotten into an accident. She survived, Tony didn't. Arissa was the doctor who worked on Lacy, that's why she saw me."

"I'm so sorry, Archer. I...I..."

He waved off her explanation, not wanting to go into it with her right now, preferring instead to have a nice evening. "Not many people know, Delicia. It's hard, but it's okay. It's been two years now."

The timer went off and she rose to pull the meal out of the oven. The kitchen filled with rich scents and his mouth watered. Delicia walked to his side instead of retaking her seat. He didn't move when she reached out to touch his face. She smoothed her hands along his features, her eyes holding his.

"I'm so sorry. For everything. I can't imagine how much pain you've gone through."

Turning his head, he pressed a kiss to her palm. "Thank you."

"Let's eat."

She stepped back and he grabbed her wrist, halting her. Her brown eyes met his and he drew her in slowly, tugging her down for a kiss. He sighed as she allowed him access to her warm mouth. Bringing her to his lap, he gripped her hips and increased the kiss.

Delicia wound her arms around his neck and pressed closer to him, tangling her fingers in his hair. His cock stiffened even more when their tongues danced and she nipped his lightly. He broke the kiss and stared at her.

"You said something about dinner."

"I did," she whispered, placing light pecks on his lips. "Are you hungry?"

"More than you could possibly know."

She rested her forehead against his. "Okay then."

He could hear the disappointment in her tone. "I don't want you to think I am just after sex, Delicia."

"What are you after?"

"You," he admitted, surprised at how easy it was to tell her that.

She leant back a bit. "Me?"

Moving his hands up and down her back, he said, "Yes."

Delicia blinked and got off his lap. "I see."

Archer followed her to the counter and stared at her. *Maybe I moved too fast.* "Delicia?"

She looked at him and smiled. "I just thought about something."

"What's that?"

"I've not really said anything stupid since you've gotten here. Normally I've said something that embarrasses the hell out of me."

He grinned. "I happen to like that."

"You would."

"Nice to know there's something that makes you a bit unsettled."

"You always have."

He brushed his lips along the curve of her neck. "Likewise, Delicia."

She rested against him briefly before turning her attention back to serving them dinner. The meal was relaxed and delicious. Afterwards they relaxed on the couch, popcorn between them and waited for the movie to start. By the end of the show, Delicia was tucked against him, her hand resting against his chest.

He held her close as the credits scrolled, not in any rush whatsoever. She felt so right along his body. Pressing a light kiss to her temple, he felt her sigh.

"What are you doing tomorrow?" he asked.

"Training in the morning then my afternoon n' evening is clear. Why?"

"I wanted to spend some time with you."

Delicia moved so her head was in his lap and she stared up at him. "What'd you have in mind?"

A whole lot of you and me with nothing on. "Nothing specific. Something you'd like to do?"

"Do you like to hike?"

"Yes."

"Want to go hiking?"

After kissing her briefly, he said, "Sounds like a plan to me. Want me to come pick you up or did you want to drive to my house?"

"I can come to your house, that way I don't keep you waiting for me if I'm running a bit behind."

"I don't mind waiting for you, Delicia. But by all means, come to my home. I'd love to have you there."

"You're a charmer, Archer Bennett."

"You think so?" He ran a finger along her cheekbone and around her lips.

"I do."

Remember those words, Delicia Wright. I plan on hearing them from your lips before a minister one of these days. He smiled. "I should get going. Thank you for a lovely dinner and for even better company."

For an answer, she reached up and threaded her fingers into the hair at the base of his neck. Drawing him flush to her lips, she kissed him. Slid her tongue into his mouth and stroked along his. Flames of primal lust rose within him and he growled low in his throat. He dragged one hand down her side, loving her curves, and sank his other into her hair and pressed their mouths tighter.

Her back arched and her breasts met his chest. He took over the kiss and thrust his tongue in and out of her mouth, sweeping through all he could reach. Her mewls made him harder than granite and he wanted nothing more than to strip off their clothing and enjoy her body. He knew she was a powder keg—beneath her calm exterior lingered a raging fire. A fire he would keep for himself.

He broke the kiss with a curse. Her gaze was slightly unfocused as she stared up at him. Sitting up fully, he cupped her face. She swallowed a few times, the pulse on her neck throbbing.

"I have to go, Delicia. I have only so much control."

She got to her feet and pulled him up. They walked in silence to the door. Before he opened it, he wrapped his arms around her again and waited for her eyes to meet his.

"I'm not leaving because I don't want you, Delicia. I'm going because I want you without a single doubt in your mind that being with me is what you want. Okay?"

"Goodnight, Archer," she whispered before pushing up on her toes to brush their lips together.

"Goodnight, Delicia."

After one more kiss, he left her there then, with a dick that could break rock, he headed home for a cold shower. Standing in the stall, he struggled with the urge to bring himself release.

"No, damn it all. I want her touch. Not mine."

Archer set his jaw and finished his shower in record time. His erection still pulsed when he climbed into bed. Sleep was a long time in coming and Delicia

Wright's name was on his lips when he awoke the next morning.

* * * *

He paced anxiously, waiting for her to show up. It was three in the afternoon when his doorbell rang. With a deep breath, he walked to the door and pulled it open. A smile lifted his lips when he gazed upon the person on the other side.

Delicia wore black shorts and a light grey T-shirt. Her hair was drawn up in a ponytail and a sparkle in her eyes.

"Hi," she said.

"Hello, beautiful," he replied. "Come on in."

Chapter Four

A thrill went through Delicia at his words. *Breathe, girl, or you won't get through the date.* She'd enjoyed their kissing, and thoughts of having his naked flesh pressed against hers had filled her all through her training. Although her focus had been scattered, she had pushed on to make sure she got her work out done. Now, as she stood before him, the image of him naked was even sharper.

Delicia turned her attention to his house. She'd driven by where he lived, often on her way to work and her own place. The outer part showed an older home with lots of character and a welcoming air. Flowers indigenous to New Mexico led up to the three steps, then the covered porch that ran the length of the front had some hanging plants. A comfortable looking swing was on one corner of the porch. After she'd entered, she noted that the interior had a welcoming feel and was full of character.

The foyer was small. To her right she glimpsed a kitchen, which had a breakfast nook. Archer led her to the left to a living room. The fabric of the couch, chairs and love seat were done in caramel. On the sofa there was a throw across the back. The centre and end tables on either side of the couch were cut from a rich oak. An Aztec style rug was under the centre table. A large entertainment centre—made from the same wood as the end tables—whose focal point was the big screen TV was on a wall that could be easily seen no matter where you sat. There was a full stereo system with speakers.

Unconsciously, Delicia headed for the wall farthest from the door they had entered. When she stood before the floor to ceiling bookcase, which was built into the entire wall, she studied the titles on the shelves. A smile curled her lips as she noted they were in a variety of topics. She went to the ladder glancing up then moved it, noting it was attached and moved along some sort of rail at the top of the bookcase.

"Oh my, this is awesome. I always wanted one like this," Delicia mumbled as she climbed the steps.

"Me too. That's why I had it built. Have one in my bedroom too."

Delicia stopped, startled and looked at Archer. "Oh...sorry I was so taken by it that I just—"

He cut her off. "No problem. Feel free to check any place in my home. I want you to be comfortable here. Think of it as yours, too. Come down a sec."

Delicia wasn't sure what to make of his statement. She did as he asked.

"To save space, I usually keep the smaller ladder down. Let me change that. Step back a few steps." Archer moved forward then pressed a button she hadn't noticed.

The ladder she had climbed slid up then seemed to fold right at the top of the bookcase leaving behind a decorative design. She returned her gaze to Archer. He had a small smug smile on his face.

"Watch." He pressed another button.

Delicia looked up. A shape started to unfold from just below another design. It came down and rested just next to Archer.

"No way." Awed, Delicia ran her hand over the ladder with handrails.

This ladder was wide enough to fit two or more people comfortably next to each other. The steps were also larger, and could fit a box on, if you had to unpack some books. She pushed it and it rolled along a mechanism near the ceiling. Delicia turned to Archer. He smirked.

"Who did this for you? And hell, can they make me one too? You said you have one in your bedroom too?"

"I designed the bookcases I wanted and then talked it over with my buddy Harmon McCurdy. And we built them together. The ladder gizmo was a pain to get right, but we did, and this is the result."

Delicia frowned. "Harmon? Didn't he play football with you in high school? I think he made Katiya's desk set at The Oasis." Delicia remembered the big bruiser of a linebacker. He was intimidating as hell.

"Yeah, that's him. He's a furniture maker. The things he can do with a piece of wood are artistic. He made most of the pieces in the house. I help him out once in a while. It's an interesting process, going from wood to a finished product." Archer was studying the bookcase.

Delicia was impressed, Archer was turning out to be a surprise. She went up the ladder and Archer joined her, pointing out some of his favourite books. Some of them were similar to her own tastes. After a bit they got down and he showed her the bookcase in his bedroom—it was almost identical to the one in the living room. Reaching for a book, Delicia again marvelled at the variety of topics.

"Delicia. We need to go." Archer's voice sounded strangled.

Delicia glanced back, confused. His gaze was lowered, but when he raised his head, the heat in his gaze made her body clench. Delicia put back the book and turned to face him, stepping down to press her body against his and Archer groaned. Delicia raised on her toes and closed her mouth over his. He gripped her waist and she kissed him thoroughly. Archer duelled his tongue with hers, then he withdrew, a harsh sound escaping him. He breathed deeply.

"We can't, Delicia."

Delicia flushed and pulled back. She lowered her head, but with blunt fingers, he tipped up her chin until their gazes met.

"It's not that I don't want to, but I want more than a roll in the sack. I want you all in with this. Sure of going long-term." Archer sounded very certain.

Delicia wasn't sure what to say to that. He kissed her gently then released her.

"Think about it. And once you know, tell me. Until then, let's do some hiking." Archer went down the steps then held out his hand for her.

Delicia let him help her off the ladder then they went out of the bedroom door, crossing the hall to the front door. She waited as Archer locked up, then headed for her Jeep.

Once they were inside, Delicia said, "I was thinking of going to the Kellava but with the time it's too late for that. We can go to the Felilta Canyon and take one of the easy trails to see some of the petroglyphs."

"Sounds good."

Delicia nodded and they drove off, chatting comfortably until she parked half an hour later. They both shouldered their packs then Archer led the way as they headed off. Delicia wondered when hiking clothing had got so sexy—Archer's T-shirt hugged his broad shoulders while his shorts stopped just above his knees, leaving the rest of his strong calves bare until his sock and boots. Delicia bit her lip, stifling a moan. She wanted him. Yet instead of telling him so in his bedroom—so close to his king-sized bed made up with pale yellow sheets—she'd been mute. The one time when she should have been babbling and blurting out what she wanted, she hadn't been able to come up with the words.

Just a few words. Take me, Archer. And you couldn't even say it. Way to go. Delicia followed his delectable ass. Soon she was pulled into the scenery of the trail and the petroglyphs. She and Archer talked about what they saw and other things. It was getting late when they decided to leave so Delicia could get ready for her shift.

"I had a great time. Next time, we can go to Kellava and maybe camp out over night at the Devil Rock Hot Springs."

Delicia frowned as she parked in front of his house. "You know how to get to Devil Rock? When I've been to Kellava, I've tried to get to it but could never find it. I've been there once before, but it was with Tarak."

"It's tricky to find. We can go there on your next weekend off," Archer offered.

"I'd like that. I'll let you know when I have one."

"Good. Are you still on the night shift at the station?"

"Yep."

"Can we meet for breakfast again at The Enchanted?"

Delicia smiled, delighted. "Yes. The same time as before."

"Sounds fine. We'll make some plans for some more dates."

"You planning on booking up my time?" Delicia teased.

"Maybe. At least when you're not working or training," Archer said.

"You could come with me sometimes when I do." Immediately, Delicia wondered if that was a good idea. The distances she did in biking, running and swimming weren't what most people could do.

"I'd like that," Archer said softly.

"We'll discuss it at breakfast." She pushed aside her concern.

Archer pulled her towards him, onto his lap and kissed her hungrily. Delicia returned it. They were breathing hard when they parted. Archer put her back behind the wheel. He ran the back of his knuckle down her cheek.

"See you for breakfast."

"Breakfast," Delicia murmured.

Archer got out, then tapped the side of the Jeep and stepped back. Delicia drove off, resisting the urge to look back at him.

* * * *

Getting out of her Jeep, Delicia stretched. It had been a rough shift—one call after another. Every part of her body ached. She had been tempted to call Archer and cancel, but she'd found herself looking forward to their morning breakfasts at The Enchanted. She thought of it as their place. For the last week and a half they had been meeting here for breakfast. It was a pattern she had come to love. Rose already knew what they ordered and had everything ready when they arrived.

Archer had stayed true to his word and when she wasn't working or training they had spent their time together. They'd been back to Felilta Canyon for a longer hike, had gone to the Lina Zoo and Gardens Park and had taken in the sights of the indoor and outdoor living museum. The park displayed more than forty native animal species and hundreds of succulents from around the world. They'd explored the sand dunes and mountainous areas while taking in all the features of the park. They'd made plans for her next weekend off to go for the Kellava and the Devil.

Each time they went out it was enjoyable—they were already so comfortable together. During the down times when not spent discovering places in McKingley, they hung out either at her house or his on the couch cuddling and kissing. It sometimes became heated, but Archer either left or escorted her out before it went too far. She wanted it to go further but wasn't sure exactly how to let him know it—she didn't want to just blurt it out again.

Delicia rolled her head, trying to relieve the tension in her shoulders, then walked towards the restaurant. She waved at Archer who was sitting in their booth. Inside, she raised her hand in acknowledgement of Rose's greeting. She kissed Archer softly before sliding into the other side of the booth.

"You look beat. Why didn't you just call and go home?" Archer studied her.

"Wanted to see you." Delicia shrugged.

"Make the order to go, Rose," Archer called.

"Sure thing," Rose answered.

"That's not necessary," Delicia protested.

"We're getting you home to bed," Archer said firmly.

Anytime, anywhere and anyway I can have you. Delicia bit back the words.

"Order is ready," Rose said.

Archer stood at Rose's word and went to the counter to pay and collect it then returned to her. He held out a hand and pulled her up when she took it. She groaned then preceded him out. Outside, she glanced around.

"Where's your truck?"

"Left it at the shop. Had one of the men drop me here on the way to a tow. Figured I would get a ride home from you."

"I'll give you a ride," Delicia said.

"I'm not going home. We're going to your house. We can have breakfast there. That way you can go straight to bed. Keys," Archer said.

She handed them over, too tired to even protest. Archer helped her into the Jeep, placing the food on the back floor before going around to get in the driver's seat. In moments he had them on their way.

"Did your mom arrive yet, or at least call?"

"Nope. As I mentioned, I didn't expect her to do either. She says she is coming and never shows up or calls to explain why." Archer shrugged.

Archer had mentioned briefly about his mom's visit. He'd said it with such bitterness she hadn't needed to wonder about their relationship. She hadn't felt it was her place to push for more details. Delicia didn't understand why the woman would promise to come see her son, then not show up or call. Delicia absently watched the landscape blurring.

She was startled awake as she was lifted. Blearily, she glanced at Archer's face.

"Wha—"

"Shh…I've got you. Go back to sleep."

Delicia trusted him and let herself float between sleep and wakefulness. She felt the shift as he unlocked her door then went inside. A thunk came as he kicked the door closed behind them. Archer carried her down the hall and to her bedroom. She sighed as he placed her gently on the bed. Delicia sat up, shaking her head then stumbled to her feet.

"Didn't get a shower. Can't go to bed this way." She went to the connecting bathroom.

Quickly she washed then donned a nightshirt. With a yawn she walked back to the bedroom. Archer stood by a chair across from the bed. She crawled in and he pulled the light quilt over her then kissed her on the forehead.

"Lower," she mumbled.

Archer chuckled then complied. His lips were gentle against hers then he was gone. Delicia slid into sleep.

* * * *

The sound of raised voices woke her.

"What the fuck are you doing in my cousin's house?"

"Damn it." She got out of bed.

Stomping to the door, she listened as she walked.

"None of your business, Justin." Archer's tone was calm.

"Get the fuck out!" Justin roared.

"I'm not going anywhere." Archer sounded unruffled.

Justin started screaming and cursing. Delicia increased her speed at the scuffling she heard. Racing down the hall, she then went around the corner to her living room where the noises came from. She slid to a stop and her mouth dropped open. Justin was throwing punches and Archer was blocking them effortlessly. He didn't retaliate. Justin lashed out with a leg and Archer blocked it, throwing out his hands and knocking the attack away. Justin threw another punch. Delicia rushed forwards and grabbed his arm.

"What the hell are you doing, Justin?" Delicia jerked him around.

His fist headed for her face, but he caught himself before it connected. Justin was breathing hard, his face furious. He lowered his arm. "What do you think you are doing?" Justin screamed.

"Don't fucking yell at me. What the hell are you doing in my house?" she growled.

"I came by and he was here. Opening the door like he lives here. Coming up in the world, Archer?" Justin jeered.

"Don't you speak to him like that," Delicia stated.

"Why not? It's true. He's n—"

"Don't say another word. Archer is welcome in my home. You, on the other hand, are trespassing. Get the hell out of my house."

"What? I'm family," he sputtered.

"Being family is the only thing saving me from decking you in your smarmy face. Get the fuck out." She pointed.

Justin eyes narrowed. "And if I don't, what are you going to do? Call the cops. I wish you would. Does

Leo know about this? How about Dimitri, or Jonathon?"

"I will. And you know Leo has no use for you. None of my brothers do. Do you really want to have to deal with them?"

Justin looked fearful. His eyes widened and he couldn't hide the shudder that shook his frame.

"That's what I thought. Now leave." Delicia sneered.

"You're going to regret this." Justin glared.

"I'm so afraid. Not. Get lost," Delicia said.

"You want me to put him out?" Archer's tone was cool.

Delicia studied her cousin then shook her head. "Nah. He's leaving. Aren't you, Justin?"

Justin left without another word, but he slammed the front door. Delicia locked it behind him.

"Damn nerve of him." She turned.

She gasped as she realised Archer was right behind her.

"I think it's best if I leave." His face was closed off.

"What? Why? Don't let him run you off." Delicia said.

"He's not. But I don't know how your family would feel about us being together." Archer shrugged.

"My family wouldn't care," she said.

Archer's look clearly said he didn't believe her.

"Okay, they would. But only because I'm the youngest and they are overprotective. They'll love you when they meet you. Be happy for me. Us," she insisted.

Archer looked doubtful. "I'll go."

"After all this about you wanting more than a roll in the sack, to be long-term. You're just leaving. The hell you are," Delicia growled.

She grabbed his hand, pulling him behind her. Archer stilled her.

"Don't make me pissed. Come on," Delicia said.

"This isn't pissed?" Archer asked.

"Not by a long shot. Now are you coming or do I need to get more forceful?" Delicia scowled.

Archer moved. She held his hand, pulling him behind her to her room. Inside, she led him to the bed then let go of his hand.

"Get comfortable and lie down."

He opened his mouth.

She put up her hand in warning. "No arguments. I'm tired, cranky and leaning heavily towards full bitch mode, so do whatever you need to do to get comfortable to sleep. Then get into the bed. We'll discuss this after I get some rest."

"Why do I need to lie down with you?" Archer sounded amused.

"Because I said so and so you don't get away," she snapped.

Delicia glared then slid into bed, turning away from him. There wasn't any sound for a moment, then his footsteps moved towards her. She smiled grimly. She saw him pass and go into the bathroom, closing the door behind him. The sound of the shower running reached her. After a bit, he came out with a towel draped over his shoulders. She licked her lips at his glistening bare chest and his unbuttoned jeans. Archer passed her again then the bed behind her dipped.

Delicia held still, wondering if she could actually sleep with him next to her.

"Del—"

"Just shut up and let me sleep," she snapped.

"God, you're a prickly woman when your sleep is interrupted."

"You'd do best to remember that," she grumped.

"I was just going to ask if I could hold you, because with your attitude I'm not sure if you won't take my arm off."

"Funny man." Delicia chuckled.

"I know," Archer quipped.

He slid his arm around her and pressed against her back. Delicia flattened her lips, stifling a moan. Her pussy flooded at his heat.

"Sleep," he whispered. His soft kiss ghosted over the side of her forehead.

How the hell am I supposed to sleep with your luscious self against me?

Archer held her, his soft breath filling the silence.

Delicia's body relaxed as she went to sleep. Arms around her, Archer smiled. Her fierce defence of him with the jerk Justin made him hard. But Justin's words had stung and brought up all his own doubts. He had thought that once he'd decided to go after her, he'd put them to rest, but Justin's words had reawakened those insecurities. Even Delicia's kicking Justin out hadn't stilled his uneasiness, though her snappiness and refusal to let him leave made him feel wanted. It was strange how he had come to think of her as his. He already knew where he wanted them to end up.

Am I willing to do anything for her? Including facing her family?

The answer to that was a resounding yes. As far as he knew, the Wright family was very down to earth. And close. They were well known around McKingley. He'd been around two of her brothers—Dimitri and Leo—often, due to their jobs and his owning the garage. Jonathon, another brother, was the more anal of them, and used his garage for anything to do with his car, demanding that only Archer work on his car, since he was the only one who knew how to treat it. And he'd commented more than once that the reason he came to Archer was because his garage was clean compared to most. Although he could do much better, but he was willing to overlook it since it didn't affect his car—Jonathon's exact words. The man had some major issues about being clean.

All of Delicia's brothers had always been personable and friendly. Dimitri was the most intense of the family and, from what he had heard, the most overprotective. Even their parents weren't as bad with interfering.

"I'm going to face whatever I have to for you, Delicia," he said softly.

He hugged her close and listened to her slight snore. Archer made a note to tease her about it. His lids lowered and he went to sleep.

Something woke him in what felt like no time at all. Brown eyes were studying him. Delicia had her hands crossed under her chin, propped up on his chest, and she lay partially on his body. There was an intensity to her study.

Her voice matched her expression. "I've been lying here going over the last week. I'm trying to understand why we're waiting to do the deed. At first, I took you at your word we were waiting for me to be sure about the long term. But now, after earlier, I realise something. It is not me who isn't sure. You're the one who is putting up barriers, Archer. I know what I want. I want you. The question now is—do you want me?"

Chapter Five

"With all that I am," Archer admitted.

"No more of that crap about running because of worrying what my family will think," Delicia said.

"I wasn't running," Archer protested.

She snorted. "You were."

Archer sighed. "I'll admit to a strategic retreat. But I'm all in."

"Be very sure, Archer. I'm stubborn and once I have my mind set on something, I don't let it go without a fight," Delicia warned.

"If I ever retreat again, don't let me go. I want you, Delicia Wright," he rumbled.

"Good... Ummm...you want to get something to eat?" Delicia lowered her lids partially.

Archer smiled. The fierce warrior was all of a sudden nervous. He stroked a thumb down her cheek. "Yeah."

Delicia moved to get off him. Archer held her, then arranged her over his body. She gasped as she cradled his erection between her legs. Delicia looked startled.

"Later. After we do the deed," he whispered.

Delicia wrinkled her nose. "That didn't come out how I meant it to sound."

"I like the sound of it. That's what I'm going to say to you whenever I want you. Let's do the deed, Delicia," he said against the side of her neck.

She shivered and moaned. Archer took that as agreement and turned her head, kissing her. She whimpered and sank deeper against him. Archer licked at the inside of her mouth. The kiss was carnal, wet and only stimulated his appetite. He rolled her beneath him and rocked against her panty-covered mound. Delicia dug her fingernails into his shoulders.

Archer pulled back then lifted her up, pulling her burgundy nightshirt over her head. He paused taking in the beauty before him. Delicia breathed harshly, her firm breasts moving with each breath. Her chocolate-coloured nipples were pointed — he licked his lips and resisted the urge to suckle them. Instead, he moved and knelt between her spread thighs, putting his hands on either side of her ice-purple coloured high-cut panties. She raised her hips and Archer pulled them off. At the sight of her bare mound, he growled, leaning down to inhale her scent.

Delicia whimpered, widening her legs. He went closer and licked from the top to the bottom of her slit. She shivered, making little sounds of need. Rising up, he let his eyes move up her body. She writhed on the bed. The flat pane of her stomach had a light sheen of sweat. Her ribs were moving up and down as she breathed and her breasts jiggled with each motion. Her full lips were wet and need blazed in her eyes. Archer kept his eyes on hers as he lowered his head. With his tongue he travelled the same path he had with his gaze. She moaned wantonly with each lick on her satiny flesh, arching as he pushed his tongue into her navel then laved above it. At her ribcage, he nibbled along the skin. The catch of her breath, then her moan, vibrated against his lips.

He nuzzled the underside of her breast teasing his teeth along it. The volume of her pleasure increased.

"Archer… pleas…e…"

He gave her what she requested. Moving up he dragged his teeth along her breast, up to her nipple, then closed over the bud. He suckled it and Delicia bucked. He held her down, taking his fill of her beauty. He slid across to the other nipple and did the same.

"Ar… Pl…Ummm…"

He moved up her neck peppering kisses along the way before reaching her lips. He blanketed her with his body, kissing her fiercely then gritted out.

"Do you have protection?"

"In…" She cleared her throat. "The bedside drawer."

Archer reached over where she gestured, finding it then sitting back. Archer reached for his briefs pausing when her hand covered his.

"Let me." Delicia's voice was husky.

He moved his hand. She sat up, legs on either side of his hips, and tugged his briefs down. He moved to kick them off. Delicia kissed his lips and he moaned as she covered his erection and began jacking it. Her fingers stroked along the hand that held the condom then she took it from him. Breaking the kiss, she lowered her head, smoothing the latex over his burgeoning shaft. Archer shuddered at the feel and sight of her hand on him.

He gripped her wrist then pushed her back on the bed, covering her body with his own. In one stroke, he impaled her. Delicia groaned loudly, shaking uncontrollably. Her pussy clenched around him.

Archer gritted his teeth at the sensation, struggling for control.

"Do the deed." Delicia's demand filled the air.

His control disintegrated and he thrust deeply into her. Going faster and faster. Her wild cries and movements matched his. They were in sync, moving towards the pleasure. Her nails dug into his back as she held him close.

"I neee... Del...icia," Archer moaned, unable to get deep enough.

"Archer."

She undulated her hips and slid her hot hands down his back to cup his ass and pull him deeper into her — he arched. Delicia tightened around him and wetness coated him. His balls went tight and he roared as he came. Delicia matched him spasm for spasm. He kissed her, swallowing her moans as she shivered. Delicia stroked along his back and Archer relaxed against her as she made soft noises over him, calming him.

Finally able to speak, he said, "Breakfast soon."

"When you wake up." Delicia chuckled.

"I'm not going to sleep," Archer slurred.

"Uh-huh."

He didn't even know when he gave in to sleep.

* * * *

Archer surreptitiously slid his foot closer to Delicia, where she was sitting on the other end of the couch. He glanced at her out of the corner of his eyes as he pretended to read a book. Delicia seemed to be engrossed in her own novel. He moved his leg closer then jerked as Delicia turned in a burst of movement and sprang until she was on top of him.

"Did you need something, Archer?" She smirked.

"You weren't reading," he accused.

"With you trying to be sneaky? Of course not. Is there something I can do for you?" Delicia straddled him.

Archer could think of a whole lot of things. Although they'd been having sex over the last two weeks, he still couldn't get enough of her. Every time they went somewhere, it was all he could do to wait until they got to one of their houses to have his way with her. Their breakfasts at The Enchanted after her shifts had taken on a whole new dimension. They ate leisurely, torturing each other into a sensual frenzy. Then went to one of their houses to relieve it. If it was one of his days to work the garage he would have to leave. The men had commented on his big goofy grin and his extra energy. They had no clue it was the idea of seeing Delicia that motivated him to finish so he could meet her. The weekend they'd planned for their overnight hiking trip was coming up in about three weeks—he couldn't wait to have her by the hot springs.

He kissed her leisurely, building the fire. Delicia moaned, grinding against him slowly. The phone ringing shattered the air. Delicia pulled back.

"Crap." She reached over his shoulder and picked up the phone. "Yeah…oh, Arissa."

Archer kissed along her face, not really paying much attention. Delicia yanked his hair.

"Let me ask Archer?" Delicia covered the phone. "Quit that. Arissa is inviting us to dinner. She wants us to meet someone."

"Me?" He was confused.

"Yeah, you. I told her about us. So is tonight good?"

"Sure," he said cautiously.

"No retreat," she warned.

Archer frowned. "I wasn't going to. Why don't you invite her over here? We can get some groceries and make dinner."

"You mean I can."

"No, we can."

"You can cook?" Delicia asked dubiously.

"Of course I can. Why would you ask that? I've made us breakfast a few times."

"We'll that was just breakfast. I've always cooked dinner."

"You get kind of possessive of the kitchen when you cook. I thought it best not to get in the way."

Delicia scowled. "I do not."

"You do," he said.

"You do." A voice on the phone echoed his.

Delicia glanced at the phone then put it to her ear. "Sorry, forgot you were there. Come over for dinner. Archer and I will cook." She paused then said, "I do not get possessive of the kitchen... Fine, I'll wait until you come and we can all cook together so I can prove it. Seven o'clock."

She hung up then threw the cordless on the centre table.

"I don't get possessive when cooking." She pouted.

"You do, but it's cute." He kissed her wrinkled nose.

"Cute?" she said in disbelief.

"Yep. Are we going to Lewis' for groceries?"

"Nope. Arissa and her mystery guest are bringing what we'll be cooking. We'll be cooking together," Delicia replied.

"Hmmm."

Delicia tapped her fingers on his chest. "Stop thinking about it."

He knew the comment of being possessive was on her mind.

"Well it is bugging me. I didn't know I got that way. Why didn't you tell me?"

"You never asked." He shrugged.

"It's a boyfriend's job to point these things out. It's in the handbook," Delicia said.

Archer kissed her fiercely. Delicia moaned into his mouth. He pulled her tight against his erection, pulled out of her mouth and licked along her bottom lip. He met her gaze.

"What was that for?" Her voice sounded thick.

"You called me your boyfriend."

"Hell, if that is all it takes to get you going then I'll call you that all the time," she promised.

Archer laughed.

Delicia enjoyed the sound and feel of his laugh. His massive chest shook where she lay on him. Archer sobered and his eyes got that glint she had come to know so well.

"You wanna do the deed," he said in a decadent whisper.

Her pussy flooded in readiness for him. Delicia didn't reply, at least not verbally. She leaned away pulling down his short pants and briefs, baring his big cock. Raising her housedress, she moved her pussy against his erection.

"You naughty woman. No panties. If I had known that I would have already had you," Archer said.

"I like being prepared," she whispered.

Delicia pulled a condom out of the pocket of her housedress and smoothed it over his cock. The heated flesh of his shaft was like silken steel. Rising up slightly she rubbed the spongy head of his erection along her slit. Delicia moaned as Archer's groan shivered along her skin. Moving forward, she lined him up and rocked forward taking him inside her. Archer gripped her ass.

Delicia moved back and forth against him, his hard length set off pulses of pleasure up her spine. She rocked faster and faster. Archer slowed the motions.

"Slower...deep...like that," Archer urged.

She struggled to move faster but he held her effortlessly, controlling her movements. The slow, measured, controlled thrust was driving her crazy.

"Archer...pl...ease...more. Damn you." She whimpered.

He chuckled, a wicked sound, moving even slower. He undulated his hips setting off a blaze of heat. Gasping, Delicia ran her fingers to her nipples, plucking at the tight buds.

"Play with them. Feed them to me," he ordered.

She leaned over, cupping his head with one hand and using the other to hold her breast to his lips. Archer suckled the nipple hard. The contrast between that and him having her made her shiver. He bit down on her bud and Delicia moaned loudly as she came, trembling against him. Archer's fingers tightened and he shuddered, coming with her. He continued to suckle her nipples as he rocked inside her. He collapsed back, relaxing. Delicia fell forward against him. He nuzzled the side of her face and kissed it gently. They lay there, calming slowly.

"I need to make a trip to my house. How does some homemade ice cream for dessert sound?" Archer said.

"Okay," Delicia agreed.

"In a little while."

* * * *

Delicia went around Archer, putting down the plates as he placed the glasses on the table. She grabbed the utensils and they finished readying the table together. She stood back and observed the table. It was laid with one of her favourite settings — cream plates with a blue and green mosaic pattern around the edge. Green wine glasses. A cream-coloured cloth covered the patio table and utensils sat next to napkins that matched the tablecloth. In the centre was a shallow earthenware bowl that served for the centrepiece of wildflowers they had picked up on the way back from Archer's house. The ice cream maker was ready to make the dessert.

"It looks nice, Delicia." Archer put his hands on her shoulder.

"It does. Thanks for helping." She turned and kissed him softly.

"Why are you so nervous?" He draped his arms over her shoulders, hugging her close.

"I'm not."

Archer didn't say anything. Delicia sighed and put her head against his chest.

"It's our first official dinner party we are hosting together," she admitted.

"Why is that important? It's just your sister." Archer sounded baffled.

"I know. I'm being silly," Delicia said.

She couldn't admit the truth. She really wanted Archer to see that her family was just like everyone else. That he had no reason to think they would not accept him. He hadn't brought it up again, but she didn't want anything to ruin what they had.

Maybe this was a bad idea.

"Stop worrying. It will be fine," Archer said.

"Okay," she breathed, hugging him.

The sound of the doorbell made her pull away. "I'll get the door. Check the coals for the grill."

Delicia left him outside. She walked to the door, running her hand over her sundress of various shades of orange, before opening it.

"Hey, Lis. Thanks for having us. This is Deiter Schneider."

From his name alone she assumed he had to be German. Delicia stared at the gorgeous man with her sister. He appeared to be over six feet. Just like her brothers. Deiter was well muscled with tanned skin, blue-grey eyes and an amazing white smile. His blondish-brown hair was a little shaggy but still close to his head. A dark blue button down shirt open at the collar hugged his chest and the sleeves ended just above his elbows leaving the rest of his muscular arms bare. She struggled not to look lower. His name niggled at her memory.

"Deiter? Are you the one who Tarak talks about in his emails? Who moved here a few months ago when he did? Working at the university or something?" Delicia asked.

"Yes, I am. It's nice to meet you, Delicia. Tarak and Arissa have told me so much about you," Deiter said.

"Lis, please." She shook his hand and studied him, wondering why Arissa wanted her to meet him.

"Honey. Go on through the kitchen and take the steaks to Archer. Introduce yourself."

Delicia eyes widened at the 'honey'.

"Okay." Deiter kissed Arissa then left.

Delicia stared after him as he walked away. His black slacks hugged a fine looking ass.

"No ogling my man." A hand smacked her on the arm.

Delicia continued to look as she replied, "I can't help it. He is fine. Not as fine as Archer, but damn, that is one sexy piece of man. What is with all of us getting such fine men? Katiya with Warwick. Now you and Deiter. How do you know him anyway?"

She returned her attention to her sister. Arissa had a rueful smile on her face. It piqued her curiosity. "Rissa."

"We met on my cruise a while ago."

"It must have been strange to meet him that way. Tarak talked about him often enough, but none of us met him," Delicia said.

"I didn't know who he was until I moved to McKingley."

"What?" Delicia could tell there was a story.

"I'll fill you in another time. Let's go out to join the men."

"You better tell me everything later," Delicia said as they walked towards the kitchen.

"I will."

She paused and put her hand on her sister's arm, stopping her before they entered the kitchen.

"Is it serious, Arissa?"

"Very. He asked me to marry him and I said yes." Arissa raised her left hand.

Delicia gasped and pulled it down so she could see the engagement ring on her finger. The starburst pattern amethyst was offset by four rows of diamonds on each side and had a band of braided white gold.

"Oh my God. That is a beautiful ring. Does the rest of the family know? I'm so happy for you." Delicia hugged her.

"Thanks. Told Mom and Dad. I wanted you to be the first of the siblings to know. Well, Tarak knows since Deiter showed him the ring before asking me. And

Deyon, since we're living in one of her apartments until we get a place of our own." Arissa returned her embrace.

Delicia squeezed her tighter. Arissa and she had been inseparable until she'd moved. Being the youngest, Delicia usually went to Arissa—who was the closest to her in age—when she had problems. She still did, in a fashion, by email when Arissa had been in Chicago. But when she needed someone closer she'd gone to Deyon, whose blunt attitude helped her immensely. At the thought, she realised she hadn't spoken to Deyon in a bit, which wasn't normal. No matter how busy they were, they kept in touch. Even if it was simply Deyon calling and leaving her a rude message on her machine for not calling her.

"Haven't heard from Deyon for a bit. I have to call her."

"Oh yeah, she mentioned she called a few times. Last time she left you a message and got no return call," Arissa said.

"She did?"

"Yep. Left it on your machine." Arissa nodded.

Frowning, Delicia walked over to the table under the phone. She checked the answering machine—it didn't seem to be broken. "My machine seems fine."

"Sometimes they mess up. Maybe you need to get voicemail instead."

"Maybe," Delicia replied.

Perhaps it had been when she'd been with Archer. But if so, why hadn't she got the message?

"The other times she left a message with Justin."

"With Justin? What was he doing in my house and answering my phone? I kicked him out," Delicia said.

"You did? Why?"

"He was acting the ass about Archer. But why was he in my house?"

"Does he have keys? If he does, you need to change the locks. He's always given me the creeps." Arissa sounded concerned.

"He d—" Delicia thought about it and cursed. "Damn, he does. I gave them to him to pick up something for Aunty, but never got them back. That was months ago." Delicia frowned, thinking of when she had come home with Archer the first time and Justin had been there. She wondered if he had been coming into her house that long.

"I'll have the locks changed and sign up for voicemail."

"I think you should tell Leo. If Justin has been coming here without you knowing, it's a problem," Arissa aid.

"No. It is fine. No big deal. I'll change the locks and it will be fine. Please don't tell Leo, you know how he is." She gripped Arissa's arm.

"Fine. If you promise to do it tomorrow."

"I will." Delicia glanced out of the bay windows to the back patio. "And no word to Archer either."

"Is it serious, Lis?" Arissa echoed her earlier words.

"I'm hoping it will be," Delicia replied.

"I'm here if you need me."

"I know." She hugged Arissa.

They walked out and joined the men. As the dinner progressed, Delicia watched the comfortable teasing and loving glances between Arissa and Deiter. She wanted that with Archer. Delicia observed him as he laughed and talked with Arissa and Deiter. He was such a sexy man. And she wanted him for herself.

"That was delicious, Archer. I've never had homemade vanilla ice cream in mango sauce before.

What do you make it with?" Arissa's comment brought her attention back to the conversation.

"It's made with —"

She didn't listen as they discussed the variations of the recipes. Delicia studied Deiter — he had a smile on his face. Deiter looked at her and leaned closer.

"She has a thing for food," he whispered.

"She does. Even as a kid." Delicia snickered.

"Tell me about it?" Deiter sounded curious.

Delicia filled him in on the misadventures of their family and food. Deiter chuckled and interjected in parts asking questions. Before she knew it, she was telling him about her job.

"Let me wash up," Arissa said.

"I'll join you. You all wrap up the extra food. Archer, make sure you give some to Deiter for them to take home."

"Yes, ma'am." Archer winked then kissed her softly.

He walked away to the plates and bowls by the grill. Deiter stood, kissing Arissa, then went to join him. She and Arissa cleared off the table before taking the plates into the house. Arissa filled the sink and started to wash. She rinsed the dishes then put them on the drainer. Deiter and Archer brought in the rest of the dishes and placed them on the counter by them.

"Here's the food for your sister." He touched her back.

"Thanks. Go watch some TV or something till we're done."

"Okay. Come on, Deiter, we're being banished to the living room so they can talk about us," Archer said.

"Behave, you." Delicia snapped a towel at him.

Archer dodged, laughing as he left the room. Deiter followed him out. She and Arissa watched for a while.

"I like seeing how you are with Archer. You all look happy."

"You do too." Delicia said.

"I am. Took some to get there, but it is worth it. Remember that, Delicia. No matter what," Arissa said.

"I will." Delicia was silent for a while then said, "I like Deiter. He knows how to get people talking and is a good listener."

"He is. I love him, Lis. I really do." There was a lot of emotion in her voice.

"I'm glad. And I can see he loves you too. I can't wait to see you walk down the aisle. Have you set a date yet?"

"Not yet. We're still enjoying being engaged," Arissa said.

"Once the rest of the family finds out, that'll change," Delicia warned.

"Mom and the aunts love Warwick being so into the wedding. It's driving Katiya batty. They're too busy planning Katiya's wedding to think about mine. Thank God."

"Please, you know the aunts love…heck…live for the planning and execution of a wedding."

"Oh, God. You're right. Maybe we don't have to tell them." Arissa mused.

"Mom probably already called them. They're lulling you into a false sense of security."

"Shit. Maybe I'll elope."

"Nope. They'll never forgive you if you do. The wedding is a better alternative."

"Probably." Arissa sounded forlorn.

"Buck up. It won't be so bad."

"I hope you say that when it is your turn." Arissa glanced towards the empty doorway. "Which might not be too much longer."

"I don't know where we are going. We're just letting it happen." Delicia ducked her head.

Arissa didn't say anything else. They finished cleaning the kitchen and headed to the living room. Delicia snuggled against Archer and Arissa sat in Deiter's lap. They watched TV and chatted. After they left, Delicia got ready for bed. The sound of Archer in the bathroom reached her. She wondered what it would be like to have him as her husband.

* * * *

Days later, she waited for Archer in his living room as he got ready for their excursion. Delicia couldn't get the thought out of her mind. The sound of the doorbell broke the silence.

"Delicia. Get that for me," Archer called from the bedroom.

"Okay." She went to the door and opened it. She spotted Archer's father first. "Hey, Mr Bennett, Archer is in the back."

"I've told you to call me Todd, Lis."

She chuckled at the familiar words.

"Why are you acting so familiar with the maid, Todd?" An imperious voice demanded.

Delicia turned her attention to the woman who came up the stairs behind Archer's dad. She looked as haughty as she sounded. Within a second, Delicia knew who she was looking at.

"Get Archer and be quick about it. Tell him his mother and his wife are here."

Delicia stiffened, glancing at the woman who joined Archer's parents. From Archer's brief mention of her, she had expected someone who looked malicious or uncaring. This woman was not only innocent looking but devastatingly gorgeous. She was a Nordic blonde with cornflower blue eyes. The woman raised one slender hand and pushed her hair out of her face. A small, warm grin curled her lips.

"Delicia, who is it?" Archer's voice came towards them.

She turned to face him as he came into view. "Your mother and wife."

Chapter Six

Archer glanced at her sharply, sure he hadn't heard her right. Then he looked at the people framed in the doorway. His dad looked amused. The two women with him were opposites. Although he hadn't seen her in a long time, he knew the woman with the haughty look had to be his mother. She had his eyes and a similar facial structure. The blonde on the other hand was a stranger. The woman smiled tremulously then pushed her hair over one ear and ran her hand down the tresses, worrying the edges. At the movement, realisation dawned.

No, that cannot be Lacy.

"No greeting for your mother and wife?" Victoria's voice was patently false.

"Ex," he snapped.

"Ex." A voice he remembered so well said simultaneously with his.

Son of a bitch, it is her. Archer studied the woman who looked nothing like the Lacy Donavon he had married or seen all those years ago when his son had died. The wild child he had married — the drunk — was gone. Or at least it looked like that externally. The soft curls of her ice blonde hair framed a face that seemed more ethereal. The cornflower blue eyes were guileless and open.

"Our bags are in the car," Victoria said.

Archer looked at her. "And they'll be there when you go to the hotel."

"I'm not staying in a hotel. Have the maid take our bags to our room," Victoria said.

Archer looked at her in disbelief, then at Delicia. "Did she just call you the maid?"

"She did. Twice already. Once more and I won't be responsible for what I do." Delicia smiled fiercely.

"Archer, why are you letting this woman speak about me this way? She's just a maid." Victoria's voice dripped with insolence.

"And that's it," Delicia said.

Archer shifted in front of Delicia, saying, "I've got this." He faced his mother.

"Vicky, stop showing your ass. This is Archer's girlfriend Delicia. Now say sorry to the nice young woman and act your age." His father's voice was steely.

"Victoria," she snapped, smoothing down the front of her blouse then said to him, "Archer, this cannot possibly be your girlfriend. I've brought Lacy with me."

He moved beside Delicia and put his hand around her waist. "This is my girlfriend Delicia Wright."

"Wright!" Her venom was even more pronounced.

"Yes. Now you can take yourself off to a hotel," he said gleefully.

"Now, Archer, I was just taken by surprise. Nice to meet you, Delicia," she gushed.

Her falseness sickened him. Archer turned his back on her, leading Delicia into the hall. Delicia was stiff.

"I'm sorry, Delicia. Let me deal with her and we can go to the Caves."

"Maybe you need some time to deal with that—" She stopped.

"Witch." He helped out. "No. Just go back to the bedroom and I'll get rid of them. Please."

Delicia stared at him then nodded. "Okay. If you need me call. I'll kick her in the shin for you."

"I might take you up on it later." Archer chuckled.

Delicia raised her face. They kissed gently.

"If she calls me the maid again I'm going to kick her somewhere else and make it hurt," Delicia whispered against his lips.

"And you have every right to," Archer said.

Delicia harrumphed then strode away down the hall. Archer returned to the door.

"I'm sorry that I insulted your lady."

"If only I could believe that, Victoria. I have plans, so go to a hotel or, better yet, leave McKingley," Archer said.

"Archer." His dad's tone was reprimanding.

Archer refused to back down. Victoria looked unsure then gave a small smile.

"Can I stay with you, Toddy-kins?" Victoria hooked her arms with his father.

Todd looked even more amused. "Sure."

Archer didn't like hearing that. "Won't your boyfriend have a problem with that?"

"Oh, Rudolph and I are through. It's just Lacy and I. Let's go to our home, Toddy-kins." Victoria was gripping his dad's arm.

Lacy was silent not watching any of them. Archer clenched his fist—he didn't want his mother staying under the same roof as his father.

"You can stay here," he gritted.

"That's wonderful. Show me to my room." Victoria looked pleased.

"I have plans. Pa will show you." He addressed his dad. "Pa, give them the rooms at the other side of the house." Archer turned to walk away.

"But, Archer, I wanted us to catch up. And for you and Lacy to talk," Victoria protested.

He ignored her and went back the bedroom. Opening the door, he spotted Delicia.

"Let's go."

Delicia followed him out. She didn't comment about his dad bringing in the bags. They got into her Jeep and drove to their destination. At the Caves they got in line and waited to be let in. Archer's thoughts returned to the mess back at his house. The thought of being under the same roof as his supposed mother and ex pissed him off.

They arrived at the entrance and were given a map of the Turquafel Caves. The caves were made up of turquoise, quartz and feldspar. Its name derived from the minerals. They were large and high. The walls created a visual delight. People went into the many cave passageways, which led to the centre where wild outcropping formations made of the local minerals and rock resided. He'd been to the cave a lot of times and usually enjoyed it, but today it lacked the joy. He trailed Delicia as she explored.

"That's it," Delicia said, pulling him into a little corner. "Where are you?"

"What do you mean? I'm here with you."

"Physically, but mentally you're back at your house. Why didn't you just stay there instead of coming here? We could have done this another time," Delicia said.

Archer rubbed his hand over the back of his neck. "Christ. Sorry. I don't want to be back at my house. Hell, I don't even want to sleep at my house with them there."

"Why'd you let them stay?"

"Victoria was going to stay with my dad otherwise." Archer shrugged.

"Your dad can take care of himself," Delicia pointed out.

"Maybe, but I don't want to take the chance. So it was my house."

"You can stay with me if you want," Delicia offered.

Archer stared, surprised, then shook his head. "You don't have to do that. I'll—"

She put her hand over his mouth, pressing against him. "Just shut up and nod your head. You're staying with me." This time it was a demand.

Her eyes were fierce. Archer nodded. Delicia removed her hand and kissed him. He tugged her firmly against his frame, but she withdrew.

"I'll drop you off later to get some of your things. Forget about them for a while. Now let's have some fun. Explore a little."

Archer let her pull him with her. "I'd rather explore you. Wanna do the deed?" He wiggled his eyebrows.

Delicia laughed. "Later. I want to explore the cave and go for our bike ride."

"And I want to ride you."

"Behave and I'll let you later. Now come on." She pulled him along.

Archer laughed and went with her. They had fun in the cave. In the centre they took pictures of each other then asked someone else visiting the cave to take their picture together. Once they left the cave, they headed to Lendro Peak for biking. After they got there, Archer took down the bikes.

"Jackson. How are you?"

"Lis, little sis, how's things," someone with a deep voice said.

Archer watched as Delicia embraced the tall, broad-shouldered man.

"Been meaning to come see you." The man smiled widely, making his craggy face light up.

"No prob. I'm sure you've been busy getting settled in to McKingley and the new job. I didn't know you biked?"

"It's a new pastime. I'm loving it." He leaned closer. "Also a good way to get a certain stubborn man out of the house."

"I heard that," someone else said.

Tarak Brady walked up to join them. He was like a brother to Delicia and her siblings.

"Tarak, you've been hiding out in your house. Shame on you not coming to see me." Delicia hugged him.

Tarak squeezed her. "I knew you were busy with work and training for the triathlon."

"Humph. That's an excuse," Delicia said.

"If you say so." He tweaked her nose. Tarak glanced at Archer then put out his hand. "Archer. How have you been?"

Archer shook it. "Good. Harmon mentioned he hadn't seen you come by the shop. He has a piece he wanted you to check out."

Tarak looked intrigued. "I'll have to make a trip to see him."

Tarak glanced at Delicia talking to Jackson, then at him. "Heard you and Delicia are dating. Hurt her and you'll answer to me." He smiled widely then joined Delicia.

She glanced at him then said, "Sorry, Archer. Jackson, this is Archer. Jackson is a friend of the family. He moved from Chicago with Arissa and is working at the hospital."

"Nice to meet you, Jackson."

"And you." Bright blue eyes studied him then the man put out his hand and they shook.

"We'll have to catch up, Lis. I've got to get home so I can get ready for work," Jackson said.

He hugged her then kissed her cheek. Tarak did the same before they departed.

"Tarak is looking much better."

"Yeah, he is," Archer agreed.

"We'll, let's get started," Delicia said.

They got on their bikes, putting on their helmets. Delicia took the lead as they rode up one of the more difficult trails. Delicia had asked previously if he wanted an easier trail, but he had said no. He followed her as they traversed the sometimes tight and twisty single track along rocky then smooth ripping paths. Delicia pulled off and he stopped, stifling a moan. He was fit, but the trail had been difficult.

"Do you want us to turn back?" Delicia looked on towards the trail.

"I do, but you can go on if you want," Archer said.

"Umm…"

"Go on." He urged.

"Are you sure?" Delicia said.

"Go ahead. I'll head back and wait for you in the Jeep," Archer said.

Delicia gave him the keys then kissed him briefly. "Okay. Meet you in a bit."

Archer watched as she biked away. He was amazed at her stamina. He'd known she was training for the triathlon, but today showed him how fit she was. Archer turned back and went back to the Jeep to wait for her.

* * * *

"Thanks for being so understanding," Delicia said for the fourth time since arriving back to his place.

"Stop saying that, Delicia. It was nothing. You are really good at biking. I'm proud of you. How much longer until the triathlon?"

"A little under two months. I'm getting nervous."

"No need to be. From what I've seen—at least biking—you are fast. I had barely made it back to the Jeep when you came behind me. I couldn't believe you had ridden to the end of the trail we were on and gotten back so fast."

Delicia smiled. "Still need to pick up my time."

"You will. I'll meet you at your house in a bit." Archer kissed her and got out of the Jeep.

Delicia beeped her horn then left. Archer stood at the end of his drive and watched her taillights disappear before he went to the front door. Opening it, he frowned at the sound of the TV playing. He bypassed the living room and went to his room, packing a few things before heading back to the front door.

"Archer," Victoria said behind him.

"What?" Archer gritted his teeth.

"I was waiting for you to return so we can talk. Do you think it is a good idea to be dating her? Really, Lacy is much better suited for you. Sh—"

"Not another word. I suggest you shut up or I'll put you out."

"I'll go stay with Todd." Victoria sounded smug.

It was what he wanted to avoid. "I'll be staying with Delicia until you get out of my house. I'll be back tomorrow for some more things."

"But, Ar—"

He slammed the door shut behind him, cutting off what she was saying. Archer strode to his truck then got in. Glancing at the house, he noticed movement on the porch. Lacy waved from the swing on the porch. Archer ignored her and headed for Delicia's. As he drove away, the tension drained from him and instead, eagerness to see Delicia filled him. In less than ten minutes, he'd parked in front of her house. Grabbing his bag, he went to the door before ringing the bell.

Delicia opened it. She was in one of those flirty housedresses he had come to obsess about getting off her. This one was blue. Archer stepped in, closing the door with his foot. Delicia backed up. He stalked towards her, unbuckling his pants and pulling down the zipper. He took out a condom and smoothed it over his cock. Delicia moaned, her breath coming fast. She swerved and her back hit the kitchen's doorjamb. Archer closed the distance between them. He lifted her up and Delicia raised her housedress—she had no panties on. She wrapped her legs around him and Archer groaned as her hot slit pressed against his aching shaft.

He shifted his hips and slid into her wet, heated slit. Delicia whimpered. He thrust urgently, gripping her butt. Delicia's nails bit into his shoulder. Closing his lips over hers, Archer swallowed the sound she made. He pounded into her, moving towards their release. Delicia countered his movements, grabbing then releasing his shoulders. The hitch of her breath signalled she was getting ready to come. Archer increased the speed of his thrusts. The base of his stomach tightened. He dug his fingers into her ass.

Delicia wrenched her lips from his and screamed. "Archer... Yes...please."

Her pussy clenched around him, rippling as she came. Archer shook as he joined her in pleasure. Panting, Archer held her as she shivered. Delicia rested her sweat-soaked forehead on his shoulder.

"What the hell was that?" Delicia asked breathlessly.

"Pent up need from waiting to do the deed." Archer chuckled.

"Let's wait more often," Delicia said.

"No," he stated firmly.

He slid his hand under her ass, holding her more firmly against him then strode down the hall.

"I need a shower," Delicia whispered.

"We both do. Then we can do the deed some more," Archer replied.

"You enjoy saying those words a little too much," Delicia groaned.

"And you love it."

"True. So come on, man. Let's wash then get to doing the deed." Delicia smacked him on the ass.

Archer sped up, taking her to the bedroom.

* * * *

Archer parked his car in his driveway. He sat there for a moment praying for some patience. For the last three weeks, whenever he'd gone to his house for clothing to stay with Delicia, Victoria had taken it as an opportunity to give her unwanted opinion about Delicia. She was trying hard to have him 'come to his senses' that they were not right for each other and that Lacy was his supposed soul mate. The only reason he hadn't pitched her and Lacy out on their ears by now was because of Delicia.

Surprisingly, she had calmed him on more than one occasion about Victoria. He didn't want any secrets between them and shared all his mother had said — usually he'd raved about it and threatened to throw his mother out and never speak to her again. Delicia was the voice of reason who talked him down. Delicia was sure of their relationship — she said nothing Victoria said could change what they had, unless he let it. Delicia's surety and calmness was what kept him from ejecting them. The one thing Delicia stated was that she was not going to be around either woman. She couldn't promise what she would do to his mother if she said the things she did to Archer in front of her. Archer was in complete agreement. Delicia hadn't been by his house or around both his mother and Lacy since that first day.

Archer glanced at the clock in the dash. He had to get his bag and get back to Delicia's. They had made plans over a week ago to go to Morrow — a supper club — for dinner and dancing. He needed to clean up at her house before they could go. He got out of his vehicle — the sooner he got his things the sooner he could get back to Delicia. He'd come straight from the garage, as he usually did. He'd even added more grease and grime to his person. It was the one thing he noticed that would keep Victoria at a distance as she spewed her crap — she didn't want to get her perfection dirty. He strode into the house ready for another round. The silence startled him. The TV was always on in the living room. Suspicious, Archer went to peek in. There was no one there.

Breathing a sigh of relief, he went and quickly packed. He returned to the kitchen to get his mail. Turning to leave, he stopped. Lacy stood just in the doorway of the kitchen. She looked uncertain.

"Ummm...sorry. I didn't realise you were here. I'll go." She backed out.

"Why don't you just pack your shit and leave McKingley? I don't want you, no matter what Victoria thinks," Archer said.

Lacy halted and snapped, "I don't want you either."

Archer stared at her. "Then what the hell are you doing here?"

"I just...wanted to talk with you. Victoria was the only way I knew I could at least make it through the door," Lacy replied.

Archer frowned. He thought of the last few weeks, realising he hadn't seen much of Lacy when he'd come by. He wondered what she had been up to.

"Say what you need to say then leave." He leaned against the kitchen counter.

Lacy came into the room tentatively and sat on a stool by the island. She played with the placemat. Her head was bent forward, her hair shielding her face.

"We never got to talk about...our son," Lacy said softly.

Archer stiffened. "There is nothing to say. You killed him with your drunkenness."

Lacy flinched then slumped even farther. "I know. I was in a bad place. And I'm sorry, Archer. So sorry for that. Sorry you didn't get to know him."

"What, you're clean now and this is one of your steps? Am I just supposed to offer you absolution? Is that what you're here for, Lacy?"

Archer crossed his arms over his chest. His heart raced and pain filled him. Lacy stood slowly, her body rigid.

"No, that's not what I want. Why I am here. This isn't about you, Archer. This is about our son." Her voice broke and she took a shuddering breath, shaking.

Archer clenched his fist.

Lacy seemed to pull herself together. "About doing right by him. I don't want or need your forgiveness. I can't forgive myself, so how could I ever expect you to? I'm here to tell you whatever you need to know about your son. Something I should have done a long time ago. When you are ready to know, to talk about him, call me. I'll be leaving as soon as I pack."

Lacy turned then walked to the doorway. She moved as if in pain. Archer watched the woman he had eventually married in a drunken rush. Although their marriage had been short and volatile, he had loved her as a friend first. He went over to her, pulling her back against his chest. Lacy stiffened. Archer put his head on top of hers, as he had done often when they were together.

"I don't know if I can ever forgive you, Lady...but...I'd like to know more about him."

"I haven't heard that nickname in a long time, Risk. It doesn't fit anymore," Lacy said tearfully.

"It does and always will, Lady." He held her.

Lacy sighed, resting back against his chest. Archer inhaled the familiar rose scent of her. Lacy patted his arms around her waist then stepped out of his embrace to face him. The impish look in her gaze was one he recognised from the past.

"You do know Victoria won't stop if you keep being a nice guy. She's a real bitch."

"Language, Lady." Archer laughed.

"It's true. She has it in her head that if we get back together she can get to your money. She doesn't know you very well." Lacy shook her head.

"Victoria only cares about herself. And nothing outside of what she wants matters. She'll get it." Archer shrugged.

"I hope so, before she does something stupid." Lacy's expression became serious. "I for one think you and Delicia are meant for each other. Even in high school I could tell you had a thing for her."

"I didn—"

She put her finger over his lips, stilling his words. "You did. All of us on the cheerleading squad knew it. Hell, they warned me to keep away from you and I did until…that night." Lacy closed her eyes briefly. "I never thanked you for saving me from him."

"Shh…that was never necessary."

"It was. You kept saying I never needed to thank you, but you didn't have to save me. And I thank you for it. It is what brought us together. First as friends then lovers. So some good came out of it. Meeting you and being together," Lacy said softly.

Archer drummed his fingers on the countertop. "It was the right thing to do. No man has the right to force a woman."

"Very true. But he isn't a man. He's a worm. I've spotted him around town but avoided him."

"Keep away from him, Lady. He hasn't changed just gotten worst." Archer said.

"I plan to. Now, off the memory train. You don't let Delicia get away from you. Promise me, Risk," Lacy said.

"You always were a bossy thing."

"And you know it. I love you and always will. I want you to be happy." Lacy cupped his cheek.

Archer smiled uneasily. "Okay."

Lacy snorted. "Not in a love, love sense you goof. In the used to be my friend and then husband, but I still care one. Please, you aren't even my type anymore."

Archer frowned. "What's that supposed to mean?"

She rolled her eyes. "Yes, you are a big strong man and I should fall at your feet and praise the gods that made you."

"No need to be sarcastic, Lady. I get it." Archer chuckled.

"Now go to your woman." Lacy patted his arm.

"I'm on my way. Where's Victoria?" Archer asked curiously.

"I have no clue. I was coming back from my walk when she left. I think it might have been just before you arrived." Lacy shrugged. She turned and walked away.

"Do you miss Tony, Lacy?" Archer said.

She put her hand next to her head on the doorjamb then whispered, "Every single day."

"Me too. I will...want to take you up on the offer of talking about him. But not yet. I'd like if you can, for you to stay a little while longer so we can talk about...Tony." Archer cleared his throat.

"I can stay for as long as you need. Took a sabbatical from my job," Lacy replied.

"Okay. Thanks. What do you do?"

"I'm a counsellor for victims of violent crimes and grief," Lacy said.

Archer was shocked. Lacy glanced back at him.

"I have lots of experience with it. Might as well use it. I'm going to take another walk. Need to clear my head a little. Have fun at Delicia's." Lacy walked out.

Archer didn't try to stop her this time. He picked up his mail and bag then headed for his car. He paused by the living room door. *Where the hell is Victoria?*

* * * *

Delicia turned on the pedestal, looking at the outfit in the various mirrors. The halter-top shirt had a handkerchief hem, the peach and white flower design of the fabric complemented her skin. A sweetheart neckline and princess cut gave definition in the right places. The matching pants had an intertwined white and peach scalloped crocheted lace at the bottom of each leg that rested just below her knees. Delicia put out one of her feet. High-heeled sandals left her toes bare—they were painted a pale peach with a white design. Frowning at herself, Delicia wondered how she'd let herself be talked into polish on her toes, for Christ's sakes.

"She looks good. And it suits her, if I do say myself," Deyon De'clare said.

"And it keeps with her not being much of a dress person," Arissa said.

"And will bring him to his knees to kiss her delectable toes. Don't you agree, honey?" Katiya Wright, her other sister, said.

A man with inky-black, shaggy, shoulder-length hair came into view in the mirrors. He was very big— muscular and intense. He walked around to where she stood on the pedestal and stopped when he faced her, studying her out of indigo eyes. He joined her on the raised platform and took her hand. He raised it to his lips and kissed it gently.

"Delicious. If Archer doesn't fall to your feet, call me. I'll gladly do it." He winked.

"Warwick, behave." Katiya sounded amused.

Warwick Taylor winked again then released her hand. He slid his arm around her waist and turned her to face the trio of women. Delicia had asked Deyon to make her an outfit for her date with Archer. This was their first date that wasn't so athletic and she wanted it to be special. Deyon had done it gladly, spending hours and working late to get it finished in under a week. Delicia was unsure what Deyon would come up with, since she wasn't into really feminine clothing—she was more a pants and shirt woman. But now, seeing the outfit, she'd admit Deyon had matched her athletic side with a sophisticated, sexy one perfectly.

"You have done an excellent job, ladies," he said.

"Like I need you to tell me that," Deyon snorted.

"You know you're fabulous." Warwick blew her a kiss.

The women glanced at each other uneasily. Delicia bit her lip, stifling a laugh. They had convinced her to use her getting her outfit to teach Warwick a lesson, which seemed to be failing.

"And now that the show to convince me to back down on wanting to take part in every step of the planning for my wedding to Katiya is over, I'll head home." Warwick got down then kissed Deyon and Arissa on the cheeks.

He pulled Katiya into his arms and kissed her thoroughly. Pulling back, he ran his finger over her cheek.

"See you at home later." Warwick strode to the door of the fitting room then paused. "Katiya?"

"Yes, honey."

"Don't honey me. It wasn't necessary to torture me with a day at the spa getting pampered with four women to have me back off. All you had to do is ask. You're going to make this up to me. Now, I need a drink." Warwick blew out a breath yanking open the door then walking out.

"I will make it up to you, honey," Katiya promised.

"Christ, who knew women could talk so much. Or there were so many places to pluck, tweak and all that shit. I didn't want to know all that. Leave some mystery on the process to the wow. Wait until Calix, her brothers, Tarak and the others hear this shit. I'll never live it down. I've been plucked and tweaked. Have polish on my damn nails and toes. I don't care if it's clear. It's polish, for fuck's sake. Yeah, I need a really strong drink." They could hear his muttering as he disappeared from view.

They waited a few moments until they were sure he was gone then started to giggle. Delicia stepped down and collapsed on the large couch with the other women. They laughed hard.

"That was so mean. Hell, I felt like I was being tortured *tooooooo*." Delicia leant back chuckling.

"He had me worried for a bit. Took it all without a complaint. And yeah, he will be ribbed about this." Katiya wiped her wet eyes.

"Serves him right. Questioning me about the type of dress and fabrics and all that. Hell, he knew more about fabric than you did," Deyon said.

"He's been researching it. He's a computer geek with unlimited access to info at his fingertips. His assistant called me and begged me to help. He was driving her crazy with showing her swatches of fabrics and wedding things. I know he wants to be part of it, but it was getting ridiculous. When he called Mom and the aunts to set up a planning session I knew it had gone too far. He had to be stopped." Katiya shook her head.

"I'm glad we did it. Maybe Deiter hearing about Warwick's experience will stop him from falling into madness. He was already making noises about wanting to be in on the process. Hopefully this will nip it in the bud." Arissa made a cutting motion with her fingers.

"Still think it was mean to poor Warwick and to me. Funny, but mean." Delicia chuckled.

"And you were a good sport about it, Lis. Thanks for going along. Now, tell us about you and Archer," Katiya said.

"Ummm…there's nothing to tell," Delicia said, standing.

Deyon pulled her back down onto the couch.

"Girl, I made a dress in a week for you. Worked my fingers to the bone. You better be giving up some details. And as graphic as possible." Deyon wiggled her fingers.

Delicia tried to say nothing, but they prodded her until she spilled about her and Archer. They listened and laughed, teased and made raunchy comments. When she discussed his mother, they got loud.

"She did not call you the maid. Did you deck her? Please tell me you decked her," Deyon said.

"No—"

"Why the heck not?" Katiya said.

"Just a little *pow* to the kisser," Arissa added.

"Hush, you violent wenches. Let me talk." Delicia laughed, then explained why she hadn't.

"Aw...I always liked Archer's dad. He is cool. Used to come by my house and change my oil when I was out of town for an extended time. Archer does it for me now," Deyon said.

"He's why Archer is the way he is," Delicia said.

"Yeah. He raised Archer right. Made him a hell of a man. So, when's the wedding?" Katiya asked.

Delicia blinked, startled. "We're just dating. Not engaged."

"Not yet. But you all sound serious. And Archer strikes me as a man who goes all or nothing. He's going to propose, I know it. Listen to your big sis," Katiya said.

"Yep, he is. And then I will make you a fabulous wedding dress and bridesmaid gowns. Just set a date after these two, so I have time," Deyon added.

"At least you'll know some of our measurements," Arissa said.

"Yep, saves some time. I'll just have to get the sizes for the other bridesmaids she picks."

Delicia let them talk around her. There was no doubt who some of her bridal party would be if she got married. That was a big if. They hadn't even got that far. Hadn't even said the three little words. Delicia stood, then went behind the curtain to the changing area to undress and put on her street clothing. She held the garment as she returned to the open area.

"Let me get a bag for you for that," Deyon said.

She left, then came back holding a garment bag with Deyon's and the shop's logo on it. Deyon put the outfit inside and zipped it up. She put the shoes in a shoebox that had the same logo then into a bag, also with the emblem.

"I'm glad you had shoes to match the outfit," Delicia said.

"You're lucky I did. I didn't design any. Thankfully the shoe maker and designer on staff had something. Now, have fun with Archer."

"Thanks." Delicia replied, then waved at her sisters.

She strode to the door. As she stepped into the hall, she glanced down the empty expanse. The room they'd used was the largest—it was Deyon's personal room. She knew there were six more rooms down the long hall, which were used for custom designs or fittings. She passed them as she left. Entering the main room of the boutique, Delicia took in the spacious floor, bustling with customers. Racks of clothing were set up throughout and there were couches along the walls for people to sit. There were changing rooms close to each sitting area, which could be used for people to try the stock from the floor.

Deyon's catered to full-figured women. Every item was designed by Deyon, including accessories and lingerie. She even did some of the shoes. She believed in outfitting from the inside out and head to toe. The shop had affordable as well as higher end clothing, and other items on the rack made in mass amounts. They changed based on availability once what was made had sold out, then if there had been a high demand for the item it might be made again. If not, another design would take its place. They also designed on a commission basis. Deyon was a sought after designer and had lines she'd created for most fashion weeks around the world. She was also an ex-full-figured supermodel. A custom design by her was worth a lot of money.

Delicia glanced at her garment bag. Deyon had refused payment for it, instead asking her to donate some money to her favourite charity—an animal habitat. Delicia peered at the time then skirted the people in the shop and answered the greeting from some of the staff and customers as she passed. Finally outside, she hurried to her Jeep. She drove out of the parking area and onto Atkins Street. This area had a mix of middle and upper scale businesses and homes. She glanced at Morrow when she passed it. People were already dining at the supper-club. Delicia returned her attention to the road and headed home.

* * * *

A while later, she was dressed and ready. Frowning, she headed for the living room. With a look at the clock over the mantle, she noted it was already after five. They had reservations for six. "Where's Archer?"

She picked up the phone on the end table to check her voicemail. The sound of the doorbell stopped her. After replacing the receiver, Delicia went to the door and opened it.

"About t..." Delicia's eyes narrowed as she viewed the woman standing in the doorway.

"Delicia, we need to talk," Victoria said.

Chapter Seven

Archer headed to the side of the house his unwanted guests were using during their stay. At the room he'd put the woman who'd birthed him in, he paused then rapped sharply two times. No response, so he opened the door and peered in. The room was immaculate, almost like she'd never even slept there.

Just like when I was growing up – she was never around.

With a disgusted sigh, he backed out and headed for the front door. The moment he got in his truck and had the diesel engine running, a work call came over the radio. He glanced at the clock and swore. *I'm already late.* He knew it would not go over well with Delicia. Especially when the reason for his tardiness was Lacy. *The ex-wife makes me late to meet the girlfriend. Nope, so not gonna go over well.*

His chat with Lacy had been enlightening, for sure. He'd always had a soft side and a crying female brought it out. So despite everything, his own anger included, he'd momentarily been quieted and he'd done what he'd never believed he would do—offered

Lacy Donovan, his ex-wife, comfort for *her* killing their son.

Would he do it again? Doubtful. However, his anger wasn't as sharp anymore. Definitely still there, just not as intense. Shaking Lacy from his thoughts, he growled low at the repeated call over the radio.

"Archer? You out there?" Dani questioned.

He took another glance at the time. "I'm here, Dani. What's up?"

"Sorry to bother you, boss."

"It's okay, Dani." He knew she wouldn't have called unless it was urgent. And absolutely imperative. "What's going on?"

"There was a big pileup on Canyon Road and they need the flatbeds."

Goddamn it! "On my way." He turned left instead of right—the direction which would have taken him to Delicia. As he drove, he called Delicia. Impatience rose up in him as her phone rang and rang. Finally, the machine picked up and he listened to the computerised voice ask him to leave the number and nothing else—she wasn't home. Then he left his message.

"Delicia, hon, it's me. Pick up if you can hear me." Nothing, so he pressed on. "I'm so sorry to have to do this, but I have to cancel tonight. I know I'm already late and that's what makes this worse. I have to go, there's been an accident, and I have to take one of the flatbeds out to the scene. I was really looking forward to tonight, Delicia," he said. "I'll call you when I'm done." He ended the call, tossed his phone down on the seat beside him, and drove the rest of the way to his shop, muttering under his breath about how unfair things were.

He parked his truck then jogged inside to claim the largest of the flatbeds. Dani sent him an apologetic look as he passed her—one that changed to a smile of gratitude when he winked and grinned at her, showing he wasn't angry. It was his business after all, and if someone was needed, it was his job to fill in.

After heading for the largest of the trucks, he opened the door and climbed up. Moments later, the bay door was open and he drove out on his way to Canyon Road.

Shit! The carnage made his stomach curdle in horror. This was the worst accident he'd seen in a long time. The sun had begun to lower in the sky and as he parked behind the row of flashing lights, his eyes narrowed against the glare. Slipping on his sunglasses, he shrugged out of his suit coat then laid it along the seat. The tie soon followed and he jumped out with the sleeves of his shirt rolled up. Habit had him grabbing the reflective vest and he slipped it on as he walked up to where people were gathered.

Sirens pulled his attention away from the group and he noticed the ambulance speed away. *Delicia.* He pushed her from the front on his thoughts and cleared his throat to get their attention.

They met his gaze and one officer stepped away, telling him what should go first. With a nod of understanding, he walked to his truck then got to work. As the powerful machine hauled the first one on the flatbed, he rolled his shoulders to try to alleviate some of the tension. It didn't work.

"Bennett."

The deep voice sounded familiar. Glancing to the right, he spied Leonardo Wright—Sheriff of McKingley—approaching. Instinctively he bristled before he got himself back under control. Basically, so far, only Arissa had been in his business about being with Delicia. Well, aside from Justin. But he didn't count that sorry excuse for…

"Sheriff," he replied, telling himself he may be here because of the accident.

"What's going on with you and my sister?"

Guess it's not work related. "Nothing that concerns you."

"Arissa said you'd say that."

He didn't reply—there was no point. Focusing back on the car, he shut off the motor and got to work securing the mangled mess of metal. Leo was still standing where he'd left him when he came back around and grabbed the hook for the next car.

"That's my baby sister."

"I'm sure there's a point there," he said dryly.

"What are your intentions?" The question was growled.

"Look, I know I'm not the type of guy you'd pick for your sister and I'm okay with that. All you need to know is she picked me."

"Of course you're not the guy I'd pick for her, hell, none of us would." Leo held up a hand, which kept Archer's mouth shut, then he continued, "But not because of what you're thinking. She's our baby. Always has been and she always will be." Leo ran a hand over his head then put his hat back on. "Lis was so sick when she was born, we never thought that she'd make it. Touch and go for the longest time."

Archer's heart clenched and he longed to hold her. He'd not known that. After quickly hooking the next car up, he moved back to the switch and threw it before giving Leo his attention.

"She hated having to stay behind and struggled to get better. It's part of why she loves being outdoors so

much. For the longest time, she couldn't be out in it."
Leo shook his head. "Look, all I'm saying is, we're
over protective of her. All of us. I know we don't
know one another very well, but I think you're good
for her. You have this calming aura around you and
that's what she needs. Lis likes to go full speed all the
time without thinking about resting."

He nodded—he'd noticed that. "So this isn't a
brother telling me to stay away from their sister?"

Leo's eyes burned with a fire that was more than a
bit unsettling. "No. This is a sheriff telling you not to
hurt his baby sister."

He got the message and sighed. Perhaps Delicia had
been right and her family wouldn't be as opposed to
them being together as he'd believed. "I don't have
any plans to hurt Delicia."

Leo shook his head. "You are like the only one who
calls her that. Even our parents call her Lis. Why is
that?"

He shrugged and answered honestly. "Lis is yours.
Delicia is mine." There was no way to hide the
proprietary tinge that drenched his words and he
didn't care. His heart had belonged to one woman his
entire life and now that he had her, he did not intend
to let her go.

Leo's eyes narrowed slightly, but again, Archer
didn't care. He didn't anger easily and had nothing to
prove to anyone other than to Delicia. He'd always
called her that, since he'd seen her and found out who
she was. To everyone else she was Lis, baby sister to
the Wright family. To him...she was Delicia. *His.*

Her brother seemed as though he wanted to say
something else, but all that stopped when the radio at
his side crackled and a voice called out to him.
"Coming," Leo said. "This isn't done between us,

Bennett. I will do whatever is necessary to keep my sister safe."

"Do what you feel you need to," he said with another shrug.

Then just like that, he turned away and focused back on his own job. He did sneak a final look at the man striding away. Leo Wright. Second oldest brother, third oldest Wright sibling. Archer wasn't well acquainted with the older siblings. Arissa was the one he knew best and accredited for his meeting Delicia. The Wright sisters had been walking through the empty halls at school when he'd spotted them and even then, Delicia had taken his heart. And since Arissa had stopped to talk to him, he'd got to meet Delicia.

Her smile—while shy—had warmed him from the soles of his feet to the top of his head. She'd looked up at him with her big eyes, the colour of which reminded him of chocolate mousse, her cheeks tinged with a blush, and that was all it took. Her mumbled 'hi' had made him forget he stood there sweaty from football practice, made him forget everything but Delicia Wright. And how she smelt of tangerines.

Over the years, none of that had changed. He wanted only her. Sure, he'd dated, but even when he'd woken up the day after he had drunkenly married Lacy he'd known his heart belonged to Delicia.

Christ, I'm pathetic. He laughed at himself and got back to work. He was there well after dark and knew it would be even longer, since he still had to unload. Dani met him with a hot, fresh cup of coffee.

"Go home, Dani," he said, accepting the cup and sipping some of the steaming brew. You've been here all day."

"I'm pulling a double. I'll crash in the backroom and keep the radio beside me just in case any more calls come in."

"Who's on the schedule to cover night runs?"

"Shaun."

He nodded, content she'd be well looked after. Shaun Jones was one of his most trusted tow truck drivers. "Go get some shut eye, I'll pop my head in before I leave."

She gave him another smile then walked away. He really needed to pay her better for all she did around here. With a sigh, he trudged outside and got to work. By the time he finished, it was bearing down on the witching hour and he no longer looked like the man who'd intended to take his woman out for a night on the town.

He was sweaty, had a cut on one hand and was exhausted. After saying bye to Dani, he climbed into his truck and headed towards the one place where everything felt right in his world. Delicia.

* * * *

Delicia stared at the woman on her porch. Hoping, praying, begging it was nothing but a horrible hallucination. *Please. Please. Please. Please!* The woman shifted and stepped closer, causing her to sigh with resignation. *Great, just what I needed. Of course, she couldn't be a figment of my imagination.*

"What do you want?" she asked, not bothering to temper her irritation. There was something about this woman that made her long to hiss or growl in warning. She flexed her fingers around her cell phone she'd grabbed on her way to answer the door. She'd just been about to call Archer.

"Let's go inside."

Seriously? Like she'd let this woman breach the walls of her sanctuary. "No. You'll stay out here. Say what you will then leave."

"You need to leave my son alone."

There it was. No beating around the bush, nothing. She ground her jaw but held her tongue. Victoria had a very familiar look about her. One that reminded her of...Justin. They both had this coldly superior gleam in their eyes. That desire to hiss slammed her again.

"He and Lacy made a great couple and they will again. So you stay out of their lives."

She glanced at her nails and recalled Warwick's complaint about his being polished. It almost made her smile. Hers were coloured as well, which was unique for her—she didn't do girly. But her sisters had wanted her to, so she had for them.

"What makes you think you know what's best for Archer?" she asked in a bored tone, finally glancing up to stare at her unwanted visitor. Definitely unwanted.

"I'm his mother!" she snapped, her eyes flashed angrily.

"Hmm, really? Because from where I'm standing you're nothing but the one who carried him. A mother doesn't run out on her family."

"You know nothing about my family!"

"You're right. I don't. I know you weren't there for Archer. That you ran away to be with one of numerous boyfriends. I know you made a young man numerous promises and never fulfilled one of them. But like you said, I know nothing about your family because from where I'm sitting, Archer and Mr Todd, sure as hell aren't part of yours." She took a step towards the intruder to her solitude. "You are a vain and selfish woman. Everyone knows you're back just to try and get your hands on Archer's money, but I don't think getting me out of the way is going to stop him from seeing through your damn charade."

"You..."

"I'm a lot of things," Delicia said. "None of which includes me being intimidated by you. So I'm only going to say this once — stay away from me."

Her eyes narrowed. "Archer is my son, I'll be damned if you get one cent of his money."

Delicia couldn't help it, she laughed. Despite the urge to hit and scream at this woman, she merely gave a sharp burst of humourless laughter. For the first time in her life, she did what she'd always hated Justin for doing, she used the power her family's name held.

She looked down her nose and said in a haughty tone, "I'm a Wright, I don't need your son's money. I don't need anyone's money."

They clashed gazes for a few moments and she saw Victoria try to regroup. Taking advantage of her silence, Delicia pressed forward. "You aren't worth that man's love, never have been and from the looks of things, you never will be. Leave him alone. Leave me alone. Leave us alone."

Victoria's eyes narrowed in anger. "My son will come to his senses and get rid of you, even if you are a Wright."

"Is that so? Well, in that case you have no reason to stay on my porch. Get the hell off my property." Turning around, she reached for the doorknob.

"We're not finished."

Delicia pivoted back. "Yes, we are. Get your ass off my property or I'll call the cops on you. And, in case you were wondering, my brother is the sheriff." She stared at the evil woman. "You set foot on my property again and I'll have you arrested for trespassing."

"You wouldn't," she seethed.

She licked her lips and leant forward. "Try me," she dared.

"This isn't over," Victoria said, stomping down the path to a waiting vehicle. "He will never be yours. Never!"

Foot tapping, Delicia crossed her arms and glared her out of the drive. Rage flowed hot and fast inside her, but she kept it in. She'd always tried to be good and stay calm, but damn if that woman didn't make her want to just...

The roar of a motorcycle brought her head up. She watched the red and black Ninja roll up her drive. With a smile, she headed down to meet her visitor. A welcome one, this time.

"Thom," she said, when the engine fell silent. "What are you doing here?"

He removed his helmet and grinned at her, then lifted a brow and delivered a wolf whistle. "Look at you. Damn, Lis, you look hot."

"Thanks. What are you doing here?"

"I came by to drop off a..." He trailed off and got off his bike. Once his helmet sat on the seat he pulled her in close. "Oh, sweetie, what's wrong?"

Until he asked the question, she hadn't realised there were tears streaming down her face. She sank against him, trusting he would keep her up. He smoothed his large hands up and down her back. She wanted to get away. Before something else happened she couldn't control.

"Come on," he said.

"Where?"

"I'm taking you home with me."

She sniffed. "Don't you have a hot date or something like that?"

"She'll keep."

And just like that, Delicia knew it would be okay. That was why she loved Thom so much. He was the perfect friend. He wouldn't ask nosy questions like her family and his loyalty was to her, not one of her brothers, so nothing she said to him would go any farther. He kissed her cheek.

"Get on the bike, I'll grab your keys."

He jogged off and she grabbed the extra helmet before carefully pulling up her dress a bit so she could straddle the bike. While she waited, she called Archer. Nothing. She hung up with a sigh. Moments later, Thom came back and got on. She slid her arms around him and soon the powerful engine turned over and he got them on the road to his place.

Once they arrived, they rode the elevator in silence to his third storey loft. She kicked her heels off by the door and padded barefoot across his smooth wooden floor. As she made her way to the kitchen, he picked up the phone and made a call. She tried to reach Archer at the same time, but it went straight to his voicemail so she hung up, biting the inside of her cheek.

"Sorry, darling, something came up and I won't make it tonight. Yes, I'll make it up to you, promise." He hung up and walked to stand in front of her.

"I am sorry I'm making you miss a date."

"No one makes me do anything, Lis. She's a piece of ass, you...are my friend. You'll always come first."

She gave him a wobbly smile and he spun her in the direction of his bedroom.

"Get changed into something more you."

She didn't argue and soon wore a baggy shirt and pair of his shorts. Thom was in the kitchen whipping up some food and she sat on one of the stools. Barely breaking in what he did, he reached into the fridge, withdrew a lager and slid it to her. Then he went back to cooking.

"Archer and I were supposed to go to Morrow's tonight," she said after a good, healthy swig of the lager.

"I figured you were going somewhere. You don't wear dresses."

She stared at her painted nails and her lips curled in disgust. "No, I don't."

"So what happened?"

"I don't know. He didn't show. But his mother did."

Thom said some words that would have made trucker blush. He knew about Victoria. "Let me guess, she wasn't exactly throwing out the welcoming mat."

Another few sips. "I don't know why it bothers me. I know she's a bitch. But Jesus, Thom, his ex-wife is living in his house. I offered for him to stay with me, but she's living there. Like she has every right."

He set a plate full of steaming food down before her. Her stomach growled at the fare. Soon he joined her at the island.

"So the bitch is at his place, Lis. He's staying with you. That should tell you all you need to know."

She sighed. "I know, it's just…missing the date, not answering calls and the mother showing up on my step is kind of overwhelming."

He stared at her so long she began to shift on the padded stool.

"What?"

"Are you okay? I know you're busting your ass for this triathlon, but are you ensuring you get enough sleep, Lis?"

"I..." She shrugged. "I don't know, Thom."

"Okay then, what you need is a night of movies and junk food. Come on," he ordered, grabbing his plate and walking towards his sofa.

With a smile, she followed him. She knew he would listen to her and even give her advice whether she wanted it or not. But, bless him, he also knew when to back off and let her have her space. Like now. Movies were non-threatening.

She sat down beside him and grabbed his remote. Flipping through the selection, she found the one she was looking for and pressed play. She took the nail polish off and felt better. The beer, food and movies helped her relax and she fell asleep, finally free of the worries that had been racing through her mind.

* * * *

Come morning, Thom had waffles, eggs and fruit ready for her. After they ate, they went down to his bike and he gave her a ride home. Her heart jumped at the sight of Archer's large white truck parked in the drive. She hopped off the idling bike and gave Thom a hug, conveying her gratitude. The slam of a screen door had her glance to the porch.

Archer stood there, arms crossed over his bare chest, pants hanging low on lean hips and enticing her all too much even from the distance he was. She swallowed, flexing her fingers in the material of her dress, then she waved to Thom before walking up to her house in heels, and Thom's clothing.

Indigo eyes watched her walk the entire way. She wasn't sure what to make of his silence. Archer was laid back and easy going but this...something screamed danger and damn if she wasn't a bit hesitant.

His look burned her and he flicked those intense eyes between her and the motorcycle. His large body blocked the door. She trailed her hungry gaze over him, his golden skin. Hard muscular physique with defined pecs and abs she'd never get tired of exploring. Powerful legs encased in jeans and he had bare feet. Back up to his stony expression. His tousled dark brown hair appeared as if he'd been raking his hands through it.

She swallowed. "Good morning, Archer."

"Are you okay?" he questioned through clenched teeth.

"Yes." And she was. She did feel much better now.

"Good."

She glanced at him. "Excuse me, I need to get ready for work."

The fire in his eyes vanished and she felt goosebumps pop up on her skin. Silent, he slipped aside and held the door for her, ever the gentleman, her Archer was. She moved by, doing her best to ignore the scents which made her think of nothing but him and her. The door clicked behind her and she'd gone three steps before he spoke.

"Delicia."

She turned and was taken aback by the emotion in his gaze. "Did you have a good night, Archer?" She didn't want to fight, just wanted to get ready for her day.

"No." His muscles rippled. Damn man truly was a work of art. "Did you?"

"After a fashion," she admitted. She tossed the dress at him. "Here, in case you wondered what I was wearing last night."

He snatched it out of the air and pain sliced across his expression. "I called you, Delicia," he said.

She rubbed her eyes. "I called you, too, Archer. I have to get ready for work."

"Shower in a minute, we need to talk."

"I don't need a shower. I did that at Thom's. So talk." She rotated to walk back to her room, only to find herself pressed against the wall with Archer blocking her in.

"You're wearing his clothes." The sentence was low and angry. "You smell like him."

Lord it was hard to think when she just wanted to kiss him. "I stayed at his house. And like you said —"

"Five seconds," he growled, interrupting her.

"Excuse me?"

"Get out of his fucking clothes, Delicia."

"Are you jealous?"

The gleam in his gaze gave the answer. "Three seconds."

Delicia stripped the shirt off and pushed the shorts down. "Better?"

"No. Not until you smell like me and tangerines like you usually do." He kissed her hard, demanding her submission. As soon as she gave it, he backed off. "Why?"

"Your mother showed up at the door when I was expecting it to be you. Then Thom arrived and I really needed a friend. I had to get away."

She could see the agony in his expression, but his touch on her remained tender, yet possessive.

"I called, but you didn't answer," she said.

"I'm so sorry, Delicia. It was the accident on Canyon Road."

"I figured it had to do with work." She shook her head. "I have to get ready to go in."

He lifted her in his arms and carried her to the shower. "Mine!" he growled as he slanted his lips over hers.

Oh, yeah. She could definitely get used to showers like this.

Chapter Eight

Archer leaned against the railing and watched as the first few males crossed the finish line. His heart was up in his throat as he waited for the woman who wore number two-oh-one. He'd been living at her house since his mom and Lacy had arrived. They didn't seem in any rush to leave McKingley and while he hated them in his house, he loved being in Delicia's with her.

It had been almost two months since their missed date at Marrow. Things had been rocky, but they'd moved passed it—or so he'd hoped. When he'd woke this morning and found her already gone, he'd called his dad in to cover for him and headed up near Taos to be there for her. None of her family was going—when he'd asked her, she'd just shaken her head and said no.

Given what Leo had told him the night at the accident, it surprised him none of her family would show. Personally, he wasn't about to miss this for anything. He'd only seen her once and knew she hadn't seen him. Pride filled him at the knowledge of what she was doing. People jostled him on each side, but he refused to give an inch. He would be at the finish line when she crossed.

"Not surprised to see you here."

The voice from beside him drew his attention away from the exhausted runners. He bit back a snarl as he looked over and saw Thom standing there in a sleeveless white shirt and a pair of shorts. He really didn't like this man, or how close he was to Delicia.

"Look, man. I know you don't like me, but don't you think for Lis' sake we should at least try to get along?"

"Why?"

Thom laughed. "Because I'm not going anywhere so you may as well get used to me. She's my friend."

"The kind of friend who you let wear your clothing and sleep over?" Anger began to grow as he recalled that morning when she'd arrived on the back of his motorcycle.

"That's exactly the kind. The kind her boyfriend should have no problems trusting her with. Because Lis and I are only friends." The reprimand was there, and not all that subtle.

Archer reined himself back in and swallowed, the dry air making him long for a nice cool drink. "Why are you here?" he asked.

"I always am. Lis never had anyone else to come with her so I always do. I was shocked to see you weren't driving her, but now that I see you here, I'm guessing she just kind of left."

"I woke up and found she was gone."

"Well, am I correct in understanding you'll be taking her home today?"

"Yes."

Thom nodded and peered around him. Archer didn't know what it was, but he felt the prickle go up over his spine and he, too, glanced off to the approaching runners.

He skimmed the men until his heart thudded loudly. There. Delicia ran behind two men, the white and green of her outfit identifying her. Her bone straight hair bounced in its ponytail and was a darker honey hue than normal. The sun glistened off her sweaty body.

The closer she came the harder his heart pounded. Her sunglasses obscured his view of her eyes so he had no clue if she knew he was even there or not. Thom began to move and Archer followed. He watched some cross the finish line and collapse. Delicia crossed amid resounding cheers, for she was the first woman to do so. Thom's arms were there and Archer almost snapped at him until he heard what he said.

"Walk, Lis. Don't fall over. Walk and cool down."

She took some water from an attendant and dumped it over her head as she did as Thom ordered then tossed the cup to the side. Archer followed and they got out of the way of those still crossing.

He stood silent as she paced around, cooling down. She stayed focused on Thom and he didn't much care for that.

"All right, Lis," Thom said. "You should be fine now. I'll see you back in McKingley."

She reached for him. "How am I supposed to get home, you dolt? I rode with you."

Thom grasped her shoulders and turned her. "You have a ride home." Then with a kiss to her cheek, he slipped off into the crowd.

"Archer?"

He moved towards her, unable to make out her expression. Was she unhappy he was there? Reaching out, he cupped her cheek and smoothed his thumb over her damp skin.

"I am so proud of you, Delicia," he murmured.

"Why are you here?"

"Did you really think I wouldn't come?" he countered.

"You were sleeping when I left."

A smile turned up one corner of his mouth. "Delicia," he began. "I always know when you leave the bed. Always." He lowered his mouth to hers and kissed her. She moaned slightly before pulling back. "What?" he asked, frustrated she ended it.

"I'm all sweaty."

Yes, she was. He chuckled and pulled her flush against him. "I don't give a damn, Delicia." He closed his eyes when her arms went around him and for a moment, the world belonged to the two of them. No racers. No spectators. No news crew. Nothing but him and her.

It was short lived, for soon people wanted to talk to her. He waited while she answered questions and posed for pictures. Then he waited some more while she went to grab her bag and take a short shower. When they finally made it to his truck, she looked beyond beat.

"Do you need to eat?" he asked as he held the door for her.

"I should, but damn it, I'm so exhausted."

"Sleep while we go somewhere."

He closed the door and hastened to the driver's side. She'd already reclined the seat back and had her eyes shut. So he started the engine and with the AC on low, he drove away and back towards McKingley.

They stopped for dinner an hour later and Delicia still looked worn and drawn, but she gave him a smile. They ate slowly and when they were on dessert, he placed his fork on his plate. He leant forward and stared at her. She took a bite of her cheesecake and lifted her brows.

"What? Did I embarrass you with how much I ate?"

"No."

"Then what?"

"Do you have any idea how impressed I am with what you did today?"

She began to wave it off, but he refused to let her.

"No. I mean it, Delicia, you were...are amazing."

"Please don't," she said.

"Why don't you like compliments?"

She shifted and didn't look at him.

"Delicia?"

"I just don't like them."

He sighed but let it go. There was something so innocent about her sitting there. He wanted to gather her close and never let her go. "Okay, Delicia." He paid and they carried the dessert with them. Once she was back in the truck, he brushed his lips over hers then got them back on the road.

It was dark when they made it back to McKingley and as he turned up the street towards her house, he reached over, and shook her awake. "Wake up, Delicia."

"Are we home?"

Three words which he'd never thought would make him so happy. "Yeah, we're home."

"I'm ready to sleep for a week," she muttered.

He smiled. Only to have it wiped away in the next second when he heard her gasp.

"What is it?"

"Something's not right. Let me out here then block the driveway so he can't leave."

He frowned but listened. She jumped out and he did as she'd ordered before shutting off the engine and scrambling after her. Delicia ran up her drive and to the front door.

"What is it?" he whispered in her ear when he caught up to her.

She didn't respond, instead burst into her house, and yelled, "Damn you, Justin! Where the hell are you?"

All protective instincts went on full alert the moment she mentioned Justin. The bastard stuck his head around the corner and there was shock on his features, which smoothed away to be replaced by false cheer.

"What's up, Lis?" Justin asked, then glared at him.

"You've been stealing from me, haven't you?" Delicia thundered, moving towards her shiftless cousin.

His eyes narrowed on her and he shrugged. "You didn't even miss the stuff. Besides, I needed the money."

"Then go out and get a fucking job, Justin." Another step.

"You're just like your brothers, always on their high horse about what I should do. You have money, I should have money."

"I have it because I work for it, dumbass. I don't drive a Ferrari and I don't live in a house I can't afford."

His expression morphed into something pathetic. "You won't tell will you, Lis?" he whined.

"Yes, I will, Justin. You've abused my goodwill for the last time. You've erased my messages and stolen from under my nose. Call Leo, Archer."

Justin looked at him with a feral glint in his eyes.

"You call your brother, Delicia. I'll keep an eye on Justin."

Justin popped his neck and sneered. "You think you can take me, boy?"

Archer moved around Delicia and held his gaze, the anger he'd had at this piece of trash his entire life flaring to the surface. "I know I can. I kicked your ass when we played football against one another and I can do it now."

Justin let out a primal cry and charged at him. Archer braced himself for the hit, more than ready to deal with this confrontation, years in the making.

Delicia cringed as she watched her coffee table—one she'd made herself, using pictures she'd taken as the top under a clear lacquer—became kindling underneath the thrashing grown men. She'd called her brother and now stood to the side waiting for him to arrive.

She didn't try to stop them—she knew this went way beyond Justin being in her house uninvited—again. However, watching them went against everything she stood for. She'd become an EMT to help people, not to stand there and watch them beat the shit out of one another.

Flashing lights and sirens grabbed her attention and she went to open the door. She cringed as Leo's car drove up on her front yard. Two others followed him and she stepped back as her brother shouldered his way into her house.

"Jeez, couldn't you not ruin my yard?"

"Really, Lis? You want to do this now?" He held out a hand to the two deputies behind him and said, "Hang on a minute. Go check his car to see if he put things in it."

"What about them?"

"I'll stop them."

The men left and Delicia looked at her brother. "Would you stop them, please?"

The look he gave her told her he'd rather let Archer continue to pummel the shit out of Justin, but he sighed and stepped closer to them. "Break it up!" he said in a deep voice that did wonders in large crowds. The men kept fighting. "Damn it, Archer, I said break it up!"

A final crunch filled the air and Delicia inhaled deeply as Archer shoved to his feet, leaving Justin on the floor. Blood streamed from the cuts on his face, but Archer definitely looked better than Justin did. Her cousin appeared to have gone through a meat grinder.

"Arrest him!" Justin squealed. "He attacked me for no reason."

"Shut up, Justin," she and Leo said at the same time.

"Sheriff?" Dave stepped back in the room. "We found some paintings in there."

"Catalogue it and then you can go. I'll handle this."

"You sure?"

"I'm sure."

Delicia walked by her brother and moved closer to where Justin stood, only to stop at Archer's touch. He pulled her to him and kept her anchored to his side. She looked up at him and said, "Let me get my bag and I'll clean you up."

"Sheriff!" the call came from outside full of urgency.

Everyone ran out and Delicia's breath caught in her throat. In her now-open garage stood Lacy, beaten and bruised with torn clothes. *Oh my God.*

"Lacy!" Archer's voice seemed torn from his chest and he shoved by her heading towards the woman.

"No!" Justin screamed, his voice high and strained to the point it was no longer human.

Time seemed to slow as Delicia saw her cousin, who even looked like a wild animal, grab a sidearm from the other cop who'd come to the door. In a split second, Leo's was on him.

"Drop it, Justin."

"Archer!" The word was laced with venom.

The other cop who'd been with Lacy appeared with his gun drawn as well. Two guns on Justin and one on Archer. Honestly, the only one Delicia gave a damn about was the one on Archer.

He turned slowly, hands outstretched. "You just had to go back and do it again, didn't you, Justin?"

Again? What was he talking about?

"You self-righteous bastard. Lacy was mine. You came between us."

Delicia frowned but stepped back out of the way at Leo's look.

"No. I stopped you from beating on a woman. I should have said something then."

"No one would have believed her anyway. I'm a Wright, she's nothing but a slutty Donavon."

"I will never stand by and watch as a man hits a woman. I don't give a damn what his last name is," Archer growled.

"Which is why I'm going to kill you."

Fear ballooned in her chest. Justin said it with such calm, so matter-of-fact, it chilled her to the bone.

"Put the gun down, Justin," Leo said again.

Justin didn't seem to hear him—he lifted the gun a bit higher. Delicia didn't think time could move any slower, but it did. The shots were almost simultaneous and she screamed, unable to stop the noise from racing from her chest.

Justin went down and Leo was at his side immediately, kicking the gun away and pushing her back. She looked for Archer and found him. Alive, holding Lacy in his arms. Radios crackled beside her and she heard them calling for the ambulance.

She ignored her cousin lying there and neared Archer and his ex-wife. "Come on, Lady," he crooned in a deep, comforting voice. "Don't leave me."

That was when she noticed it. The large bloodstain growing on Lacy's chest. Her training kicked in and she ran all out, despite her exhaustion, to her house where she grabbed her bag from its resting place by the door and headed back out to Lacy.

"Lay her back, Archer and get out of my way," she ordered.

He did as he was told only to settle by her head and stroke her face. "Why, Lacy? Why?"

"I miss Tony so much," she wheezed. "Now I can go be with him."

She flicked her eyes to Archer's face. He was totally focused on the woman who'd both borne and taken his son from him. Shutting them out, along with the pain the emotion on his face caused her, she got to work.

Five minutes later, she skimmed her lower lip with her tongue and sat back on her haunches. She'd failed. Lacy Donavon lay in her front yard, dead. She wanted to scream, cry and yell, but she did none of those things. She closed the woman's eyes and drew a sheet, given to her by one of the cops, up over her.

Archer knelt beside her, head down, bloodied hands resting on his thighs. She wanted to touch him, to offer comfort, but he seemed to be within himself.

"I'm so sorry, Archer," she whispered when the cop left.

He lifted his head, but those amazing indigo eyes seemed to see right through her. "I know you did everything you could, Lis."

Her heart broke as he pushed to his feet and headed for his truck. Leo reached out a hand to stop him only to drop it when she shook her head. She didn't move as he got in then drove away.

Lis. He'd called her Lis.

Leo approached and helped her to her feet. "You okay, Lis?"

"I tried to save her, Leo."

He pulled her close. "I know you did. You always do." He kissed her cheek. "I have to go take care of the Justin thing."

She stared at her dead cousin with dispassionate eyes. "Good. Get his fucking car off my property as soon as you can." With a heavy heart, she went to gather up her things.

Delicia sat on her porch until all the flashing lights left, all the lookie-loos went back inside their own homes and all that was left was her and her exhaustion. She'd spoken to her family and told them not to come over — all she wanted to do was sleep. But now that she sat there alone, she realised alone was the last thing she wanted to be. She wanted Archer, but him calling her Lis and staring through her, didn't inspire much confidence.

Exhaustion pushing her, she stumbled to her feet and went inside her house. After a long hot shower, she crawled into bed and was asleep before her head hit the pillow. When morning came, she was still alone and there was no sign of Archer.

With a groan, she got up and ready for work before walking slowly to her Jeep. She could still see some of the blood on her rocks, but she ignored it, making a mental note to clean it up.

* * * *

Over the next five weeks, things progressed in the same way. Yes, she saw Archer, but he'd become different. Distant. His mother had left—where, she didn't know or care, but Archer had withdrawn into himself. And honestly, she didn't have the energy to fight right now. When they did spend time together, he was subdued and quiet.

Saddened and feeling alone, she met Thom at the ambulance after a very uneventful weekend. Thankfully, he was as he always was, just what she needed. When they were on the road, he handed her a card and she looked at it before glancing back to him.

"What is this for?"

"Remember the two men I introduced you to about a year ago? The Kline brothers?"

She nodded her head. "Yes. They had the training facility in Washington State."

"They're here in town and want to talk to you."

Delicia swallowed once then nodded. Last year had been extremely rough on her and she'd debated whether she should even stay in McKingley. Thom had got her in touch with these two men. Maybe it might be worth talking to them.

"Set it up."

Thom smiled. "Already did. Meeting them tonight at Bella's."

"Thank you, Thom."

He reached across the interior and squeezed her leg. "You know I love you, Lis. I just wish you'd tell me what's wrong and what I can do to help you get through this."

It was tempting to tell him, but she kept it to herself. She was private. Always had been. Always would be. "I love you too, Thom. And thank you. We just have to get over this hurdle." However, she wasn't even sure that would be enough.

The day passed with surprising quickness and soon she found herself heading for her brother's law office. When she was waved back, she cracked the door open and peered around the edge. "Got a minute?"

"For you, Lis, always." Jonathon closed the file and gestured her in while getting up to greet her. After sharing a hug and kiss, he gestured her to the leather couch and sat nearby on a matching chair. "What's up?"

She licked her lips and forged ahead. "I need to borrow your car."

He gave a short, disbelieving bark of laughter. "My CL600? Are you serious?"

She held his gaze and gave him her patented baby sister plea. Jonathon had never been able to say no to her, especially with her eyes shimmering with tears, just poised to flow over. It didn't matter he knew they were crocodile tears—he hated to see her cry.

"I just got that car, Lis," he said.

"I won't hurt it, Jon," she said indignantly.

He ran a hand over his head. "Why do you feel you need my car?"

She wouldn't meet his gaze and she knew he was suspicious. "It would just be for the rest of the day. I'd bring it to you late tonight or early tomorrow morning."

"Why, Lis?" He added the tone he used in the courtroom when a witness was treated as hostile.

Her hands rubbed along her legs. "Can't you just lend it to me?"

"Did your Jeep break down or something like that?"

"No," she replied immediately. "I just want something classier for tonight."

"Dimitri has trucks."

Her sigh said it all. She didn't want to go to her eldest sibling. Dimitri had a way of acting like one of their parents.

"Tell me why."

Her sigh was one of resignation. "I have a dinner meeting with some people and I didn't want to take my Jeep."

"Dinner meeting? And you need my car."

"Yes."

"So this isn't with Archer?"

She wouldn't meet his gaze. "No. It's a job offer."

"Look at me." She did and he narrowed his eyes. "Are you leaving McKingley?"

She shrugged. "Nothing's concrete yet. Please don't say anything to anyone. I just want a vehicle other than my dirty Jeep to climb out of in my dress."

He pushed to his feet. "Don't keep this from everyone, Lis. Including Archer." In that sentence, she realised he really liked Archer.

When he exhaled heavily, she knew she'd got her way. After he took her to his vehicle, she left him with a kiss and a wave then headed off to prepare for her evening.

Chapter Nine

Archer stared at the box on the table before him. It had arrived today and he'd yet to have the courage to open it. He knew what it was—stuff from Lacy she'd kept of their son's.

Lacy. He couldn't believe she was gone. Justin had done it, he'd actually killed her. Moreover, he hadn't been able to save her. She'd given her life to save him, stepping in front of the bullet Justin had meant for him. He felt like he'd failed her again. He couldn't manage as her husband and he couldn't save her.

"I'm sorry, Lacy," he said, reaching for the box.

Lifting a knife from beside him, he slit the tape and folded back the flaps. His hands were shaking as he reached in and withdrew a few aged photos. The boy even looked a bit like him, same dark brown hair as opposed to Lacy's Nordic blonde. Tears stung as he flipped through all three of them. There wasn't much stuff in there. Just a letter addressed to him telling him how sorry she was for her actions and what she could remember about Tony.

In the bottom lay a toy soldier, a dinosaur and a tow truck. He sat there for a few minutes staring at the items, and mourned the loss of his son. The son he'd never had a chance to know.

The house was silent as he grieved and when he finished he carried the contents of the box to his office and put them up so he would always have a connection to Tony. His mother was gone. After Lacy had been murdered, he'd come home and kicked her out, not in the mood to deal with her. So with the promise of retaliation if she ever went near Delicia again, he showed her the door and told her with no equivocation that she was never welcome at his place again. Where she went, he didn't know. Didn't care either.

He picked up his phone to call Delicia, only to hang up when the doorbell rang. With a groan of disappointment, he snapped it shut and walked to the front of his house. He missed her—there was this chasm growing between them. Even when they made love there was something missing. Yes, it was amazing as all get out, it always was with her, but the connection he'd felt before was gone.

He needed to get in touch with her for a talk. After reaching for the doorknob, he swung it open. He arched one eyebrow as he stared at his visitor.

"Can I help you?"

"What the hell did you do to my baby sister?" Jonathon Wright demanded.

Archer took in the youngest Wright brother. Six feet tall, he was well dressed in an expensive suit and had a serious expression on his face. Correction—he had a fierce scowl on his face.

"I'm sorry?"

Brown eyes bore back at him. "Don't play dumb, Bennett. Why else would she be interviewing for another job—an out of state one at that—if you hadn't done something to her?"

His stomach clenched and he felt nauseated. *Leaving?* "What are you talking about?"

"She's interviewing for a job in Washington State right now with two guys. So I'll ask you again, Archer Bennett. What the hell did you do to my baby sister?"

"I didn't do anything to her. Where is this meeting at?" He needed to go. He needed to stop her from leaving him.

A harsh chuckle. "I'm not telling you where it is. I debated even telling you period, since she told me she'd not mentioned it to you. So I figured you'd done something to run her off and that, I don't like. Our family is supposed to be here, not leave. We just got Arissa back and I'll be damned if I lose my baby sister because you two are having some kind of lovers' quarrel. So get your ass to her house and fix it."

"How do you know about this?"

"She came to borrow my new Mercedes." He scowled. "My brand new Mercedes."

Archer kept his shock contained. He'd heard that Jonathon was buying a new one, but he'd never known him to let his siblings use any of his cars. "Thank you for telling me."

"Don't make me regret having done just that. Fix this. Make my baby sister happy again. I hate to see her sad. And I promise you, if I know she's sad, so does the rest of our family."

He got the message. While the Wright siblings might be okay with him dating their sister, they wouldn't put up with him hurting her. Not that he wanted to. With a nod, Jonathon walked back down to his

Mercedes SUV and drove away without another word.

Glancing at his watch, he noted the time. Eight-thirty. He hurried back inside and showered before dressing in jeans and a T-shirt. Keys in one hand, he made sure to have his phone and wallet in the other as he headed for the door. Once in his truck, he made one stop before driving to her place. It was almost ten by the time he arrived and saw there was only the outside light on.

Pulling in the drive, he parked next to her Jeep and smiled at it as he got out. This vehicle personified everything he loved about Delicia. Real. Earthy. And a trooper. He trailed his fingers along the dirty, scratched and dented vehicle as he moved around it towards the steps.

He unlocked the house and walked inside. After putting his bag down in the bedroom, he made his way back up to the front and sat out on the porch in her rocker-glider. He was antsy, yes. But he'd waited for her for a long time and he would keep on waiting. So, feet propped up, he did just that. He waited.

It was close to midnight when headlights crossed the house as a low car swung into the drive, its powerful motor purring. He sat up a little bit. The engine shut off and the door opened, warm light spilling out into the night.

His cock jerked in his pants as he stared at her. *Damn!* She hesitated when she looked at his truck before she shut the door and locked it. Seated where he was in the darker corner of the porch, he watched unobserved as she walked up to her house. The outside light framed her and he found himself with a mouth drier than the desert.

The asymmetrical steel-grey dress clung to her body like nothing he'd ever dreamed. She looked almost ethereal. Yet he sensed her exhaustion beneath all that poised perfection.

He spoke when she reached out to unlock the door. "You look beautiful, Delicia. Where've you been?"

She started, but recovered quickly. Anger began to grow in his gut when he saw the expression, which had been on her face since the night Lacy was murdered. Her 'I'm keeping the world at arm's length' look. He didn't like that. Archer wanted his Delicia. The one who blushed when she said something off the wall or impetuous. Not this one, who had a mask on to keep an emotional distance.

"Out with some people I know."

He wanted the one who didn't keep secrets from him. Pushing to his feet, he prowled towards her, watching how her eyes never left him. Desire pooled in them, but it was quickly masked.

"Can we talk?" he asked, stopping before her. With her heels on, her lips were even closer to his.

"Sure. How about tomorrow. I'm tired."

"No, now."

She narrowed her eyes slightly before all expression smoothed away. "Fine."

Have I said how much I hate that impersonal look? "What's going on?"

"Nothing," she replied. "I was going to change and go to bed, but you said no."

He reached out and cupped her chin in his fingers. "You're running."

Retreat was all over her face. "No, I'm not."

Archer lowered his head until their lips were a miniscule distance apart. "Bullshit!" He kissed her hard and so possessively she almost melted into him then lifted his head to stare at her. "Bull-fucking-shit."

Delicia stared up at Archer. Her belly was a mangled mess of jumbled nerves. She wanted him so much, but she wanted everything or nothing at all. Her lips still tingled from his dominating kiss.

"What?" she asked, more aware of his large body than his words.

"You heard me," he growled. "You're running."

Maybe, but so was he.

"You're one to talk," she snapped, hating how she felt so defensive.

"What are you talking about?" he demanded. "I'm right here, trying to talk to you."

She opened the door and stomped in, tossing her purse to the bench beneath the coat hooks. Having a row on her porch at midnight wasn't her style. "Don't play dumb with me, Archer Bennett. You've been just as distant ever since your precious Lacy died."

His expression hardened and those indigo eyes darkened with escalating fury. All it did was further her own. Had it all been a lie with him?

"I did what I could and I'm sorry I couldn't save her life. If I had maybe you'd be happy again." She crossed her arms desperately trying to contain her feelings.

He seemed taken aback by her comment and the rage drained from his gaze. "Is that what you think?"

She shrugged and put her hands on her hips. "What else would I think? I try to offer you comfort and you look through—not at—*through* me and...and call me Lis!" After whirling around, she managed to take two steps before he grabbed her and whipped her back around to face him.

His expression shocked her. Never had he looked so imposing, not even in confrontations with Justin. Flames flickered in his eyes and his face appeared carved from marble for all the emotion it had.

"I don't call you Lis. Never have. And even if Lacy were alive, I'd still be here with you."

She ignored the burgeoning bit of hope that sprouted within her. "Yes, you did. You did call me Lis. The night she died. You held her close and looked at me like I didn't even exist."

He shook his head. "I never wanted you to—" He raked his hands through his hair.

Delicia watched him pace wanting to touch him, her anger dissipating at the sight of his own personal distress. Instead, she forced herself to remain immobile.

"Is that why you met two guys about a job in Washington? In that dress and with your brother's expensive car?"

Damn you, Jon! "I was exploring my options."

His gaze narrowed and froze her to the spot. "You, Delicia Wright, belong here in McKingley." He paused. "With me."

Archer stalked towards her with such purpose, such determination, all she could do was back up until the wall prevented her from going any farther. He pinned her in, strong arms on either side of her head.

"Why?" she managed to ask through dry lips. Her tongue sneaked out to dampen them.

His gaze smouldered. "Because you love me and I love you." He trailed his knuckles down her cheek and along her bottom lip. "I've loved you since the day I met you, Delicia. And I will love you past the day my life leaves my body."

Her heart clenched and she was at a loss for words. He'd never said those words to her before. "Lacy?"

His finger followed her neckline before drifting towards her breasts. "I protected her from Justin in school once. I felt like I failed her. But I've never loved her, not even remotely close to how I love you."

Words still wouldn't come. The tears, however, had no problem. They leaked over her eyes and ran down her face. He swiped them away with his thumbs.

"I'm not letting you run, Delicia."

There it was. The bassy, seductive and unhurried way he drew out her name. The way it made her feel so safe and protected. So...*his*.

"Things have changed," she protested.

"Do you love me?" he asked.

She nodded.

"Tell me," he whispered the command.

"I love you, Archer Bennett."

His smile was just as seductive as his voice and she found herself melting all over again. "I've waited years for you to say that to me." He kissed her until she nigh forgot her own name. Desire burned in his gaze when he pulled back and looked at her. "Don't leave, Delicia."

Don't leave me, were the unspoken words. She wrapped her arms around his neck and pulled him as close as she could. She didn't want to talk, not right now. Her body was sending her an entirely different message right now.

"Archer," she moaned as he cupped a breast and teased the nipple to a turgid point.

"I need you out of this dress, Delicia, or I won't be responsible for what happens to it."

Her body flamed even hotter. "I don't care." And she didn't. The price didn't matter. All that did was the man touching her. He loved her. Moreover, he'd told her so.

So when the sound of ripping material reached her ears she only shook to help it fall to the floor, the beads bounced and scattered all over. Her thong followed and all she wore were her heels. He undid his jeans, lifted her and she groaned in pleasure when he lowered her back down on his thick shaft.

Archer took her hard and fast against the wall, her heels digging into his back and their screams loud and unchecked. She lost track of everything but the man with her.

"Mine," he uttered as he pistoned deep within her.

Her only answer was a scream of raw pleasure as she came around him. Delicia had a vague sense of them moving to the bedroom, but everything aside from Archer and his touch was a blur.

* * * *

She woke in bed, the sun streaming through her sheer curtains. Every inch of her was sore and as she rubbed her eyes, she felt a large, warm body shift behind her. Archer draped his arm over her waist, keeping them anchored together. She knew she needed to move it in order to get out of the bed but, honestly, she couldn't quite summon up the energy.

"Why are you thinking of running already, Delicia?" he murmured, his shaft stiffening and pressing against her ass.

"I can barely move, Archer. Running is the last thing on my mind," she replied.

"Good." He moved her, rotating her so they were face to face.

His sleepy eyes simmered with passion and she knew it would be so easy to let him whisk her away again to the place where nothing but the two of them mattered. "What happens now?" she asked.

"We get married."

She blinked and stared at him. He held her gaze unflinchingly. "I'm sorry, what?"

"Marry me, Delicia."

That was her Archer. Straightforward and blunt. She sighed. Yes, hers. He was the one she wanted more than anything else. "Yes."

His gaze warmed her from the inside out. "I'm never letting you go, Delicia Wright."

"I don't ever want you to." She pressed her mouth to his and whimpered as the kiss melted her.

"I'll get you a ring today."

Ring. Her heart sank. She knew how things were for Arissa and Katiya with the planning of their weddings. Well, technically only Katiya, for Arissa claimed there was no date, but she knew what would happen once it was announced. His fingers tipped up her chin.

"What's wrong?"

"I was thinking of the wedding."

He smiled, a flash of white against his tanned skin. "Let's go to Vegas."

She bit her lower lip. "Really? Would you?"

"I don't need a big wedding. All I need is you. Your sister's wedding plans are driving you crazy now. I can't imagine what you'd do if it was yours."

"I just..." She shook her head. She'd always hated people making a fuss over her, she'd had enough of that as a child. "You don't know my family, eloping will be risky."

He kissed her until she forgot her own name. "What did I tell you about risky pleasures?"

"What?"

"Risky pleasures are usually the best kind." Another spine-tingling, toe-curling kiss. "In this case, I know so."

Her heart sang with joy. He was right. Other things were minor, Archer was her future. "Shower first, then we leave?"

"In a rush to become Mrs Archer Bennett?"

She slid from the bed then sashayed to the bathroom. "Been waiting since the day we met. Come on, scrub my back so we can get going."

His deep laughter followed her as he jumped up and came after her. It took them over an hour to get to his truck, but as he drove them from McKingley towards Vegas, she realised that yes, doing this may be risky, but it was always worth it when it came to Archer 'Risk' Bennett. He loved her and she loved him. The rest would work itself out.

PURE
HARMONY

Dedication

To my sister, whose love of reading made me pick up my first book, which ultimately led me on this path to become an author. Thanks for passing on your love of reading and your support.
— McKenna Jeffries

To all the grandparents out there who help their grandbabies to find what moves them. I know all mine are looking down from Heaven on me. Thanks for always watching over me. I love and miss y'all so much!
— Aliyah Burke

Chapter One

Jonathon Wright groaned and shifted against his cool sheets. As he'd been doing every morning for the past two months, he reached across the expanse of his king-sized bed to find...nothing. No warm body waiting for him. No soft silken skin to slide along his as they made long, slow love.

He was alone in bed.

Again.

A frustrated grunt left him as he ignored his rock-hard shaft and climbed from the bed. Once in the shower, he braced his hands along the sandstone-hued tiles and allowed icy cold pellets to pound his skin. The temperature encouraged him to hasten through his shower and soon he stood on the thick rug towelling off. It didn't take much to get dry — being in New Mexico with such low humidity, it seemed the water evaporated from his skin.

Rubbing the towel over his shorn head, he tried to ignore the flashes of memory that insisted on popping up. *Get a grip, Jon*, he reprimanded himself. After hanging up the towel, he made his way to his bedroom and got dressed. He had a piece of toast for breakfast then walked out of his condominium with a coffee in one hand, his briefcase in the other.

He headed for the college where he'd agreed to give guest lectures for first year law classes. As he drove through McKingley, his racing mind began to slow. He loved it here, had grown up here, and had graduated from the very college he was on his way to. His entire family lived here, and, while sometimes they made his life miserable, for the most part he was thrilled to have them so close.

In fact, he'd worked with a friend of his eldest sister Katiya a few times. Yurandol Blake was an attorney for the local FBI field office and they had occasionally done things that caused their paths to cross in the legal world. She was sharp, lethally so. In fact, she had been the one to ask him to cover the class today. Something had come up on her schedule and she wasn't able to make it.

He pulled into the parking lot and drove through to find an empty space. Locating one, he whipped in and shut off the engine. He sipped his coffee and watched the students stroll by.

A bit later, he strode across the well-manicured lawn towards the law building. Pushing through the door, he felt he was swept back to when he'd been a student here. Ever serious, he'd been very focused — on his studies, living at home and saving his money. After he'd passed the bar, he'd purchased his condo as a gift to himself.

He nodded at people he went by as he made his way to the auditorium. Entering, he walked down to the front and placed his briefcase on the table nearest the podium. Opening it, he organised his papers. He took another drink to finish his coffee and settled the mug by his case.

Grabbing the back of the chair, he manoeuvred it so he could sit and watch the students continue to stream in. When the clock indicated the time was right for the class to begin, he stepped up to the podium, turned on the microphone and introduced himself before beginning the lecture.

* * * *

By four in the afternoon, the last of his students had left his final lecture. After piling his things back in his satchel, he snapped it closed and headed for the exit. A storm had rolled in, dampening the ground. He eyed the ominous clouds hovering overhead. As he walked across campus, the rain began again. The sky opened up and fell in a torrential rush.

Muttering a curse, he dashed for the nearest building. *Damn it!* He noticed the water droplets on his silk suit. He wiped off his briefcase and fought a frown. New Mexico weather was unpredictable at best.

The halls were mostly empty, which made it very easy to hear the haunting melody that poured from a room. His skin prickled and, of their own accord, his feet took him towards the sound. Never had music drawn him with such intensity before.

He paused at the door and stood there, allowing the notes to flow over him. Unable to resist, he proceeded into the large room. The lecture hall was mostly dark, except for the lights upon the stage that illuminated a large gleaming black piano on centre stage. A woman sat there playing. His heart pounded erratically in his chest as he stared at her. His palms grew sweaty and he swallowed repeatedly as he walked closer.

It's her.

His extremely analytical brain worked out the percentage of likelihood that it could be her. On the other hand, his body already knew. He grew hard and lust coursed through his veins.

Harmony.

She was alone, as far as he could tell, and unaware of his presence. Her long, thick black hair hung down to the middle of her back, clasped at the base of her neck by a simple barrette. She wore a long-sleeved coral shirt that complemented her skin tone. She moved in time with her playing.

Captivated, he continued closer until her face was clear. It *was* her. He'd never forget her face. The smooth skin, delicate features and large eyes framed by doubly thick curled lashes. She was slender with a tiny waist and breasts that, he recalled, fitted so perfectly in his hands.

He knew when she noticed she was no longer alone—her fingers faltered and eventually she halted playing. Her dark brown eyes flashed with reminiscent passion before it faded and her gaze cooled. A flush skated up her cheeks, though.

"That was beautiful," he said, ignoring the powerful impulse to touch her.

Her cheeks reddened further. "Thank you." She ducked her head. "What are you doing here?"

Not the issue at hand for him. "You left." He fought a chill from the ice in her eyes. Then, like the passion, it vanished to leave behind a blank slate. His gaze moved to her hands, which remained on the keys, then back to her face. The signs were there. Blatant and obvious. She was about to bolt. He moved closer and watched her eyes grow wider.

"Harmony," he said, her name falling familiarly from his lips.

"Excuse me, Jonathon. I must go."

He reached out for her arm. She stilled beneath his touch. "Wait."

"Why?"

He wasn't sure but he'd been unable to get this woman out of his mind since their one date and night of shared passion. Jon felt a bit out of control and it disturbed him. He liked neat, orderly, controlled situations. Even in the courtroom, he was always as prepared as he could be to ensure surprise didn't take him. She unsettled him, rattled him, but damn it, she visited him every single night in his dreams. Now he had her, he didn't want to let her go.

"Let me take you to dinner." When she hesitated, he added, "We've been out before."

Her flush told him she recalled exactly what had happened on that date. How it had ended up — clothes strewn all over the floor and moans the only sounds in the room.

"When?"

"Now, if you can leave." His phone buzzed in his pocket and he ignored it.

"Okay."

Her soft, lyrical voice had the power to make him crazy with lust. He stared as she got to her feet and slid the bench in under the piano. She wore charcoal grey slacks that hugged her hips. As he observed her, he noticed she allowed her right hand to be swallowed up by her sleeve until just her unpolished nails were visible.

He waited for her to gather her stuff and walked slightly behind her as she made her way up to the door. Close enough so the gentle scent of gardenia could be smelt and far enough to ogle the natural, seductive sway of her hips.

They paused at the door leading outside and stared at the continuing downpour. He grumbled under his breath — getting soaked and ruining his suit were not in the plans of the day. He slanted a glance at Harmony and noticed the sparkle in her eyes as she gazed out over the campus.

"Perhaps we should wait it out," he suggested.

Silent, she led the way to a small sitting area. He claimed the chair across from her. He couldn't take his eyes from her.

"You're staring," she mumbled.

"I'm sorry. I can't seem to help myself. You look so different than you did...that night."

A small smile lifted one side of her mouth. "Teaching a music class is hardly the place to wear a cocktail dress."

He grinned broadly. Perhaps not, but she'd looked damn good in it. "Why didn't you tell me you were coming to McKingley to teach?"

She pursed her lips and glanced up when thunder rocked the building. "When exactly would I have done that? During our bidding war over the vase? Or after, in your hotel room?"

He flashed an arrogant grin. "So you do remember."

Her brown eyes narrowed. "What are you doing here?"

Stretching out his legs, he made sure to touch her foot with his, craving the physical contact.

"I was here giving lectures all day. Over at the law building."

"That's right, you mentioned something about being an attorney."

He was pleased she remembered. "Yes. How long have you been teaching music?"

She tensed, her entire body did. Her right hand completely disappeared inside her sleeve. Not for long, but he did notice.

"About a year or so."

There was a story there. "Why were you so determined to get the vase?"

Her eyes sparked and he realised he'd just erred. Grievously. "Just because I'm not a lawyer doesn't mean I don't appreciate fine things."

Harmony Oshiro seethed inwardly. The handsome, arrogant and stuffed-shirted Jonathon Wright never failed to do two things to her. One, make her forget all common sensibilities and want to spend the night with him, engaging in all kinds of erotic endeavours. Two, get her dander up with nothing more than a simple glance from his medium brown eyes.

The look he'd given her when they'd begun to bid on the same vase was as if he didn't believe she could afford such a thing. True, she'd gone over her intended budget to acquire said item, but his smug, over-confident look had spurred her into the rash action. So she'd won the vase, and consequently, she'd been eating noodles and peanut butter and jelly since. Nevertheless, it had been worth it. She'd secured the final item in the set her grandmother had begun for her.

"I'm sorry," he said. "I didn't mean for it to sound that way. I was just curious as to why you wanted it so bad. Does it have a special meaning for you?"

"My grandmother gave me the first few in the collection. The one offered that night was the only one I didn't have." She cocked her head to the side. "What about you? Why did you want it?"

His entire countenance softened and her heart skipped more than a few beats.

"My mom. She loves little knick-knacks like that. And the robin's egg blue colour is one of her favourites."

She smiled and his gaze heated. "So you did it for your mom."

His grin made her heart race. "Yes." He glanced away briefly then said, "The rain appears to have stopped."

He assisted her to her feet and let his hand linger afterwards. Then he slid it around to her back, the heat from his palm warming her through her shirt. Outside, the air smelt clean and fresh. The dark clouds rolled away off in the distance, leaving the sun free to shine down.

"Where did you want to meet?" she asked.

"We can go in my car and I can bring you back here to collect yours." He spoke as they walked.

"I don't have a car."

He stared at her, brows raised and a bit of a shocked look on his face. "Is it in the shop?"

She chuckled. "No. I don't own one."

He inhaled sharply. "Then I will take you and bring you home."

Her insides trembled a bit at that statement. He'd *taken* her for sure already. Over and over that night. She stumbled slightly at the memory.

"Okay." She wanted to be around him—perhaps it didn't make sense but being with Jonathon Wright allowed her to *feel*. "Where are we eating?"

"Are you, like, a vegan or something?"

She shook her head.

"Then we can go to a small place on the outskirts of town. Great food. One of my favourite places."

They walked to the parking lot and she sighed when he unlocked a Mercedes. A metallic iridium silver coupé. *He must really be loaded.* At least the car didn't sport any vanity plates.

Jon held the door for her and she slid into the interior, across the tan, butter-soft leather seat. The inside had a beautiful wood trim and she was afraid to touch anything for fear of ruining it. She tried not to fidget, but she was growing more nervous with each passing moment. Not for fear of what could happen, merely because she was a much simpler person. Her vehicle, when she'd had one, had cost about five thousand dollars. It wasn't a model that started at over one hundred and fifty thousand.

He got settled and she hid a smirk when she spied him wipe a piece of fuzz off the dash. Mr Jonathon Wright, attorney at law, was a neat freak. The powerful engine turned over and they were on their way. As he drove, another storm rolled in and began to drench the earth.

Eventually they pulled into a place called Hattie's. Jon grabbed an umbrella from the back seat and had it opened, offering him shelter, before he got out. She stifled another laugh—personally, she loved the rain. He came around to her door and together, under the umbrella's protection, they hastened to the door.

He escorted her to a table in the back as they followed the attendant. Again, he rested his strong hand against the small of her back and took her mind back to their shared night. She blinked away the thoughts and focused on what he was saying.

Her meal was delicious and he said as much about his. They both lingered over dessert and coffee, and she imagined he was in no rush to go back out into the fury of the storm. Then again, neither was she.

"What about your family?" he asked, stirring creamer into his coffee.

"My parents live over in Japan—that's where I grew up. I have an older brother, who's married with one child. They also live in Japan."

He stared at her. "So you're the only one who came to the States?"

Memories of concert tours flashed and she forced them away. "Yes. I had been over here for a while and decided to stay." Better that than to see all the disappointed faces of her family.

His eyes were sharp and assessing as he moved his gaze over her. As if he knew there was more to it than what she'd told him. "And now you teach music at the college?"

"That about sums it up."

The look he gave her told her he didn't believe it for a second.

"And you?" she asked quickly, wanting the attention off her.

"Me. Well, my family is bigger than yours is. There are six of us kids in all, but also the town is full of our cousins, aunts and uncles, so it feels larger most times. I have two older brothers, an older sister, then there are the two youngest sisters."

"Wow." Things had been crazy at times with just her solo brother. To have five siblings—it must have been a zoo.

He chuckled, a deep warm sound. "Yes. It had its moments." A shrug. "Still does."

She ducked her head and finished off her final piece of fried cheesecake. Stuffed, she rested her fork on the plate and leant back. "Thank you for inviting me to dinner." She gave him a smile.

His gaze grew predatory and she felt an answering tremble in the pit of her belly.

"Why did you leave?"

Her protective barriers shot up immediately. "What does it matter?"

A loud rumble of thunder outside echoed the lightning in his eyes. "Why?" he asked again.

"I had my own room and my own plans."

He didn't approve of her answer—that much was obvious. His jaw flexed before he calmed down.

"Are you ready?"

The abrupt change in conversation threw her momentarily. "Of course." She reached for her purse.

"You're not paying."

She jerked her gaze to him and realised it wasn't a battle she'd win. "Thank you, then."

He paid then escorted her back through the rain to his car. She hid her laugh as he muttered under his breath, cursing the rain. "I looked for you," he said once he'd begun to drive. That surprised her and she was unsure of how to respond. "Even the next night at that auction. I searched everywhere for you."

"I left after getting what I wanted. There was no reason for me to stay longer." The moment she spoke the words she realised how they sounded, and she blushed. "Oh my goodness, I didn't mean it like that. I... I...was talking about the vase."

He gave a short bark of laughter. She looked at him and reached out a hand to lay it on his arm. It never got there. Through the windshield, headlights glared and Jonathon yelled, "Shit! Hang on!" then swerved off the road as an oncoming truck in the wrong lane barrelled past, showering them with even more water.

With her breath lodged in her throat, she gripped the edge of the seat and the door handle. The coupé bounced and skidded until they finally came to a halt.

"Are you okay?" he demanded, touching her as if he needed to ascertain it personally.

"I'm fine," she said over the pounding of her heart. "Are you?"

"No," he bit off. "I'm fucking pissed off. He could have killed us. Not only that, he didn't stop to see if we were all right or not."

Well, that was true. The road seemed to be deserted. She took a couple of deep breaths only to realise she was gripping his hand. Releasing it, she ran her palm over her mouth. That had been too close. Much too close. He started the engine, which had shut off, and put the car back in drive. The rear tyres began to spin.

He scowled, cursed and gunned the engine again. She could feel the car sinking further. She unbuckled her belt and reached for the door only to halt at his stare.

"Where are you going?"

"We're stuck. All you're doing is sinking us deeper. I was going to push."

He stared at her as if she had three heads. "No way. I'll go push, you drive."

She pursed her lips to keep from asking the question she longed to. Him out in this weather didn't make sense. Hell, he'd used an umbrella to get from the car to the restaurant. The man flicked pieces of lint off his immaculate dash. Now he was suggesting that he go out in a silk suit and push his car free of the mud?

Harmony didn't want to bruise his pride so she said nothing. Besides, he could do with getting a bit dirty.

He shrugged out of his dark blue jacket, which left him in a vest and white shirt. Her mouth watered a bit as she stared at his powerful torso.

He opened the door and vanished into the rainy night. She slid over into his seat and adjusted it to fit her shorter stature. Shifting into the lowest gear, she waited, her eyes flashing between the rear-view and side mirrors.

"Go!" he hollered.

Harmony gently gave it some gas and could feel it pulling free of the mire. The car lurched forward when the front tyres found solid purchase. She made sure to stop on the firm part of the shoulder and double-checked to ensure the hazards were flashing. Checking the mirrors, she frowned when she couldn't spot Jonathon.

The passenger door opened and her eyes widened in shock at what entered. Mud covered him. Head to toe. The scowl on his face would have sent the Devil into hiding.

She had to bite the inside of her cheek in order to keep the laughter inside. He released a continuous litany of curses as he lowered his soaked and muddy body into the seat.

"Not a word," he growled.

Holding up a hand in agreement, she shut off the hazards and got them on the road. She couldn't help but keep looking at him, he looked so miserable and yet…so cute and rumpled. Not the stuffy man he normally portrayed.

"I see your grin, Harmony," he said.

"I'm sorry… It's just that…that… Well, you look" — she burst out laughing—"adorably miserable."

His low rumble echoed in the small interior.

She did her best to compose herself. "Where am I going?"

"My house."

A flutter appeared in her belly. "I don't know how to get there."

"You will." His words were drenched with more than just a fleeting promise.

After he gave her directions, she concentrated on driving and not on the handsome yet mud-soaked man in the passenger seat. However, it didn't escape her attention that the sexual tension between them seemed to increase the closer they got to his place.

Chapter Two

Jon sighed with relief as he stepped from his large shower and wrapped a blue towel around his waist. He was clean again. Rubbing his chest and face with another towel, he paused at the mirror and stared at his reflection. For a few minutes he stood there until he remembered he had a guest. After drying off quickly, he dressed in a pair of grey slacks and a tan, mock neck sweater.

He left his bedroom, fastening his watch on his wrist, and stopped abruptly at the top of his stairs. Staring over the edge, he found Harmony pretty much where he'd left her. By his large windows, beyond which the storm continued to make its presence known.

Harmony stood there, her left hand absently rubbing her right forearm in a continuous motion. A vague memory of a scar appeared in his mind but he couldn't recall with absolute certainty — after all, there had been other things to think of at the time.

He made his way silently down the stairs and moved up behind her. She truly was beautiful. A perfect blend of African-American and Japanese. Black hair fell in long, thick, silken waves around her. He stared at her reflection in the window and took in her slight stature. She made him want to gather her close and protect her.

She barely reached his shoulder and he had personal knowledge that he could span her waist with his hands. Yet, despite how petite she was, they had fitted perfectly together in bed. Her body had cradled to his as if it had been made specifically for him.

"You seem like you feel better."

Her warm, lyrical voice surrounded him. Instead of moving closer to her and pressing along her body, he stepped to the side and leaned against the window. He noticed she'd stopped rubbing her arm.

"Much. Can I get you a drink of some kind?"

"No, thank you." She smoothed her hands down along her hips. "I really need to get home. So, thank you again, for the meal, but—"

He captured her shoulders and turned her directly towards him. It took a bit to remember to focus on talking and not what the feel of her body touching his did to him. His cock hardened and he counted to ten before he felt he was in enough control.

"Why are you running? *Again.*"

He groaned under his breath when she dampened her lips. Her large eyes narrowed and he got the feeling he'd just messed up. Again. But if she had any anger it didn't linger, nor did it show when she spoke.

"I am not running. I have things to do before I can crash for the night. I've been up since...well, really early."

Stay here. With me. "I want to see you again."

She shook her head. "I don't believe that would be wise."

Words he despised hearing. "Why not?"

"I... I am not looking to be involved with anyone else."

He flashed a grin and drew her in closer. "Good. I am not into ménages."

"Very funny." She glanced at her watch. "I really need to get home."

"Why? We were good together. *Really* good."

She got this look in her eyes he recognised. He had sisters. Walls were going up and he would get nowhere.

"Let me get my keys and I'll take you home."

"Nonsense. I can call a taxi."

He pinned her with a look, prompting her to snap her mouth shut. Reluctantly releasing her, he stepped back to get his keys. Harmony still stood by the windows, although her gaze was upon him.

"Come on," he said, waving her over.

Together they headed for the kitchen and through to his garage. He ignored his car, which he would have detailed tomorrow, and headed for his SUV. Holding the door for her, he struggled not to pluck her from the seat and carry her back upstairs to his bed.

It's like she has no clue how she affects me.

Locking up his libido, he climbed in and started the vehicle. He backed out of the garage into the continuing deluge and asked her where she lived. He didn't need to ask for directions when she gave the address — he'd grown up in this city.

The ride to her place was done in silence. He manoeuvred to the kerb and put his SUV in park before facing her. She was in the process of unbuckling her seatbelt and he took the opportunity to stare. Her profile was serene and composed, yet there was a haughty air about her.

"Goodnight, Jonathon Wright."

He freed himself from his own seatbelt and grabbed for the door.

"No, there's no need for you to get out."

"I will walk you to your door."

Her musical laugh gave him pause. "No. I wouldn't want you wet again."

She gathered her items and jumped out before he could say another word. He watched her go up to the door and enter with a wave over her shoulder. Memorising the address, he pulled away. His body was almost rebelling against him for being so close to the woman he'd dreamt about nightly and letting her walk away.

In the rear-view mirror, he caught a glimpse of his expression. One he wore in court when he had the trap laid and just needed to spring it. Harmony Oshiro wouldn't get away.

* * * *

For the first time since he'd met the unforgettable Harmony, he didn't wake reaching for her. He'd found her and this was his city. She couldn't hide from him, not in McKingley. Therefore, when he left his condo for the office, there was a smile lingering in his soul and a jaunty whistle in his head.

"Mr Wright, you have a visitor."

Elisa, his administrative assistant, dragged his attention from the case he was currently studying. Glancing at the clock on the wall, he was pleased to know it was almost time to leave for the day. *Could it be?* Even as he wondered, he knew it couldn't be Harmony. Elisa only said things like that when his family stopped by.

Sure enough, a few moments later, the door cracked open and a familiar face peeked around the edge. "Got a minute?"

"For you, Lis, always." He closed the file and waved her in while getting up to greet her. After sharing a hug and kiss, he gestured her to the leather couch and sat near on a matching chair. "What's up?"

"I need to borrow your car."

He gave a short, disbelieving bark of laughter. "My CL600? Are you serious?"

She held his gaze and into hers leeched his downfall, the patented baby sister plead. He'd never been able to say no to her, especially with her eyes shimmering with tears poised to flow over. It mattered not that he knew they were crocodile tears—he hated to see her cry.

"I just got that car, Lis," he said, trying to find some strength to resist. *Brand new and it's already in for a detailing.*

"I won't hurt it, Jon," she said indignantly.

He ran a hand over his head. "Why do you feel you need my car?"

Something flashed in her gaze and he immediately grew suspicious. "It would just be for the rest of the day. I'd bring it to you late tonight or early tomorrow morning."

"Why, Lis?" He added the tone he used in the courtroom when a witness was being treated as hostile. Her hands rubbed along her legs and he knew she was hiding something.

"Can't you just lend it to me?"

"Did your Jeep break down or something like that?"

"No," she replied immediately. "I just want something classier for tonight."

"Dimitri has trucks."

Her sigh said it all. She didn't want to go to the eldest sibling. He had a way of acting like one of their parents.

"Tell me why."

Her next sigh was one of resignation. "I have a dinner meeting with some people and I didn't want to take my Jeep."

"Dinner meeting? And you need my car."

"Yes."

"So this isn't with Archer?"

She wouldn't meet his gaze. "No. It's a job offer."

He narrowed his eyes. "Are you leaving McKingley?"

She shrugged. "Nothing's concrete yet. Please don't say anything to anyone. I just want a vehicle other than my dirty Jeep to climb out of in my dress."

He pushed to his feet. "Don't keep this from everyone, Lis. Including Archer." He liked the man his sister was dating.

Lis glanced up at him, hope shimmering in her eyes. "Does this mean you'll let me use it?"

He gave an exaggerated big brother sigh. "Yes. I'll take you to the detailers to get it. But, Lis — not one scratch."

She jumped up and wrapped her arms around him. "Thank you. Thank you. Thank you! I promise I'll be gentle with it." Drawing back, she frowned slightly. "One question, though — why is it at the detailer?"

Because I was covered head to foot with mud inside it.

"It was time," he muttered. "Let's go."

He drove Lis and they chatted easily. At the dealership, they got out and made their way to the desk. A slender redhead sat there and grinned at them.

"Good evening, Mr Wright."

"Evening, Fiona. Are we ready?"

"Yes, sir. All the mud has been removed. All clean again."

"Mud?" Lis asked, turning to look up at him.

"Not now, Lis."

Her chuckle didn't make him feel any better. She would be asking about it later, he'd bet she would. He paid for his car and they walked out together to his waiting vehicle. He smiled at the man there before opening the door and sighing with relief that his car was, once again, spotless. The outside as well. Even the tyres shone.

He took a deep breath and glanced at his baby sister. Honestly, he expected her to be chomping at the bit to get in his car. She wasn't even looking at it. Her gaze was fixated off in the distance and he could see the bags under her eyes. She fingered her necklace and he knew something was wrong—she only did that when worried or stressed. Still, when she looked at him she tried for a smile.

"Are you okay, Lis? Really?" he asked, reaching out to her.

"Yes. Thank you for letting me use your car. Did you want me to bring it to you tonight?"

Images of Harmony came to him. He smiled. "Tomorrow is fine." No reason to interrupt his plans for the night.

"Okay." A quick kiss. "Thank you, and I promise I'll be very careful."

You'd better. Although truth be told, he didn't give a rat's ass about the car, as long as his sister was okay.

Jon watched Lis slip behind the wheel and drive away with a wave. He headed to his SUV while checking the time. Harmony should be done by now, so he figured he'd take the chance to pick her up for dinner. Well, after he did a couple of things first.

* * * *

"Come on, Harmony, it won't kill you."

Harmony glanced at her friend who had an oyster on a half shell outstretched in her hand. "Get that nasty thing away from me," she ordered, nose wrinkling in disgust.

Lana Kanseah sighed with her usual dramatic flair. As Harmony watched, she sucked it down. Harmony's belly heaved with the thought of doing such a thing.

"So nasty," she said at the look of pleasure on Lana's face.

Lana winked. "So tasty." She sucked another down. "You seem a bit quieter than usual. Are you okay?"

Harmony peered out of the window, staring across the street. Bella's was over there. One of, – if not *the* – most prestigious restaurants in McKingley. She and Lana ate here, at Kell's, every week knowing they'd never get in over there. Not that she wanted to – it was the beauty and majesty of the building that drew her. Bella's was a place that called out to her – she longed to go in it and play. *The acoustics must be amazing.*

"Harmony?"

"I'm okay, Lana." She sighed. "No, I lied. I'm not. Remember I told you about the guy I met at the auction in Las Cruces?"

"Oh yes. The hot yet arrogant attorney who turned your world upside down with his masterful caresses and his huge – "

"Lana!"

Thankfully, her friend shut up. She peeked around, hoping no one had heard Lana's outburst. From the looks she received, it was a safe bet they'd heard. *Damn actors. Always with the carrying voices.*

Lana Kanseah was an actress. One who'd come back to McKingley to live instead of residing in Beverly Hills. She was of the Chiricahua tribe. They'd been friends for a long time and when Harmony had told her she was leaving Japan, Lana had told her to come here to McKingley. So she had.

"What about him?"

She fiddled with the knife. "I saw him yesterday."

"So you're tired?" Lana asked with an impish twinkle in her eyes.

"You are such a bitch."

"True enough. Now dish."

So she did. Right up to driving his car for him back to his place. She even mentioned the huge piano he had downstairs in his condominium. Lana was leaning close by now.

"He let you drive his car?"

"I don't think he wanted to continue spreading mud all over. He was filthy. Filthy. And, Lana, it was so funny. He's like a clean freak and to see him like that... I wanted to laugh so hard."

"I don't care how dirty he was. This man let you drive his car. That is something. Now, did you join him in the shower?"

"Of course not!" *Thought about it, though.*

"Why not? You two have already done it."

"It's different now."

Lana scoffed and sent her a scowl. "How so?"

"My entire apartment could fit in the downstairs of his condo. He drives a car that starts at over a hundred and fifty Gs. Oh yeah, and his name is Jonathon Wright."

Lana was at a loss for words. For once. Her mouth moved but nothing came out. With a sigh, Harmony turned her attention back out of the window and stared at nothing, waiting for Lana's speech to return.

"Why the hell didn't you say this to begin with?" she demanded.

"Was his name really that important? I mean, I thought the fact I'd had a one-night stand would have trumped that."

"Well yes, but... Damn it, do you know who he is?"

"Yes. I'm the one who told you." She frowned as a silver Mercedes coupé pulled up to the door across the street. It was very familiar to her. In fact, she'd bet it was his. "Why?"

"The Wright family is one of the families equated with McKingley. Rich. And Jonathon made a name for himself right out of law school when he took on a case for his sister. No one thought he would win it, but he did and... Well, I don't know what he got for her, settlement-wise, because it wasn't made public, but since then, Christ, he's been known as a man of ice. And you...get him in bed at an auction. I hate you."

That all bore more thought but the door was being opened. "I think he's here, Lana. That's his car, across the street. That's the one I drove last night."

It wasn't a tall, strong man who exited the Mercedes. Not even close. This was a beautiful woman and Harmony felt a punch to the gut sitting there staring at her. The one emerging from the vehicle was tall with long legs and amazing curves. She had on a floor-length, strapless, steel-grey dress. It looked like beadwork was on the breast and one swathe near her waist, making it asymmetrical. She was gorgeous. The woman's honey-blonde hair, arranged in an elegant coiffure, only added to her looks. The dress even had a slight train to it. Classic Hollywood style with the train and lace-up bodice.

"Who's that?" Lana asked.

"I... I don't know." She felt ill, knowing she'd been lusting after a married man. This had to be his wife. *How could I not have known? And why did I fall for his lines a second time? I almost went to bed with him again.*

"Hey now, don't jump to conclusions," Lana said. "Maybe it's not his car."

"Right, there are tons of cars like that floating around here. I mean, I see at least five to ten a day."

Lana reached for her hand and squeezed it, offering silent strength. "Well, you want to go see who she is?"

That brought a wry chuckle from her. Leave it to Lana to run at things head-on. "No thanks."

"For what it's worth, hon, I've never heard of him being married. He's always been one of the most eligible bachelors in McKingley and around. Possibly in the Southwest."

"Great, so it's not his wife but his girlfriend." She reached for a breadstick. "That makes me feel so much better."

"I've lived here longer than you have, Harmony. Honestly, I've never heard things like that with him. There are a few Wrights that kind of behaviour is linked to, but not him."

Her shoulders lifted in a careless shrug. "And he asked me why it was a bad idea we shouldn't see each other again. Guess it didn't take him too long to get over that." Bitterness coated her words.

Lana didn't comment, she just sat there. With a groan, Harmony pushed all thoughts of Jonathon Wright to the back of her mind and focused on her friend. Even so, for the rest of the dinner, she couldn't help but wonder. Who was that woman? Moreover, what did she mean to Jonathon? More importantly, why did it matter to her?

"Are you sure you're okay, Harmony?" Lana questioned as they left the restaurant.

"I'm fine, just tired is all." She climbed in Lana's car and buckled her seatbelt.

"Get some rest, hon. I'm starting to worry. You're beginning to look frail." Lana drove her home, music the only sound in the car. Once Lana had parked in front of her apartment building, she turned to her. "I'll see you tomorrow. Thanks again for agreeing to help us out."

"My pleasure," she said sliding out of the car. "Night, Lana."

"G'night, hon. Sleep!" she hollered after her.

Harmony acknowledged her yell with a wave but didn't turn back. She rubbed the back of her neck and groaned tiredly. She trudged up the stairs to her fourth floor apartment, wishing there was an elevator for days like this. Rooting for her keys, she sighed.

I want to go home. Her stomach was already in knots at the prospect of playing for Lana's drama club.

Get a grip, Oshiro!

It didn't help that her hands were shaking when she managed to locate and withdraw her keys. She stumbled slightly and reached for the wall to brace herself. Her hand never encountered it. Strong arms encircled her, ensuring she stayed on her feet.

One whiff and she knew immediately who held her. Jonathon. He had this amazing masculine scent about him. *What is he doing here?*

"Easy there," he murmured.

Lord help her, she wanted to let her legs give out so he'd just hold her. Digging deep, she forced steel into her limbs and stood on her own. "What are you doing here?" she asked, not really sure she wanted to know.

"I came to see you. I told you yesterday, Harmony, I wanted to see you again." He plucked her keys from her hand and fitted them into the lock on her door. Then he swung the door open and led her in.

"How did you know my apartment?"

"Your name is on the mailbox for this one. I've been waiting for you for a few hours. Where have you been?"

The click of the door behind them made her realise just how alone she was with him. He guided her to a chair and pressed her into it before leaving her alone. Moments later, he showed up with a glass of water.

"Are you okay, Harmony?"

"I'm fine," she bit off. "What do you want?"

He glanced around her small yet clean apartment before he sat down in the chair nearest her. "Have I done something to offend you?"

"Why?"

"Your tone is angry."

"I don't like being played for a fool."

He narrowed his gaze. "Explain." The word fell like ice.

"I saw your car tonight at Bella's. A beautiful woman got out. Do you have a wife or girlfriend you didn't happen to mention? Because I will not be another woman for any man!"

"Bella's? I wasn't at Bella's tonight. I don't even have my car. It's with…" He trailed off and seemed to think over something.

"Well?" Harmony got to her feet and glared at him. Lana would be so proud of her for standing up for herself.

Jonathon also stood. He dwarfed her and she swallowed when he neared her. Gazing down at her, he trailed a knuckle along her face. "I don't have a girlfriend and I definitely don't have a wife."

She wanted to believe him but, damn it all, common sense seemed to vanish around him, and she couldn't let it go. "Who was she then? I don't see you as the kind of man who would let just anyone drive his car."

"I let you drive my car," he said without missing a beat.

Up and down, his touch moved on her face. She licked her lips trying not to beg for more, and his eyes followed the movement of her tongue. "That was a unique situation."

"You're a unique woman." He lowered his face and she was having a hard time keeping track of the conversation.

"No I'm not."

"Yes, you are." A brush of his lips along the corner of her mouth. "Very unique."

"Then she must be as well, for you to let her drive it alone." Damn, she couldn't keep her mouth shut. She sounded like a whiny, clinging woman.

"Oh, she is." She didn't want to hear that. "Her name is Delicia."

He nibbled on her lower lip and she moaned, curving her hands into his suit coat. Harmony opened her mouth to respond but he kissed her. His tongue swept deep, coaxing hers to play and dance with his. They stroked and slipped along one another. She gave all he asked for and whimpered longingly when he took even more than that. Her body was on high alert as her blood burned and her skin was aflame.

He ended the kiss and stared down into her eyes. "She's my baby sister."

Chapter Three

Jonathon watched the woman in his arms. Passion-glazed eyes, flushed skin and kiss-swollen lips. All he wanted to do was carry her to her bed and have his way with her. She was jealous. That made him want to smile. She may claim they should stay away from one another but her jealousy over his sister told him something different.

He'd been concerned when she had walked up the steps and into view. Her body had seemed almost unable to hold itself up. Her stumbling had proven him correct. Now, she was in his arms again and he had no wish to release her.

"Your sister?" Harmony queried.

"Delicia Wright. We all call her Lis. Now, where were you?"

She shook her head. "I was out with my friend Lana. We go out once a week." Seeming to regain a bit more of her wits, she moved back from his touch. Jon held in his growl of dislike. "Why are you here again?"

"I was going to take you to dinner, but that obviously didn't work."

"And you've been just waiting here for me to come back?"

"Yes." He shrugged as if it wasn't a big deal.

"Have you eaten then?"

"No."

He expected her to offer to make him something.

"You should get going then. I'm sure you're hungry."

Well, that was anything but what he'd expected. "Trying to get rid of me already?"

"I told you this wasn't a good idea."

He rolled his eyes. "What's not good about it?"

"I... You're Jonathon Wright."

He quirked a grin. "And you're Harmony Oshiro. Great, introductions are over. Can we do something more fun now? Like kissing?" He loved kissing her. Her full lips felt so good against his. Moreover, her responses to his kiss, to his touches, were amazing. "Or perhaps an activity which requires no clothing at all."

Desire flared in her eyes and he knew she was weakening. She shook her head. "No."

He plunked back down in a chair and crossed his legs. "Then tell me why you look so beat."

A look of astonishment filled her features. "Really?"

"Really. Don't try it—I'm not leaving until I get the answers I want."

She sighed heavily. "Are you always this pushy?"

"Yes." His response was immediate.

Harmony sat back down and watched him from weary eyes. His concern grew. Something was bothering her and he wanted to know what it was. He longed to help her.

"I'm just tired, that's all. Nothing more than that."

He barely blinked. "You're lying."

"What?"

"I'm an attorney, Harmony. Do you really think I haven't learnt when someone is lying to me?"

"Why are you doing this? There must be plenty of other women who would love your attention."

"Probably are. I don't care about them." He uncrossed his legs and leant forward, resting his elbows on his thighs. "Now, answer me honestly."

"Excuse me," she said, getting to her feet before running from the room.

He heard a door slam and sighed. Perhaps it hadn't been his smartest move. Alone, he got up and walked to a small table by the window, which had two pictures on it. He picked one up and smiled. Her family. Handsome Asian father, gorgeous African-American mother. Even her brother was good-looking.

In the other were Harmony and another woman. Native American, by the looks of her. The women were standing before a building with huge smiles on their faces. This Harmony looked full of joy and life. Unlike the one who'd just run from the room.

Photos back on the table, he glanced around her place. Small. Quaint would be a better word, but she made it work. It wasn't crowded and had a welcoming feel. There weren't a bunch of knick-knacks and he didn't see the vase she'd outbid him on.

"You're still here."

"I am. Where's the vase you got at the auction?" he asked.

"In my bedroom."

Pivoting on his heel, he glanced at her. Her face flushed again and she said, "I'll get it for you."

"Actually, I was wondering if I could see the entire collection."

"It's in my bedroom," she mumbled.

"I gathered that when you said that's where the one was." He held up a hand. "I'll be very good."

Her eyes narrowed and he knew she didn't buy it for a second. "Fine."

Containing his grin, he followed her back to her room. There wasn't much more space back here but he did see the collection along a wall. She had twenty of them. He walked past her and moved to get a closer look at them. All intricately detailed, they were amazing.

"Wow. This is incredible," he said.

"Thank you."

"How long did it take you to get all these?"

"My grandmother started it for me when I..." She cleared her throat. "When I was younger. She passed three years ago and I tracked down the rest of them."

There was something she wasn't telling him but he let it go. He reached for one only to pause and peer at her. "May I?"

"Sure."

He lifted one the colour of the sea and stared at it before putting it back. "You have a beautiful collection, Harmony."

"Thank you."

His gaze took in the rest of the room and lingered on the double bed. A cream-coloured comforter covered it. He sneaked a peek at her and found her gaze transfixed to the bed. She jumped slightly when he cleared his throat.

"Harmony?" he asked, reaching for her.

"I... I need to get some sleep. Long day tomorrow. I'm sure you have one as well."

"I do." He stepped towards her only for her to take one back. They continued the dance until she could go no farther, having run into the hallway wall. "Why are you running from me?"

"You could hurt me."

"What is life without risks?"

"Safe."

He shook his head at her. "Boring. I don't take you as a boring person, Harmony. I have no plans to hurt you." He'd seen the spark she had for life—it had shown when she'd looked at the rain and in the sparkle in her eyes as she'd tried not to laugh at him covered with mud. However, she tried to hide it. He wanted to know why.

He cut off her next statement by kissing her. The taste of honey flooded his mouth as he swept through and touched every part he could reach. She whimpered before sinking into him and returning the kiss with fervour. He caught her about the waist and lifted her up, holding her flush against him.

Sinking one hand into her hair and wrapping around it, he tugged her head back. "You don't run from passion like this, Harmony." He placed her back on her feet and released her hair. "I'll see you tomorrow." One more hard, fast kiss then he left her there before he gave in and took her to bed.

* * * *

Harmony could feel his touch on her even as she showered and went to bed. Her dreams were so real, and his touch so tantalising, she just wanted to allow it and never question. She was still tired come morning when she got ready for college. The day dragged and when she'd finished helping Lana, she made her way home as quickly as she could.

She sat on her bed and pushed up her sleeve, staring at the scar on her right arm. One finger traced it idly while she remembered how things had been before the incident. The concerts, the pride her family had had in her.

Harmony bit her lip as the tears began to fall. Ignoring them, she curled up on her side and let them slip free. Eventually, her exhausted body fell into a deep sleep. When she woke, she felt a bit better and washed away all trace of tears. She was ready when Jonathon came to her door.

"Hello," she said, swinging it open.

"Didn't you think you should ask who it was?"

"I looked through the peephole," Harmony retorted.

She stared at him. He was dressed impeccably, again. Nothing out of place and a look on his face that bordered on condescension. This man was excessively serious.

"Hungry?" he asked. His gaze fixated upon her mouth.

"A bit."

He kissed her and she melted into him, her arms twining about his neck. Short and powerful. Her nipples were tight when he ended the kiss and her slit was wet — she wanted him back between her legs.

"Hi," he said, his entire countenance softer.

"Hi, yourself."

"Come to dinner with me."

She shook her head. "Too early for me to eat. Take a walk with me instead."

His eyes widened a bit and he wanted to refuse, she could see it in his gaze. "Fine. A walk it is."

Yep. A man who worked out indoors. "Wonderful," she said.

Swiping her keys off the hook, she followed him out of her place then locked the door behind them. She slipped her arm through his and led him to the stairs. Once they reached outside, she tipped her head back to catch the sun's warmth.

"Where do you walk?" he asked, gazing at her.

"There's a park up the street. I walk there."

He obediently turned that way and they headed off. The wind was warm and she could feel what remained of her tension floating away.

"How was your day?" she questioned.

"Busy. Spent most of it in court."

"I'm sorry. I hope it went well."

"It did." His tone had become more serious.

"What do you do for fun, Jonathon?"

"Fun?"

"Yes. Fun. When you're not in court or working, what do you like to do?"

His silence spoke volumes—it was as if he hadn't had fun for so long it was taking him a while to think about what he did.

"This and that."

She laughed. It may not have been a nice thing to do but she couldn't help it.

"What's so funny?"

"You. Your answer. You haven't had fun in so long you don't know what you do for it. Do you remember what fun is?"

"I had fun in a hotel room with you. I remember all about that night." His words were low and drenched in seduction.

So did she. Ignoring the responses her body gave, she focused on the matter at hand. "Not what I'm talking about. When was the last time you had a picnic outside? Lay on a blanket and watched the clouds. Rode a bike in the mountains. I don't know, played pool with your friends. Bowling. Anything like that?"

"I don't have time."

She snorted. "That's crap."

"What?" He glared at her.

She wasn't intimidated in the least. "You are making excuses. You work too hard and are too serious."

"I'm an attorney. I have clients counting on me."

"Right. And no other lawyer ever takes a day off?" She shoved him with her shoulder. "I bet you even work weekends."

"If there's a case—"

"There's always going to be another case. It's the way of the world. Doesn't change the fact you are a workaholic."

"I've taken weekends off," he protested.

"When was the last one you had off?"

Jonathon stopped walking and pulled her in front of him. His eyes blazed with heat. "The auction."

"Well," she said, swallowing. "Nice to know you took time off to get something for your mother."

"I didn't think of any briefs or cases while I was with you," he continued as if she'd not said a word. "I had one thing on my mind. Keeping you naked all night and the next day. Would have worked too, if someone else hadn't run away."

She shifted and shrugged. "I had to get home."

"You want me to take some time off, you know exactly what will do it."

"I'm not paying for you to have a hooker," she said indignantly.

He laughed. Not a snicker, but a full-throated laugh. His head tipped back and his Adam's apple fascinated her. Sparkling brown eyes met hers when he'd stopped laughing.

"Not funny."

He leaned in for a quick kiss. "Very funny. I meant you, Harmony. You spend a weekend with me and I'll be in no way thinking about work."

Her belly trembled at the thought. A full weekend with him. "I don't think —"

"You're the one who said I work too much." He slid his hand around to cup the back of her head, his fingertips massaging her scalp. "Come on. Spend the weekend with me," he coaxed.

She shouldn't. But she wanted him again. And again.

"One weekend?"

He grinned. "For starters."

The grin did her in. She knew she was lost. It didn't matter that it might not be the smartest thing for her to do, but damn it all. She wanted him. Hadn't been able to forget about him since their night in Las Cruces.

"Okay."

The glint in his eyes made her wonder if she hadn't just bitten off more than she could chew. He reminded her of a predator stalking its prey.

The air split with sirens and they both glanced back to see if they could see anything. Fire trucks went by, followed by ambulances and police cars. They shrugged and continued with their walk.

As they headed back to her place he said, "I'll be by to pick you up on Friday night then. If you're going to keep me busy all weekend, I have to put in some extra time."

"I don't have to keep you busy at all."

"Oh, yes you do. I'm looking forward to it, too."

She snorted and rested her head briefly against his arm. They turned the corner and her heart jumped up into her chest. The trucks they'd seen flying by had been going to her apartment building. "Oh no," she breathed, pulling away from him and beginning to run.

She barrelled into a firefighter who caught her. "Sorry, ma'am. You can't go in there."

"I live here!"

Jonathon removed her from the fireman's arms. His hold kept her pressed against him.

"I'm sorry, ma'am," the fireman said. "I can't let you in there. It's too dangerous."

"What happened?" Jonathon questioned.

"Boiler blew in the basement."

They continued talking but all her attention sat focused on the rubble that used to be her home. Gone. It was all gone. Wrenching free of Jonathon's hold, she made her way on shaky legs over to the kerb and sat.

Everything's gone. The tears streamed down her cheeks. She could have been in there. Hell, she'd *just* been in there. Harmony lost track of time, she just sat there and stared, realising she had nothing now.

"Harmony," Jonathon said, crouching before her. "Come on, you need to get something to eat."

"Gone," she mumbled. "It's all gone. Everything. My pictures, my things from Grandma. Gone."

She barely noticed that he'd swept her up in his arms and started to walk until another fireman stopped him. When she struggled to be put down, he merely tightened his grip on her, effectively and swiftly telling her she wasn't going anywhere for the moment.

He took her to an SUV. A Mercedes and just as nice as his car, the one he'd taken her home in that night after his car had got all muddy. After setting her down in the passenger seat, he buckled her in. Her head lolled on her neck and she stared back at the smouldering building.

"Where are you taking me?" she finally asked. "I just need a phone and I can call Lana."

"No."

"No what?"

"I'm taking you home."

She coughed. "My home just burnt down. I have to call Lana so I have somewhere else to go."

"No need."

"I really don't want to sleep on the street, so if you could just let me use your cellphone."

He tossed her the phone. "Feel free to tell her where you are but you don't need to stay with her."

"What?" she asked sarcastically. "Taking me home with you?"

Jonathon rotated his head and met her gaze squarely. "That's exactly what I'm doing."

Chapter Four

Jonathon briefly studied the surprise in her gaze then focused back on the road.

Harmony was silent for a bit then said, "Fine, but I need to get some things since this..." She paused then said slowly, "Is all I have now."

She sounded so lost. Jonathon was glad she didn't try to fight him on coming home with him.

Jonathon placed his hand on her thigh, squeezing gently. "You've got me. I'll help you. I can give you money—"

She cut him off. "I don't need your charity. Thank God it's habit that I always put my bankcard, ID and a few dollars in my pocket. I have money. I just need you to take me to Karltons so I can pick up a few things."

Jonathon knew the department store she was referring to. He found a place to turn, since it was in the other direction. Harmony was talking lowly to someone on the phone. Jonathon didn't listen. Giving her privacy, he started thinking of what he needed to do to make her stay in his home comfortable.

"Thanks for giving me a place to stay. Hopefully it won't be long. I'll contact the landlord to see if he can get me another place." Harmony spoke, bringing his attention back to her.

Jonathon clenched the wheel—he didn't want her to leave so soon. She wasn't even in his home yet and she was already planning not to stay. Jonathon relaxed his hold and tried to be rational. Of course she would be looking for a new place to live, that was what she *should* be doing. It wasn't what he wanted her to do, but he knew she should.

"Stay as long as you like. At least you should get something from your renters' insurance. That'll help you to get started getting stuff for your new place." Jonathon turned into the parking lot of Karltons.

See that's good, I'm being supportive even if I hope it takes her a while to find a place.

"I don't have renters' insurance," Harmony admitted.

Jonathon pulled into a space, parked then glanced at her. "Why not? Everyone shou—"

"I don't have any. I'm going to start from scratch." Harmony unbuckled her seatbelt, opened the door then exited the vehicle.

She closed the door gently but to Jonathon it could have been a slam. He heard the underlying reprimand in her voice. Jonathon got out, clicked the alarm on his keys and followed Harmony. She had already retrieved a cart and was pushing it towards the entrance of the big department store. Jonathon jogged to catch up with her and he reached for the cart. Harmony turned her head—her face was in that closed-off expression he hated. She shifted and let him take the cart. They went inside and started to get what Harmony needed.

Jonathon was silent as he trailed her while she shopped. He frowned, noting that she didn't pick up much. Soon they were back at the counter. Jonathon helped unpack the cart that wasn't even a quarter full. He made a mental note of what she had got, and the sizes of the limited items of clothing. He bagged her things as they came down the conveyor then stood and waited for her to pay. Once she had joined him, he pushed the cart back to his SUV. In moments, they were on their way to his condo. Harmony was still not speaking and he could feel the distance building between them. He wanted to say something to change it, but couldn't think of what would accomplish that.

Harmony sighed. "Look, Jonathon, I know you mean well, but I'm sure many of us who lived in the building didn't have insurance. That's the last thing you think of getting when you're on a limited budget. I can only imagine what the other tenants are feeling right now. I know a few of them and they are hard-working people with very little disposable income. What are they going to do now?"

Her caring for the others rather than herself moved Jonathon. "First, the report on the fire will be filed in a few days. From what the firefighter at the scene said, the boiler in the basement blew. If this is the fault of the landlord then there is recourse for that."

"We've been complaining to the company who handled the property that there was a bunch of things that needed fixing. We even mentioned the boiler," Harmony said.

Jonathon considered what she had stated then said, "Did you all put this in writing?"

"Yes. A few of us did and that's how we sort of became friendly. The building, even though it had problems, was much better than most for the price.

There are some older tenants who live only off their social security and were glad for a reasonably good building and low rent. Now it's all gone. I'll have to check and see who I can get in touch with." Harmony sounded even more lost.

Jonathon didn't ask any more questions—he was already thinking about what the firefighter had stated and Harmony's comments. He'd have to do some digging into the building and after what Harmony had said, he'd bet there was something there to find. Neither spoke for the rest of the drive. At his condo, he helped her with the bags, taking them into the house. She had got so little that they were able to take it all inside in one trip. He frowned, remembering what she had—there was no way that would be enough. Inside his condo, he showed her around the ground floor pointing out the various rooms. On the way, he retrieved a key and gave it to her. Harmony took it without comment but he could see she was amused for some reason.

"I hate to ask, but can I use your computer?" Harmony asked when they were in the office.

"Sure, let me set you up your own access." Jonathon put down the bags and did just that.

Once they'd got her all set up, he led her upstairs and gave her a quick tour of that floor. At one end of the hall was his room, which had its own bathroom, then two guest rooms, a bath that was on the wall facing those guest rooms and a linen closet. At the other end of the hall was another guest room, which had its own bath.

"This room is yours for as long as you're here. Wait, let me get some linens." Jonathon placed the bags he held on the chair by the door and hurried back out.

He went to the linen closet, retrieved the items needed then returned to the room. Taking the fitted sheet, he placed the rest of the items in another chair that was by the nightstand. Jonathon started to make the bed.

"I ca—"

He raised his head and made her know he wasn't going to stop. Harmony smiled then took the other side of the sheet. They quickly made the bed. Jonathon picked up the items for the bathroom and took them inside. He fixed them neatly on the shelf built into the wall. Jonathon adjusted the items on the other three shelves then stepped back. Pleased it was all in order, he turned then stopped as he saw Harmony leaning against the doorjamb, watching him with the same amused expression.

"What?" He crossed his arms over his chest.

"You're very organised. A key for me, and this room for me to stay in is clean and immaculate. This bathroom is...wow. I haven't gotten a good look at the outside surrounding area of this place, but even that is a generous size. Last time I was here I just saw the living room and I thought that was a good size, but seeing it all now inside—this is a big place. The ground floor is quite spacious with the living room, entertainment room, den, home gym, office and that massive kitchen. Then this second floor is also spacious. Why do you need a place with four bedrooms and three bathrooms? Or a place so big for one man?" Harmony studied him.

Jonathon didn't like being the one at the other end of questions. He passed by Harmony, going out of the door and answering her when his back was to her.

"I like order and space. I didn't want to do the building-type condo. I bought in this area of

McKingley because of the location and they offered individual condos with land space, which gave you a little distance from your neighbours. This one was at the end of the block and it called to me." He was not about to admit that he'd bought this place with the intention of eventually having a family.

More recently, he'd started imagining the woman he wanted here was Harmony. Jonathon continued across the room and to the bedroom door.

"The phone lines are similar to the way they are in offices. There are multiple lines so just press a number on the phone to get one out. If it's lit, someone is using it. Feel free to use it as you like. If you need me I'll be downstairs."

"Thanks, Jonathon," Harmony stated.

"No problem." He went down the hall then descended the stairs.

Jonathon strode to the window and looked out at his manicured lawn. Remembering he wanted to make a call, he quickly made it then went back to studying the view. He peered at his watch and noted an hour had already passed. Jonathon glanced towards the entryway for the living room but didn't go to check on Harmony.

She's just staying with you. Give her space.

Jonathon went to his office and retrieved his laptop before returning to the living room. Soon he was immersed in work.

"Jonathon... Sorry, I didn't know you were working," Harmony said.

He looked at the time on the laptop and noted he'd been at it for four hours. He lifted his head—she had changed into one of the things she'd bought. As he saw the time, he wondered where they were. The doorbell rang and Jonathon put down his laptop, stood and walked towards her. Harmony backed up and started to retreat back upstairs.

Jonathon caught her arm. "Wait, the door is for you."

Harmony turned and stared at him, confusion on her face. Jonathon noticed she had on shoes. He led her towards the door before opening it and smiling at the man and woman there.

"Dey—"

"Hush—making me shop in such a short time has made me cranky." Deyon De'clare's melodious voice indeed did sound put out as she pushed past him carting many bags.

"She's also hungry. I brought us all dinner." Leonardo Wright, his brother, followed holding even more bags. He paused and handed him a key before trailing after Deyon.

Jonathon nodded then tugged Harmony out of the door and down the walkway to the dark blue Toyota Corolla. He clicked the button to unlock the door then opened it before stepping back beside Harmony and gesturing to the vehicle.

"Get in and check it out."

"Why? Who are those people and why do they have all those bags?" Harmony asked.

"The car is yours to use. I realised on the way here it's a longer trip for you to the college from here so I got you this car to use." Jonathon gestured towards the house. "That's my family, Deyon and Leo."

"You have another sister?" Harmony's tone was clipped.

"I have three in total and two brothers including Leo. You know this, I told you so earlier. Deyon isn't my sister—she's family, though. Maybe will even be a sister-in-law—she and Leo recently started dating. Enough questions—now get in the car."

"You can't just give me a car." Harmony stepped back.

"I'm not giving you a car. It belongs to my cousin. She's away at medical school and left it here. I called and asked her if you could borrow it. She was glad to lend it to you. Said it was just sitting there anyway," Jonathon said.

Harmony turned on her heels and went back to the house. Baffled, Jonathon followed her. Her back looked rigid as she moved before him. Inside the condo, he caught her arm and turned her to him.

"Harmony, what—?"

"Come on, Harmony. Let's make sure you like this stuff I got. After all, I had to depend on Jon for your sizes and what you might like. I want to get this done so we can eat," Deyon called from upstairs.

Harmony glanced from the stairs to Jonathon. Her face was even colder than before. "You bought me clothing too."

"I—"

"Jon, shut up and let her come upstairs. Get the rest of the bags from the car. I don't have all night." Deyon's footsteps headed towards Harmony's room.

Harmony's eyes narrowed then she turned on her heel and went up the stairs. Jonathon watched her, wondering what was wrong.

"Boy, I know that look. You have some grovelling to do." Leo spoke from behind him.

Jonathon glared at his older brother. "I don't know what you mean."

"Haughty works on people who don't know you. What is she to you? Heard you were asking around about the fire at her apartment building." Leo pushed his hands into his pockets.

Jonathon didn't even wonder how he knew—Leo was the sheriff, and their older brother Dimitri was an arson investigator, so he would have heard about it from him.

"You all are a bunch of gossips." He headed back outside to retrieve the bags.

Leo followed. Jonathon opened the back door of his brother's truck. He stared at the bags then remembered what they'd already brought inside.

"Christ, did she buy the whole of Karltons?"

"You're the one who sent Deyon to shop for things for Harmony. And you said, and I quote, 'She needs everything'." Leo chuckled. "You should have known better than telling a clothing horse like Deyon something like that."

"Damn it, you could have controlled your woman," Jonathon stated.

"Mind your business. What's between us is our business," Leo stated and pulled out some bags, pushing them into his hands.

Jonathon didn't ask him outright what was going on. They all had at some point, but Leo was being strangely mum about what he and Deyon had going on. Their parents had decreed them not to ask about the two. Jonathon accepted the bags and they headed back inside. Upstairs, he strode into Harmony's bedroom. She glanced at him then away. Deyon pointed to the bed and they put down their bundles. She pushed them out of the room, closing the door in their faces.

"What the hell is Deyon's problem? Why is Harmony looking at me like that? I didn't do anything wrong," Jonathon said.

"Deyon is just being ornery because you told her that Harmony wasn't as flamboyant as she is. She saw that as an insult to Harmony and took exception to it."

"But she doesn't even know her. I didn't mean it as a bad thing." Jonathon walked down the hall.

"It doesn't matter. You know Deyon. She has a big heart, although she tries to hide it below that sassy mouth." Leo smiled a roguish grin.

"I don't even want to know what that grin is about." Jonathon descended the stairs.

"Back to the question of why Harmony is looking at you the way she is. Well—she's probably pissed off you bought all that stuff for her and lent her the car. I bet you didn't even tell her." Leo headed for the kitchen.

Jonathon followed. "I didn't, but she has no reason to be mad. I'm helping her out. How much was everything?"

"I have no clue. Deyon has the receipts. I left her shopping and went to get the car. I took it to Archer to check over to make sure it was working okay."

"Thanks. No wonder you took so long. It's already after ten." Jonathon glanced at the wall clock.

"Nope. That didn't take long. I was waiting for Deyon. It's a good thing I went into Karltons when I did—she'd already got the store manager to help her. He was pushing around a cart along with two others employees who also had filled wagons. Deyon was about to get a cart of her own when I got there. Told her we had to go. Boy, was she pissed. When we went to the counter, I realised she had another cart there already waiting. That woman is a shopping manic." Leo chuckled.

He pulled out a hero sandwich and handed it to Jonathon then took one for himself. They sat at the island and started eating. Eventually the women joined them and they got their food. Harmony ignored him and conversed with Deyon and Leo. Soon they were finished and Deyon and Leo were getting ready to leave. At the front door, Jonathon hugged Deyon and shook Leo's hand.

"How much do I owe you, Deyon?" he asked.

Deyon raised her head. "Nothing. Harmony and I worked it out."

She pivoted and strutted out. Jonathon shook his head and glanced at Leo. He was watching Deyon walk away. The lust on his face was evident. Jonathon smacked him on the back of his head.

"Stop ogling her ass."

Leo rubbed his head then pushed at his shoulder. "But it's a great one. What's going on with you and Harmony?" Leo stared at him.

Jonathon glanced back then frowned when he didn't see Harmony, though she'd come into the hall with him. He faced Leo again then crossed his arms over his chest.

"Just like you and Deyon—it's none of your business."

"Fair enough. But you know the family will wonder why she's staying with you." Leo left with those words.

Jonathon knew they would. He pulled the key for the car out of his pocket and pointed it at the vehicle, armed it then stepped back inside. He heard footsteps and turned to see Harmony coming down the hall from the direction of his office. She headed to the stairs.

"Harmony, here's the key." He held it out.

She took it then went up the stairs. Jonathon stood at the bottom of the staircase watching her retreating figure. He was curious about what Harmony and Deyon had worked out but didn't think it was a good time to ask. Jonathon locked up then went upstairs to bed. He decided he'd talk to her in the morning before they both headed out to work.

* * * *

The next morning, he came down early so he could make her breakfast and they could talk. In the kitchen, he noted something on the island countertop. He frowned, picking up the key for the car. Jonathon went to the front door, peeked out of the window and saw the Corolla was still there. A suspicion formed and he stood at the bottom of the stairs.

"Harmony," he called.

There was no sound upstairs. Jonathon returned to the kitchen then realised there was a paper under a magnet he had on the fridge. He went over and took it down. Jonathon read the note from Harmony, which informed him she would be home late. He crushed the note in his hand, wondering where she was going. Jonathon fixed the magnets back to how they should be, then went to get ready for work. Throughout his workday, all he thought about was Harmony and what she was doing. When he arrived home he got comfortable then paced, waiting for her. Finally, he heard the key in the lock. He saw it was nine thirty and, from their conversations, he knew Friday was her early day at the university so she'd finished at twelve. He went into the hall and waited for her to open the door.

"How did you get to work? Where have you been?" he demanded as she entered.

Harmony glanced at Jonathon. He was standing with his feet braced apart and arms crossed over his chest. She had noted before that that was his 'trying to be calm while actually pissed off' pose. Harmony closed the door, stifling a smile. She faced him again and got the zing of need. She was mad at him and should not be thinking of how fast she could get him naked and inside her. Harmony passed him and went into the kitchen. She heard his footsteps behind her. Harmony put away the food from the bag she'd brought in.

"Well."

Harmony moved to the island, looking at Jonathon across the surface. She had already seen the key for the car and knew they had to talk.

"I took the bus to work. I've been with Deyon. We made arrangements for me to help her out at her store. I need to pay off the things she bought for me."

"But I was go—"

"Pay for them. No and that brings me to the point. You can't just buy me stuff and give me a car. People don't just do things like that, Jonathon." Harmony thought of all the things Deyon had bought.

She was set for replacing her clothing and other essentials. Deyon had been through and had even bought her shoes. At first, she'd been pissed off and embarrassed that Jonathon had done such a thing, thinking of her as a charity case. Deyon—in what Harmony realised was her blunt way—had quickly dissuaded her of being a charity case. At least to Deyon. She'd told Harmony she didn't look like a woman who let a man pay for her and since she— Deyon—might have got a little spend happy, Harmony could work it off in her store. Also, for some additional money, she wanted to use Harmony's petite frame to fit for a special order she was making for a model friend. As well as a shoe and hand model for some shoes and jewellery that she had recently made for her store. There would be no pictures of her face, thankfully. Deyon hadn't cared that Harmony had no experience in modelling—she'd said she would do it and that was that. When Harmony had first met the exquisitely dressed woman, she'd had trepidation she would be stuck up, but Deyon was anything but.

Arriving at her store—which Harmony had heard of but had never shopped in—she'd been again intimidated, but Deyon and her employees had all made her feel welcome. After working with Deyon today, she'd seen that the woman was highly efficient and dedicated to her business. No wonder it was so successful. Deyon's store didn't carry her size, but the shoes and other accessories had tempted her.

"It's something I do. Any one of my family would have done. It's the way we were raised. To help when someone needs it." Jonathon ran his hand over the back of his neck then lowered his hand, clenching his fist. "It's not charity if that's what you're thinking. I didn't expect you to just take and not pay me back. But you could have done that in time. The car was because, as I mentioned, I realised that from here it's longer to get to the university. I figured it would cost you more in transportation and it would be cheaper to put gas in a car so you can go to and from here to there. Or wherever you needed to go. As well as take less time. None of that's charity—it was helping another human being who might need it. Why won't you just accept my help?"

His frustration was evident in his tone and mannerisms. Harmony thought of what he had stated then realised she'd automatically become defensive. The difference in their lifestyles had inserted itself into her subconscious and she hadn't even noticed it. Harmony recognised that since she'd met Jonathon, she'd been making lots of assumptions about him. She made a mental note to check the Internet to find out more about what he had been referring to when he'd said his family helped others. In her gut, she knew that if she asked Jonathon, he'd make it seem less than it was.

"Okay. I'll use the car. You're right—it would be cheaper and take less time. Thanks for letting me use it. Well, thank your cousin too."

"I'll give you her number so you can tell her yourself." Jonathon stared then asked, "I'm glad you're accepting my help. How much do you owe Deyon? I—"

"No, that I won't let you do. I'll work it off at Deyon's." Harmony smiled.

"I don't want you to have to work there if you don't want to."

"But I want to. Deyon is an interesting character and she has a lot she's showing me."

"Are you a sales person?" Jonathon sounded appalled.

Harmony laughed at his politically correct words. "Nope, I'm more like a Girl Friday at Deyon's beck and call. She's showing me a little of everything. It's challenging keeping up with her."

"Okay. But if you want to stop then you can and I'll pa—"

"Give it a rest, Jonathon. I'm going to pay off my own debt. Besides, for how much Deyon is paying me, it won't be for too long." Harmony shook her head.

Deyon demanded the best and paid for it. At first, Harmony'd thought Deyon was giving her more so she could work off the money she owed quicker but Deyon had assured her it wasn't, and had given her the pay scales she had for employees—one of the things Harmony would be helping out with was payroll. Harmony moved around the island and stood before Jonathon. This close, she inhaled his intoxicating scent. She ached with her need to have him. Even mad at him, as she'd been last night, she'd wanted him. Had been aware of his every movement.

"I'm heading up to bed, are you coming?"

"Yes. I'll just lock up. Night." Jonathon turned.

Harmony could tell he didn't know what she'd meant. He'd figure it out soon enough. She strolled upstairs. She leaned against the wall just by the steps and soon she heard Jonathon coming up. When he was at the top of the steps, he went towards his room.

"I thought you were coming to bed?" Harmony stifled a smile as he jumped then turned to face her.

"I am." His brow furrowed.

"Okay, then." She sauntered towards him, passing him as she headed for his room.

"Where are you going?"

Harmony faced him and walked backwards. "For a lawyer, you really are slow. To bed with you. And I don't plan on us sleeping for a while."

Harmony let the desire she had for him seep into her voice. Even before the fire, she'd decided she was going to stop resisting and have him. Losing everything had derailed that momentarily, but she needed to be near him. Jonathon's face changed and she saw the hunger on his face. He moved towards her, his movements predatory, arrogant and precise.

All the things that made up who he was. Harmony's pulse quickened and her pussy dampened

Chapter Five

Harmony shifted when her back touched the wall and she searched with her hand behind her to find the edge of the doorjamb. When she did, she used it as a guide to step through the door while her gaze was still locked on Jonathon's. His stroll was slow and made her heartbeat accelerate as she moved backwards away from him. Suddenly he moved faster and caught her, yanking her against his bigger frame. He lowered his head and kissed her, clearly marking his ownership, and Harmony met him, revelling in the possessiveness of his touch. The texture of his kiss was different from those they'd shared recently — this one was as she remembered from their one night together. It made the throb of her slit increase and her body prepared for his taking.

Jonathon loosened his hold and his fingers touched her throat then lowered as he undressed her. Harmony suckled his tongue as he worked on getting them naked. She cradled his head and stepped back, moving towards the bed. Jonathon matched her step for step. The cool air on her skin made her shiver slightly and she moaned as she felt him cup her breasts, kneading them then plucking at the nipples. Harmony kicked off her sandals and kept pulling him with her as she moved back. Jonathon's hands on her hips stilled her then he grabbed her ass, pulling her tight to him again. She whimpered as his bare skin touched her naked flesh. His engorged shaft pressed along her sternum. He moved his hand down her hip then under her leg, changing her hold and lifting her leg up. Jonathon rocked rubbing against her, Harmony arched, countering his motions. Jonathon lifted his head and stared at her.

"Harmony." The harsh need in his voice made the heat in her belly increase.

Holding her leg, he lifted her off the floor and stepped forward. Jonathon lowered her to the mattress and covered her with his body. He pushed open her legs and surged into her. Harmony writhed, whimpering as his sheathed erection filled her. She closed her eyes, smiling. Jonathon was very efficient at donning protection without her ever realising it, just as he had been that night. Her thoughts scattered as he set a hard, fast rhythm. Harmony held his shoulders, squeezing them in time with his thrusts. She moaned continuously as he took her without any mercy. Her body was on fire with need and she wanted...no, *needed* his masterful taking. She blinked then opened her eyes and stared at his face, which was carved in harsh lines of pleasure. The muscles in his throat stood out as he pumped deep and twisted his hips.

"Jonathon," she whimpered.

His gaze focused on her as he moved quicker and his lips pulled back in a snarl. Harmony's pussy gushed at the sight of him so out of control. Jonathon was usually so contained in everything he did. Even on their one shared night, he had been meticulous in driving her out of her mind. Yet now this untamed man made her pulse jump and canal clench with the pleasure he was giving her. Harmony couldn't decide which version of his sensual conquering she preferred.

"Come for me." His harsh demand was punctured by thrusts.

"Jonathon," she groaned, arching as she flooded with her release.

Tightening her legs around him, she rocked against him, demanding that he give her his own pleasure. Jonathon's breaths puffed out and his sweat-dampened face was hard. Harmony lifted her head and licked along his lips from top to bottom then bit down on the centre of the bottom one before letting it go with a pop.

"Now," she screamed.

Jonathon stiffened then shuddered, grunting as he came. He jerked, shaking, then relaxed, collapsing against her. Harmony held him and kissed the side of his face. Her heart beat frantically as she inhaled his scent. Jonathon was limp against her, his body sprawled over her.

"You're a chameleon—a contained man one moment, then this fierce conqueror. When I think I have you figured out you change on me. Who is the real Jonathon Wright?" Harmony mused.

Jonathon lifted his head and his serious dark brown eyes were unfathomable. He studied her then rolled off her, disposing of the condom. He reached for another and quickly put it on his revived erection. Jonathon returned to his previous position, gliding into her canal. Harmony moaned as he filled her again.

Jonathon watched her, pumping lazily. "All of them. I'm a versatile man but at the bottom of it all I'm just me."

"And I want to get to know all sides of you." Harmony moaned, gripping him, as he thrust in a maddeningly slow pace.

"I want to know all your secrets, Harmony. Get to know the woman who has been in my thoughts all these months." Jonathon's gaze was steady.

Harmony gulped at what he was asking. There was so much she didn't...couldn't...share with him, and she wasn't sure if she ever would be able to.

Jonathon's face softened. "Not all at once — when you're ready you can tell me. Just give me...us a chance," he assured her.

Harmony studied him then nodded, hugging him.

Jonathon inhaled the scent that was them and rocked into her wetness. She clenched around him, creating a delicious friction as they strived towards another fulfilment of their passion. Harmony made him lose control and he didn't know how she did it. One look at her captivating face and all he could think of was finding someplace to have her — horizontal, vertical or sideways didn't matter. Groaning, he thrust slowly and deliberately. The hitch of her breath sounded with each motion, guiding him on. Her nails dug into his back as she moved her head back and forth against the pillow. She was so very beautiful. The quiet dignity and grace she portrayed in everything she did left when she let loose the passion inside her. The memories of their one night paled in comparison with now and somehow he knew each time they were like this, she'd surprise him.

He couldn't wait to enjoy each and every moment with her. Lowering his head, he kissed her hungrily and pumped his hips. She tightened around him, moaning and babbling words he didn't understand, which made him smile. Harmony was vocal and, even if he couldn't understand the language she was speaking, he enjoyed knowing he made her lose her senses enough that she forgot to speak English. He hitched her leg up on his hip and rolled them, moving inside her grasping canal.

"Jonathon—" Then a spatter of an unrecognisable language.

He moved in quick, deep thrusts and felt her clench then she gushed arching her head as she came again. Jonathon groaned and joined her in pleasure. He shifted off her to dispose of the protection then cuddled her against his side. Sated, he held her as he drifted off to sleep.

* * * *

Jonathon enjoyed the view outside his front window and in the glass he could see the smile on his lips. Three weeks spent with Harmony and he couldn't stop smiling. Even at his office, they had noticed his happier countenance and Jonathon didn't care. Harmony was a breath of fresh air and she had such a zest for life. In and out of bed, they had so much to talk about and he'd found she was even nicer than he'd thought, smart and had a wicked sense of humour. He chuckled at the thought of her humour, which sneaked up on him. Arms slid around his back and he was hugged from behind.

"What's got you laughing by yourself? Better be careful or someone will think you're crazy."

Harmony's warm lyrical voice made him hard, as it typically did.

Jonathon turned in her loose hold, lowering his head and kissing her gently. Then he couldn't resist and deepened their kiss. Harmony opened, moaning. He lifted her into his arms and her legs wrapped around him as they usually did. This hold was becoming his favourite. Harmony pressed against him, her legs open for his taking.

Too bad we're not already naked. Jonathon stepped forward, intent on getting them both that way immediately. A chiming ring tone interrupted them. Harmony pulled her lips away and turned her head then she released the hold of her legs and slid down his body. She moved away to the cell on the side table. Jonathon clenched his fist, tempted to throw the cell against a wall. Harmony had bought it a few days after moving in with him so that she wouldn't be giving out his phone number to other people. He hadn't minded, but she'd insisted that she was here temporarily and once she moved to a new place he wouldn't have to worry about getting calls that were intended for her. As he had then, Jonathon glared at the phone she was talking into. The idea of her leaving was making him ornery.

Although they slept together each night in his room, Harmony still kept her things in the guest room. Jonathon had mentioned she could move her things into his space but Harmony had laughed and said he had everything so organised in his room that her more relaxed way of keeping her things would drive him daft. Jonathon knew she was partially right—it would bug him but he'd accept it *for her*.

Harmony lowered her hand and faced him. A wide smile was on her face and she was almost bouncing in place.

"The landlord found me a new place. Same rent and everything. I'm going over now to meet the representative from the management company to check it out and get the keys."

She spoke so fast in her excitement that it took a moment for what she had said to register. When it did, Jonathon's smile faded and he stared—he was not pleased that she'd already found a new place so soon after moving in with him. Jonathon knew she'd been discussing things with the landlord but not that he'd been looking for a place for her.

You knew she wasn't going to be here forever. Jonathon spoke, "Great, I'll take you, let me get my keys."

He turned and went to the kitchen to get his keys and to give himself time to pull himself together. Jonathon took a few deep breaths then returned the way he had come. Harmony was already waiting for him. She didn't have a purse, which he knew was because when she went out casually she didn't walk with one but put her things in her pockets. Harmony always had clothing on that had pockets and Deyon had even fixed some of the clothing she'd bought, putting in pockets. If Harmony went to work or out somewhere to shop or dinner she carried a bag. He watched her, realising he knew that little quirk as well as others he'd observed of her in the last few weeks. Jonathon jingled his keys as he joined her by the door, then opened it. Harmony exited and he followed her. In moments they were in his SUV. Harmony gave him the address and Jonathon frowned.

"Are you sure that's the correct address?"

"Yes, see, I wrote it down and he gave me directions if you don't know how to get there." Harmony showed him a piece of paper.

"I was born here. I know all the nooks and crannies of McKingley." Jonathon pulled onto the street and drove towards their destination.

As far as he knew, the place they were going was in a less than savoury part of town. Although, it had been a while since he'd been there so maybe it had changed. They were silent on the drive and Jonathon's frown deepened the closer they got. The area had changed and he saw that it wasn't for the better. The buildings looked abandoned and in his opinion the area was dangerous. He kept his thoughts to himself, found the correct number and parked in front of the structure. Jonathon exited before going to Harmony's door and helping her out. Harmony's expression was blank so he couldn't tell what she was thinking. She lifted her hand and placed her fingers over where he knew the scar was on her right arm. She traced it idly as she stared at the building. Seeing that, Jonathon realised she was in deep thought. Harmony moved forward and he followed her.

Jonathon noted there was no security door and the front door lock was busted. As they went in, he made a mental list of all that was wrong with the place and they hadn't even made it to the apartment. Harmony stopped before an apartment at the end of the hall. She knocked and almost immediately the door swung open, revealing a smiling man. Jonathon took an instant dislike to the smarmy-faced, immaculately dressed man.

"Harmony, it's nice to see you again," the man said, holding out a hand.

"Vince, I didn't expect it would be you again. Haven't seen you since I got my old place." She shook his hand briefly.

"It's a shame about your place and all your things. We've been working to get all our favourite tenants into new places." The man laughed heartily.

Jonathon raised an eyebrow, hearing the falseness behind the sound. The man glanced at him and Jonathon could see he'd dismissed him as he focused on Harmony. Jonathon narrowed his eyes then contained his expression of disdain. Jonathon didn't even need to see his face to know it was his genial 'I'm harmless' look. The same one he used before he went in for the kill and ripped apart the opposition. In his eyes, the opposition was this man, Vince, who with very few words Jonathon could tell was selling a load of shit. He glanced at Harmony, wondering if she was buying it, but she still just had the same blank expression. Vince guided Harmony through the apartment, talking up the wonders of the place, which Jonathon could clearly see were visually untrue. Vince's salesman's voice was getting on Jonathon's nerves so he tuned it out and headed off on his own. As he viewed the apartment, Jonathon couldn't believe that they were trying to give this dump to Harmony.

Her old place had been small but a hundred per cent better than this one. The building she had lived in had been older but it had been much better than where they were now, even though—from what he could tell—this was a newer building. Even if the neighbourhood was bad, Jonathon would have accepted her moving here had the place been nice. Even if he had hated it, he would have supported her, but bad neighbourhood and such atrocious living conditions? No way, no how. He retraced his steps to find Harmony and Vince, whom he was beginning to think of as a weasel. They were back in the living room by the counter that separated the area from the kitchen.

"Just sign this indemnity for us against the loss of your things in the fire at your old place and this new place is all yours," Vince was saying.

Jonathon strode over to them and pulled the paper from under his finger.

"Hey, wha—?"

"Shut up," he stated calmly and read the paper.

Vince sounded furious when he spoke a few moments later. "I don't know who this guy is, but take this or nothing, Harmony. And if you don't accept this replacement place you will be in violation of your lease. We *will* take you to court for it. Our lawyers—"

"Are idiots and so are you." Jonathon lifted his head.

Vince glared at him then moved around Harmony, getting in Jonathon's face. "Who the hell are you?"

"Jonathon Wright," he stated.

In the flicker of fear in Vince's eye, he could see he recognised his name. That was good and Jonathon would use it to his advantage. Jonathon folded the paper and put it in his pocket for proof. Vince reached for it.

"Touch me and I'll have you arrested for assault." He gave the threat in a silky tone, his promise very clear.

Vince stilled then slid his hands in his pockets as an arrogant expression came over his face. "There is nothing you can do, Mr Wright. Our lawyers have already checked and there is no criminal recourse for the tenants affected by the fire. Harmony had best accept this as most of the tenants of her old apartment building did. Or else."

The threat only made Jonathon smile. Vince gulped then held his gaze. Jonathon had to give him points for guts. Many had been unable to withstand his look.

"Since I know you're the lackey sent to do the dirty work that the building owner wouldn't do so he could claim plausible deniability, I'm going to give you all one chance. Both you and I know that he knows all about the pressure you're putting on these hard-working folks who have lost everything." Jonathon paused, letting his contempt show. "This little piece of paper means nothing once I line up all those tenants you harassed into signing —"

Vince interrupted. "I didn't —"

Jonathon put up his hand, stilling him. "Shut up. I'm not done." He continued as if Vince hadn't interrupted and he hadn't answered him, " — in order to get a new place to live. There's a lot I can do and will. I'm going to get in touch with each and every one of those tenants. Even those you haven't strong-armed yet. Then we will meet you and your boss in court." Jonathon turned to Harmony who had been silent during their exchange.

He put his hand on her waist and started to escort her out.

"You can't do that. There are no criminal charges you can file. And this isn't some corporation or negotiation. I know who you are, Mr Wright, and there is nothing for you to gain here." Vince spoke behind him.

Jonathon stopped, pivoted on his heels. "I didn't say criminal. I meant civil. And if you did know anything about me you'd know I wouldn't need anything to present the tenants' case. This I would do pro bono, just for the joy of fucking up your company and the building owner. You know what I hate more than liars?" By the time he had finished he was in Vince's face and he didn't wait for a response as he gritted out, "Bullies who prey on others they think are weaker or don't have a way of knowing what their legal rights are. I will be dragging you all into court. Unless…" He let that trail off.

Vince gulped. "What?"

"Your management company and the landlord of the building come up with a number I like. Make me an offer on behalf of the tenants." He lifted his index finger. "A good one that will cover them finding somewhere better to live, the emotional damage they went through because of the fire and your harassment. And although there is no money that can cover their memories of the things they lost, add that in. You have one week."

He turned and walked back to Harmony. Her expression was the same as it had been.

"But… We need time. I can—" Vince sputtered to a stop.

Jonathon smiled, knowing it was his fierce grin, the one he used when he smelt figurative blood in the water of an opponent that was ready to give in.

"A week, or be prepared to meet me in court."

"I'm not afraid of you. You don't know civil court and our lawyers can beat you." Vince seemed to get his bearing.

"You say you know me but obviously you don't. Do your research. I'll have my secretary put you all on the books to meet me a week from today at ten o'clock."

"We won't be there," Vince stated.

"I hope you don't show up because I'm going to have a good time ripping apart everything I can get on your company and the owner of the building you manage." Jonathon glanced over his shoulder at Vince and saw him pale. "I love paper and finding everything. See you in one week." He focused forward and escorted Harmony out.

In his SUV, Jonathon gripped the wheel, still seething at Vince's arrogance and his trying to intimidate Harmony. He glanced at her and she was silently watching him. Jonathon returned his attention to the road. He couldn't discuss it now with her—he needed to calm a bit first. Jonathon rarely lost control as he had back there with Vince, but the man and Harmony being in the mix had made him see red. A hand touched his thigh, squeezing gently.

"Did you mean what you said back there about taking them to court for all the tenants if they don't meet with you?"

"Yes," he answered in a clipped tone, trying to regain control.

"But you don't even know them." Harmony sounded baffled.

"I don't need to know them to care they are getting fucked over by that egotistical bastard back there." Jonathon pounded his hand on the steering wheel.

"Is it because we're sleeping together?"

"I'm not even answering that because it will be lots of bad words and not polite." Jonathon glared at her briefly then looked back at the road.

"Even pissed off as hell and you're still being courteous. Until you dropped a few F-bombs, I didn't even think you could curse." Harmony laughed.

Jonathon winced, realising she was right. He never cursed in front of women.

"I—"

"If you're going to apologise, don't. That was awesome. I'm glad you were there because if I had spoken I would have ripped him a new one. Imagine trying to give me that shithole. Asshole," Harmony stated.

Jonathon barked out a laugh. It was the first time he'd heard her curse too.

"I don't swear often either but this is a cursing occasion. Trying to intimidate me because of my size and thinking I was dumb enough to fall for it. Bastard." Harmony clenched her hand on his leg.

Jonathon covered it and she turned her palm up. He held her hand as they drove. The rain started to fall then came in a deluge. Jonathon frowned out of the windshield as the wipers swished on the glass. At his house, he parked and turned to Harmony.

"We can wait for it to stop."

"Why? We can get rid of our anger. Come, let's jump into puddles and scream." Harmony turned to the door.

Jonathon stilled her with a hand on her shoulder. She glanced back at him.

"Are you crazy? It's pouring out there. We'll get wet."

"That's the point." She pulled away and opened the door before getting out and slamming it shut behind her.

Stupefied, he watched her as she made her way to the front of the vehicle. Harmony did a twirl in the rain then faced him. She pounded on the hood, making a 'come on' gesture with her hand. Harmony put her hands on her hips and he could clearly see her expression was daring. With the water slicking back her hair and soaking her clothing, she looked like a wood nymph. A tempting one. Jonathon opened his door, got out then closed the door. He glanced down at his shoes, which were coated in mud. A hand slid into his, pulling him.

"Come on, puddle hop."

Harmony tugged him along and Jonathon followed. She stopped, letting him go, and jumped into a puddle, sloshing the water. Jonathon stepped back, shifting uncomfortably at his wet clothes as he watched Harmony play in the puddle. She faced him with a huge smile on her face and rocked on her heels.

"So, stuffed shirt, are you able to puddle jump?"

Jonathon narrowed his gaze then hopped up and splashed, kicking water at her. Harmony shrieked and ran. He chased her, laughing and spraying her. Harmony retaliated and they ran in the rain, jumping puddles.

"Puddle jump!"

Jonathon glanced up, startled. One of his neighbours he didn't know well came out with his kids and wife. They smiled at Jonathon and joined in. Harmony pushed at his side and he joined the family. Soon more neighbours came out and they all played in the rain. Jonathon watched Harmony laughing with another neighbour. He glanced around at the neighbours closest to him, whom until today he hadn't even spent time with. A child held up his arms and Jonathon picked him up. Mud coated the little boy and Jonathon didn't even care. His father came over and they chatted. By the time everyone went back to their respective homes, Jonathon had accepted invitations to a barbecue that a few of them were having, bowling and other outings. He waved, holding Harmony's hand as they headed back to his house. Jonathon was thinking how she had brought such unexpected moments to his life. He glanced down at his clothing then hers.

"This is going to be hell to get out."

"But it was fun."

"It was and thanks," he agreed and hugged her.

At his home, they went onto the porch. Since they didn't have any neighbours close enough to see them, Jonathon kicked off his shoes and stripped on the porch. He balled up his clothing then put it by the door, planning to get it later. Jonathon took Harmony's clothing and shoes, putting them by his before they headed inside. Harmony went in first and he followed, closing the door. Harmony turned to him and dropped to her knees.

"What—?" Jonathon gasped as she gripped his cock and sucked him in with one gulp.

He braced his legs apart and groaned, watching her face and hollowed cheeks as she lapped at his rapidly hardening shaft. Harmony worked his erection, bringing him quickly to a frenzy of need. She cupped his sac, squeezing gently as she moaned wildly, moving up and down on his member. Jonathon put his head back against the door, rocking his hips and sliding his cock into her welcoming mouth. Harmony took it and made a purring sound in her throat, vibrating his cock. Jonathon curled his toes and grunted as he came. Shaking, he pushed into the wet heat of her mouth then relaxed against the door. Jonathon tried to catch his breath and calm his racing heart.

Harmony stood, a wicked grin on her face. Jonathon lifted his hand and stroked down the side of her face, rubbing her lips.

"Not that I didn't enjoy it. But what was that for?"

"You looked sexy earlier when you defended me and the tenants. I've never seen you in lawyer mode but, if that's how you look…whew." Harmony moved closer. "And outside in the rain jumping in puddles. That was too darn cute. All of it needed to be appreciated." She stroked his cock. "Now let's go to the shower where you can appreciate me."

Harmony turned and made her way to the stairs. Jonathon followed her naked ass, already thinking of ways he would have her. First against the shower wall, then later, slower in bed, all night long.

Chapter Six

Jonathon leant back in his chair and smiled as his thoughts, as they seemed to do a lot the last two days, turned to Harmony. Since the night in the rain, they had seemed to get closer and he enjoyed their time together. A buzz came then Elisa, his administrative assistant, spoke.

"Mr Wright, a Miss Oshiro is here to see you. She is insisting you will see her even though she doesn't have an appointment." Elisa didn't sound pleased.

Jonathon pressed the button on the phone and stated, "Miss Oshiro is always welcome to see me, Elisa."

There was a pause then Elisa replied, "Okay, I'll send her and her guests in."

Jonathon frowned at the *guests* but released the button and stood. The office opened and he spotted Elisa, then Harmony came in behind her. The sombre expression on her face made him come around the desk. He stopped as the office filled with other people. Jonathon counted—there were over thirty people in his spacious office. He focused on Harmony who was in the centre.

"These are the tenants of my old building. I told them what you're doing for them but I thought it best you hear from them directly," Harmony stated.

Jonathon studied her then glanced at Elisa. "Harmony did our work for us and tracked down the people we've been trying to find. Show them to a conference room and then call the investigators and tell them we don't need them found." He focused on the people around Harmony. "I'll be right with you in a moment."

Elisa led them out. Once they were alone, Jonathon went to the door and closed it. He faced Harmony, putting his arms behind his back.

"From the surprise on your face, I see you didn't believe me when I said I would help everyone. You should think about why that is. I'll get your info another day. See you later." Jonathon turned, opened the door and left.

On the way to the conference room, he knocked on the doors of his paralegals and gestured to them to join him. He continued on but his thoughts were on Harmony and the constant distance she put between them. Although they'd had a lot of fun recently, every time he thought they had got close, the chasm between them or some obstacle she put up would get in the way. Jonathon pushed his personal problems away and focused on the task at hand. He was in control when he entered the room for his new clients.

Harmony had clearly heard the dismissal in his voice and it hurt while filling her with shame. He was right—she hadn't been sure if he would do as he'd stated, so instead of talking with him she'd got the tenants and ambushed him.

Shame on you, Harmony, for not trusting him. The one thing you know about Jonathon is he's a man of his word.

She walked back the way she had come and went outside to her borrowed car. Harmony called Deyon and told her she wasn't coming in, then continued to Jonathon's condo and parked. She rested her head back against the cushion and tried to understand what she was feeling. Harmony mechanically exited the car and went inside. In the condo, she wandered to the one part of the house she typically avoided. In front of the piano, she placed a shaking hand on the polished wood. As she did, she realised what the feeling she was having was—fear and exhilaration all at once. It was what she used to experience every time she performed. Harmony closed her eyes, resting her hand on the piano and analysing why she was experiencing this. Her lids opened and she breathed out.

"I want him even more than I ever wanted to perform." That thought frightened her so bad she shook.

In the next moment she calmed, centring herself, as she did when she knew what she had to do to perform a piece that was particularly challenging. Harmony moved beyond the piano and headed to the office. She had research to do and later she had an apology to make. No matter what she found out about Jonathon or his family, she already knew she had to apologise.

* * * *

Harmony glanced at the clock again, tapping her foot. Now she knew how Jonathon felt when he waited for her. Usually he was the one already at the house when she arrived. It was nerve-racking waiting for him. Suddenly she heard a key in the door. Harmony stood and made her way to the door to wait by the entryway table. Jonathon stepped inside and spotted her—he paused briefly then closed the door before facing her.

"I'm sorry, Jonathon. You were right—I didn't trust what you said. But not for the reason you might think." Harmony gulped then ploughed ahead. "When something is important to me I get nervous about believing in it. I'll work on it."

Jonathon studied her, not saying anything, then he moved closer to her. "You're important to me too. And I accept you're working on it but someday soon you'll need to share with me the story behind this." He took her hand, holding her captive, and rubbed his finger from his other hand over her scar.

Harmony instinctively went to pull away. Jonathon held her, stroking the puckered flesh, his gaze trained on hers.

"Someday you'll actually trust me enough to tell me." Jonathon touched the skin once more and released her.

Harmony cleared her throat. "I made dinner for us. Go get changed and come down. Meet me in the backyard."

Jonathon looked curious but didn't ask. He kissed her gently then headed for the stairs.

"I looked you up on the Internet. You have quite a reputation for helping people to fight when someone is taking advantage of them. You're a nice man, Jonathon Wright."

He paused by the stairs, looking over his shoulder and putting his index finger by his lips. "Shhh...don't tell anyone. I have a rep to maintain. I'm a hard-hearted bastard and make the opposition quake."

"I won't." Harmony laughed.

Jonathon winked and continued upstairs. Harmony hurried to the kitchen then through the open glass door to the backyard. It was spacious and very well maintained. She stood watching the blanket with the picnic basket in the centre. Harmony thought of all she'd learnt about Jonathon and the Wright family. Many of them were in some sort of profession that helped people. But they went above and beyond that to help people. From what she'd read, it wasn't for any other reason than that they wanted to. Harmony had also learnt that Jonathon and his siblings had worked hard for what they had. Their educational endeavours and accomplishments were well publicised.

The complex man she had started to become enthralled with was even more than she had thought. Hearing a sound, Harmony moved towards the kitchen doorway. She grinned when she saw Jonathon. He was cleaning the kitchen, muttering. Harmony hadn't put things back as she'd prepared their meal but she'd planned to after they'd eaten. Going inside, she took the cloth from him and tugged him behind her.

"But—"

"I'll clean it afterwards." She continued moving them out of the door.

At the blanket she gestured for him to sit and he did. She sat beside him and unpacked the basket then handed him a sandwich. They chatted easily as they ate.

"I got a call from Vince—they are stalling for more time. But I expect they're just trying to test the waters.

If I don't see them by Friday I'll go ahead and file the case."

Harmony lowered her hand after tucking some hair behind her ear. "Do you really think there is a case?"

"Yes. There are a number of fines for fire violations and other things on your building. Including one for the boiler."

"I didn't know that," Harmony said.

"You wouldn't. Most tenants wouldn't, unless you outright asked. Your landlord has been warned before. Yes, there are no criminal charges to be filed but civil is a different thing. And they knew that and will not want themselves put under a microscope. As I told Vince the other day, I love paper and I will ask for every piece, go over it thoroughly and find something they don't want me to. They are going to avoid that. Yeah, they will give me a number—a good one—or they'll have to pay even more." Jonathon flashed a fierce grin.

Harmony's breath caught as she watched his face. He enjoyed what he did and it showed. It made her hot looking at him with that spark in his eyes. She lowered her gaze and finished her sandwich. They shared the fruit salad, feeding it to each other. Harmony replaced the remnants of their meal then pushed the basket away. She lay down on the blanket and patted next to her. Jonathon joined her, his shoulder touching hers. Harmony stared at the starlit sky.

"Isn't it beautiful?" she whispered.

"You are," Jonathon stated.

She turned her head to him. Jonathon was watching her and not the sky. Harmony smiled, touching his cheek.

"You're a sap."

"The proper term is romantic." Jonathon sounded snooty.

Harmony chuckled. Jonathon joined in, turning to face her. Harmony mirrored him, staring into his eyes. Jonathon slid his hand over her hip and tugged her close to him. Harmony lifted her leg over his and pressed against his erection. She moaned, wishing they were bare. Jonathon moved under her skirt and pulled it up. Harmony shifted, helping him as he pulled off her panties and he opened his pants. She pulled out a condom from the pocket of her skirt and in moments she'd slid the protection on his cock then put her leg back where it had been. She moaned as the blunt length of his cock slid along her nether lips. Jonathon cupped her ass, tilting her, then pushed into her heat.

"Harmony," Jonathon groaned.

She whimpered, canting her hips and matching his motions. They kissed tenderly as they fitted together. Harmony moaned deep in her throat as he thrust harder. Jonathon held her ass and rolled onto his back. Harmony straddled him, rocking and whimpering. His cock filled her up, making her crazy with need. She sat up, shivering as he slid deeper. Bracing her hands on his chest, she moved fast, striving towards the sensation that was just out of reach. Jonathon gripped her hips, fingers tight, guiding her.

"Jonathon." She gazed at his face, seeing the strain there.

His jaw was clenched and his Adam's apple worked. Harmony arched, pressing down on his chest. She raised herself until she was almost off his erection then dropped down. She repeated it over and over. Each time he grunted, his hands holding her tighter. Harmony moaned in accompaniment to his sounds, heat pooling in her belly. She clenched around his embedded shaft then gasped, quivering as she orgasmed in pleasure.

"Harmony," Jonathon shouted as he too came.

His body jerked under her, almost unseating her. Harmony cradled him between her legs, holding on. Jonathon went limp under her and she collapsed against his chest breathing hard.

"You wicked woman. It's a good thing I'm on a corner lot and have a privacy fence." Jonathon chuckled.

"Hmmm…exercise is good to work off your meal."

Jonathon smoothed his hands down her back. Harmony blinked as tiredness started to overcome her.

"Now, about my kitchen." Jonathon said.

"It's going to bug you until it's clean." It was a statement.

Jonathon didn't respond. Harmony slid off him, removing the condom and tying it. She stood and held out her hand.

"Come on then. After, you'll tire me out again." Harmony wiggled her fingers.

Jonathon stood, taking her hand, and they made their way back to the house.

"Go and get started. I'll clean up out here." He stopped and retraced his steps.

"My neat man," Harmony said.

Jonathon paused before responding, "All yours, for as long as you want."

Harmony watched his back as he moved away. She liked the sound of that…a lot. She continued to the kitchen to clean up so she could go back to bed with her man.

* * * *

Harmony entered the condo, closing the door with her hip. "Jonathon?"

Not getting a reply, she frowned and placed her things on the entryway table. It was then she noted that the condo was dark and silent. She frowned — Jonathon should have been home by now. Harmony reached in her purse and pulled out her cell. She frowned when she realised that it was off. She turned it on and noticed she had a missed call. Harmony listened to Jonathon saying he was caught up in the office working out something. She clicked off the messages and wandered into the living room. As always, her gaze was drawn to the piano. She hadn't played it but was tempted to. Harmony remembered the time of Jonathon's call and that he'd said he'd be a few hours.

With trepidation, she approached the piano. Harmony unconsciously reached for her scar on her right arm and traced it idly, battling memories of before the incident. She pushed them away and sat on the bench, opening the lid. Harmony trailed her fingers over the keys then closed her eyes, setting her hands in place. Her mind filled with the notes of a piece she hadn't played since before things had changed. In moments, the sound filled the air as she stroked the ivories, recalling the piece as if she'd played it yesterday. Her fingers remembered the motions and the timing.

Joy filled her as she played, filling her soul and resonating through her and out into the piano. Her arm ached but she refused to stop, pushing through the pain, tears flowing from her eyes — they were for the pain and for the memories. At the height of the song, she performed the intricate clash of notes then slid into the ending, moving from side to side as it overcame her. Harmony set her hands down on the keys, holding that last note, then raised them slightly. She breathed out, shaking, pain filling her, but she felt exhilarated.

"I've gotta get into Bella's and play their piano." Harmony murmured.

"Why do you want to play their piano?" Jonathon asked.

Harmony gasped, jumping back.

"Whoa." He caught her, righting her then setting her gently back on the bench.

He sat beside her. Harmony tugged on the sleeve of her shirt, pulling it over her scar.

"Ummm...the acoustics in there must be fabulous."

"It sounds good when the piano player performs. But he sounds nothing like you. You should play professionally. That was fabulous." Jonathon gazed at her.

Harmony stood then replied as she made her way towards the living room door, "I used to."

Jonathon stared after her, confusion filling him. He'd heard the clear dismissal of continuing the conversation in Harmony's voice. When he'd come in, the tears streaming from her eyes and the joy on her face had confused him. The music she had been playing was beautiful—a haunting melody that had resonated in him, making his breath catch. Curious, Jonathon thought of Googling her. If she had performed professionally, there should be something on her. Immediately as the thought formed, he shoved it away. He wanted to hear whatever it was directly from her. Jonathon stood and followed her. He found

Harmony in the kitchen preparing plates from the food in the crock-pot. Silently, he retrieved drinks from the fridge then returned to take the plates. Harmony picked up utensils and came with him. They sat, then said a quick prayer before starting to eat.

"Did what you were working on turn out well?" Harmony lifted her fork to her mouth.

"It did. The management company and landlord came in as advised, made an offer and I accepted. They will stall actually paying, but you and the other tenants will be duly compensated for your loss. I was hashing out the details with their attorney." Jonathon smiled, pleased at how things had turned out.

Harmony lowered her fork, shock on her face. "They did? That's it? It's all settled?"

"Yep. Now we wait for the cheque. Which I'm expecting they will drag their feet to actually pay but I'm not going to let that happen."

"You really are a miracle worker. You got all the tenants who had accepted the crappy accommodations new places to live. Even those who hadn't been contacted by the management company yet, you found places for. Now you've negotiated financial compensation. You really are a nice guy." Harmony stared at him.

"Katiya helped out with finding affordable housing for everyone." Jonathon looked around playfully then whispered. "Shh...I've told you not to mess with my rep."

Harmony chuckled, rising and coming to him. He pushed back his chair and she sat on his lap.

"The only one who you haven't found a place to live yet is me," Harmony stated.

Jonathon sobered. "If you want me to, I'll ask Katiya."

Harmony studied him then shook her head. "I'll wait for the settlement money first."

Jonathon breathed out a sigh, glad she wanted to stay. Harmony hugged then kissed him. Jonathon returned it, not sure if he wanted the settlement to come through quickly or not.

* * * *

Weeks later, Jonathon pushed back his chair and rubbed his hand along the back of his neck. He'd been on the phone again with the attorney for Harmony's old apartment building. They were indeed stalling on payment. Although he knew if they got it Harmony would be leaving, he was still pushing for it. He had a job to do and his work ethic would not let him do otherwise.

Jonathon faced the office window, not really seeing the view as he thought of the past six weeks. Living with Harmony had become so familiar that he ached to think of when she left. They had got into habits of cooking together, watching TV and just having fun. Now he was eager to get home and not linger at work. His productivity at work had even increased, since he had someone to get home to and didn't want to miss out on anything. Because of Harmony, he'd got to know his neighbours by spending time at the barbecues, bowling and other things they had invited them to. On rainy days, they went out and played in the rain and were joined by the neighbours. Since that first day, it had got bigger to include the whole block on both sides of the streets. It was almost like a party. One time they had got so loud, someone in the other streets had called the cops. Leo had come himself and teased him mercilessly for getting dirty — they all knew he was anal with how he looked. But around Harmony he sometimes let go his restraint and just had fun. His clock alarm beeped and he turned, noting the time. Jonathon quickly stood, grabbed his briefcase then headed out. He waved at Elisa who was on the phone.

Half an hour later, he was waiting at home for Harmony. Jonathon glanced at his watch, checking the time. The key sounded in the door before Harmony came in. She stopped when she spotted him.

"Jonathon, what are you doing home so early? Are you sick?" She came and pressed her hand on his neck.

"Nope, I'm fine. I left something on your bed for you to wear. Get changed and come back." He gently pushed Harmony towards the stairs.

Harmony glanced at him questioningly. Jonathon shooed her upstairs, then went out and pulled out his surprise.

"Jonathon?" Harmony called from inside.

"Out here." He raised his voice.

She opened the door and came out. A wide grin curled her lips.

"Bikes. We're going bike riding."

"It's not in the mountains, but we're going to ride them to our destination. Now close the door and let's get moving."

Harmony complied and ran down to the bike. He handed her some protective gear. She put it on, donning the helmet last, then got on and glanced at him.

"Where are we going?"

"Not saying, just follow me." Jonathon started off.

Soon Harmony was peddling alongside him on her bike. Her joyful laugh made him smile. As they rode out of the neighbourhood and onto the street with more cars, he could see people watching them—some doing a double-take as they recognised him.

"Pull over, you are impersonating my brother," a loud speaker blared behind them.

Jonathon almost crashed but caught himself and stopped, scowling. Harmony was laughing hysterically. The cruiser pulled up beside him and the passenger side window lowered. Leo leaned across the seat, smiling.

"You on a bike. I need this for prosperity." Leo snapped a photo with his cell before Jonathon could speak.

Jonathon scowled. "Are you having fun?"

"Yep, and I'll be sending this to the family, which is even more fun. Harmony, you're good for this old stuffed shirt. Keep it up." Leo honked his horn as he drove off.

"He's funny," Harmony said.

"Yeah, a laugh riot." Jonathon glanced at his watch. "Come on, we don't want to be late." He set off again.

Harmony biked up beside him. Fifteen minutes later, Jonathon stopped in front of a building and Harmony parked beside him. She glanced at the building then back at him. Jonathon got off his bike, put down the kickstand then waited for her to do the same. He led her towards the door but Harmony pulled back, shaking her head.

"I can't go into Bella's dressed like this."

"Why not? It's closed," Jonathon said.

"On a Friday afternoon? Why?" Harmony scrunched up her face.

Jonathon kissed the tip of her nose then straightened. "They usually close for about two hours before their evening rush. Come on."

He gently led her towards the door. It opened and he smiled at the owner.

"Thanks for doing this for us."

The woman winked then retreated inside. Jonathon entered, pulling the door closed behind Harmony and himself. He ignored the people moving about getting the restaurant ready for the evening.

"What are we doing here?"

Jonathon didn't answer until they stood by the piano. "You wanted to hear how it sounded with the acoustics here."

He gestured and Harmony glanced at him then back to the piano. She looked around, uneasiness on her face.

"Take a break, everyone." The familiar voice of Bella — the woman who'd been at the door and the owner — sounded.

The noise behind them faded then the dining room was empty. Harmony bit her lip and stared longingly at the instrument. Jonathon waited, not saying a word. Harmony approached it and slid across the bench. Jonathon pulled a chair up close and sat.

"I don't even know what to play."

"How about the song you played the other day? It was beautiful and I feel I can still hear it — it stays with you. I want to buy a copy of it. What was it called and who wrote it?" He leant back against the chair.

"There is no place to buy it, I never recorded it." Harmony met his gaze. "'Reverence of Forever' is the name. I wrote it before I realised that there is no such thing as forever. Everything ends." She flexed her hands then closed her eyes and started to play.

There was a tinge of bitterness and finality to her tone. Jonathon wasn't sure what it meant — however, he didn't think it was anything good. As it had before, the music drew him in but it was the woman swaying as she played expertly that enthralled him. It was obvious Harmony loved playing, though yet again he spotted the tears flowing under her closed lids. She blinked, opening her eyes, and Jonathon held his breath at the anguish he viewed in her gaze.

"What has you so devastated?" he asked.

He knew she had heard him because there was a split-second pause as she played before she continued. Slowly, her lids lowered as she shut him out. Jonathon crossed his arms over his chest—it was time they had a serious talk about Harmony's secrets. This time he was not going to be pushed away and he would get answers out of her. Jonathon studied the stubborn enigma of a woman who had captured all of his attention from the start.

Chapter Seven

Jonathon watched her expressions and knew she was searching for a suitable way to get out of answering him. Right now, her features portrayed something much different from when she'd been totally consumed by her music. This was definitely an escape plan. He exhaled and rolled his shoulders. Surely she didn't think she would be able to outwait him.

"Harmony."

Her lashes rose and he found himself willingly drowning in those brown orbs. She turned her left wrist and stared at her watch before blowing out a sharp breath. "I have to get going. I told Deyon I would be in to help her with some things. This is the last day and will even us up."

He was pleased to hear that, but he had to admit, the sound of her settling things didn't necessarily sit well with him. It was like someone who'd decided to leave. Finishing up accounts with other people.

"I know she likes you."

She nodded even as she continued to play with her left hand alone. "She's very nice."

"But?"

"But nothing. She's very nice. A bit much at times for me, but I'm her opposite." She sighed and stood. He could read the reluctance in her body language. "I have to get going."

"You're not getting away with walking out on this conversation, Harmony."

"I'm not. I have to get to work. I'm really tired, Jonathon. Working for Deyon as well as working at the university is hard. Let me get through this last day and then we can talk."

He searched her face. She held his gaze without blinking and eventually he nodded.

"Okay."

She took one last lingering look at the piano before she moved away, picking up her helmet. He walked after her, his eyes drawn to the swell of her ass as it moved in her cotton pants. After sharing a kiss with her, he waved as she rode off towards Deyon's, having promised to swing by and pick her up in his SUV when she was done. Then he got himself on his bike and headed back home.

By the time he went to pick her up it was after eight. Harmony fell asleep almost immediately in his vehicle and so he skipped going out to dinner, just driving back to his condo.

He walked around to her side after parking and opened the door. She barely stirred as he unbuckled her and lifted her into his arms. So small and slight— she felt so perfect in his grasp. Moving carefully so he didn't wake her, he carried her inside and up to his bedroom. He stripped her and covered her with the blankets. After locking up, he ignored his growling stomach and joined her in the bed, holding her close as he drifted off to sleep, thinking tomorrow would be as good a day as any to have that talk.

* * * *

That was something he said to himself for the next five weeks. They simply had very little time with one another. Work for her at the college exploded and her hours available to spend with him decreased significantly. He grumbled and sipped from his coffee cup as he sat in traffic.

"Five blasted weeks. Not only that, but she's moving out today."

The money had actually come in and she had found a place to live. He understood her wish to get back out on her own but he also hated that she was leaving. One of the reasons he had left work early was that he'd wanted to give her a hand. Unfortunately, court had run late and now he was about two hours past when he'd wanted to be there.

"Come on," he grumbled, smacking the steering wheel. "Get this God damn circus moving."

It was no use. He was good and stuck in this mess. He called Harmony's cell.

"Hello?"

As always, her soft voice gave him this warm feeling no one had before.

"Hello, gorgeous."

"Jonathon, are you okay?"

He frowned. Why wouldn't he be? "I am. Sorry to not be there, court ran late. How's everything going?"

"Fine. We're all finished up here. I'm just waiting on you to come back. Thought we could have one last dinner together."

"Baby, there will be more than one dinner for the two of us." Come hell or high water, he'd find a way to make that work.

"I'll see you when you get here," she said before hanging up."

He ripped his Bluetooth out of his ear and tossed it on the seat beside him. *Shit!* He hated this. All of it—her moving out, the fact that they'd yet to discuss her scar, and yes, had he mentioned her moving out? If not, it was worth a few more mentions.

It wasn't like he didn't know where she was moving—he had gone with her to check the place out. In his estimation, she could have got a bigger place, but she had opted for the smallest unit there. On the fourth floor and in a corner. It was what she'd wanted and she'd ignored everything he had said about her getting a larger apartment. It was only by some miracle that he'd managed to keep from asking her to stay with him. *Forever.*

It took him an hour to get home and he was in a foul mood when he finally arrived. Travel mug in hand, he climbed out and entered his condo. Smooth jazz played through the area. Soft candlelight could also been seen.

"Harmony?" he called out, setting his briefcase down and making his way to the kitchen.

"Right here," she commented from his left. She walked out of the pantry area with some boxes in her hand. "You look really tired."

"Not so much anymore." Cup down, he approached her and took his kiss. "What's going on?"

"I was going to give you a nice dinner but it's not done yet." She skirted beside him and placed the boxes down on the countertop. "Well, the dinner is but I have to make another cake. I gave the first one to the movers."

He drew her close and wrapped his arms around her. "Forget the cake."

"Are you sure? I know how much you like your sweets."

"I'm sure."

He brushed some hair from her face and cupped her cheek. Swiping his thumb along her lower lip, he held her gaze. Damn it all, he could grow used to seeing her every single day—he already had.

It was as if she had no comprehension of his turmoil. Her smile grew and she backed away before leading him to the table. While she brought the dinner, he poured the wine. It was a cosy and intimate meal with the talk hushed and easy.

He helped her clean up and, as she went to the door, he tried to think of a way to get her to stay.

"You sure you have everything?" God, he wanted to carry her upstairs and never let her leave.

"Yes. What I don't have I'll pick up with Lana."

Her best friend, a Native American actress. He'd met her a few times and had liked her, even if she was more than a bit prickly. Very professional, but like a mama bear when it came to Harmony. His patented Wright smile was well known to charm the socks off ladies, but it had gone over like a lead balloon with Lana. She'd been unimpressed until Harmony had told him to just be himself and stop trying to be anything else. She'd warmed up a bit after that—however, he knew she only cared about Harmony's well-being.

"If you need—"

"I don't need anything more from you, Jonathon, you've done more than enough." She opened the front door and he halted her exit with a hand on her arm. "Yes?"

He didn't know what to say. All his fancy talk wasn't worth a dime at this moment when he needed to tell her how he felt.

Her gaze was open and trusting. "I'll call you for dinner once I get set up."

He could feel her trying to edge him out and he refused to go so easily. "I'll be calling you too, Harmony Oshiro."

"Goodbye, Jonathon. Keys are on the counter." She touched his cheek and gave him a soft smile. "Thank you, again. For everything." She rose up on her toes and tugged him down to give him a kiss. Then she walked away without looking back.

Wait. She said keys. Whirling around, he checked what she'd meant and swore. The key to the Corolla was there as well as the one for his condo. Dashing back to the door, he opened it to see her climbing into another vehicle.

Damn it! He would have taken her. Instead, she'd called Lana to pick her up. Mixed emotions flowed through him at that knowledge. He stood there, watching until he could no longer see the tail lights. Then and only then did he go back inside.

He could feel the change immediately. Something was missing. Or, rather, someone. Specifically, Harmony.

Tomorrow—he would go see her tomorrow. For the first time in a long time, bed wasn't what he wanted. No longer were dreams of her going to be good enough. He wanted her petite frame in bed with him. He loved how ready she was for him, any time. Not to mention the joy she brought to his life.

His plans to see her the next day were thwarted. Like it had the previous day, court ran over and he got shoved behind. No matter how much he wanted to see her, he had a job to do and that came first. So he took another cup of coffee from his assistant and got back to work on the pile of stuff on his desk.

* * * *

Harmony shook her head as she looked around her new place. Lana poured them some saké to celebrate. There wasn't much in her apartment yet but it was a start. She had her own place again, which she loved. It was much nicer than the previous apartment she'd had, and still in the same price range.

"Here."

She took the drink from Lana as they shared grin then tipped it back. She blinked back the sting of tears as it went down.

"Thanks for helping out, Lana."

"You're my best friend! Besides, I've missed you."

She nodded. "I know, I'm sorry. Just with working the two jobs I didn't have the time to have our weekly dinner so much."

"She shouldn't have bought you so much if she was going to make you pay it all back. That's bullshit," Lana snapped. "Half the stuff isn't your type of clothing anyway."

She smiled gently. "I know, but she was trying to help. And it's done now. The stuff I won't wear, I'm shipping to Japan for Reika. They'll fit her—she's my size."

Lana rolled her eyes. "If not smaller—she barely weighs a hundred pounds." She took another drink. "Why did she have you helping out with payroll?"

Harmony shrugged. "I have no clue. It's not something I like doing, that's for sure. I don't have a head for figures. Luckily for all involved, she didn't give me too much to do on that." She touched her friend's arm. "It's okay, Lana. Everything is paid back."

Her friend scowled and sighed. "I know, it's just bull. All they would have had to do was call me and I could have brought over the things you keep at my place."

"They live a bit differently than we do." That was the only explanation she could come up with. She didn't mind her protectiveness—Lana was her one true friend, the one who saw past the child prodigy, the scarred woman, to who she was at her core.

"I know. I've seen his place. How are you doing with that, by the way?"

"I'll miss him, I know this, but I'm glad to be back on my own."

"I know you are. Have you heard from your parents?"

She shook her head. "No. But then I also didn't tell them what happened."

Bless Lana, she didn't comment, just squeezed her hand in silent support. Then her eyes widened and she jumped up, hastening to her bag.

"I forgot—I got you a housewarming gift."

She sat back on the couch and handed her a rectangular item wrapped in homemade wrapping paper. She recognised it—she'd helped make ones like it before, where they used cut potatoes to create the print design. Placing it on her lap, she rubbed her hands together and carefully opened the wrapping, ignoring Lana's comments on how she should just tear into it.

A new wave of tears sprang to her eyes as she stared at the gift. Inside a gold frame rested a picture of her and her grandmother. She remembered the day as if it was yesterday. Lana had actually been in the shot as well but had cropped herself out and blown up the image.

"Oh, Lana."

She found herself in comforting arms as Lana held her while she cried. There was no need for words — the picture right there was worth more to her than anything necessary for the apartment.

They crashed on the floor and woke bright and early to walk down to a restaurant to grab some breakfast. She told Lana about playing at Bella's while they ate. They ordered coffee to go then walked out of the door and headed back up the street, enjoying the cooler morning.

Turning a corner, they both halted when a horn sounded behind them. She glanced over her shoulder to see a dirty green Jeep pulling up. The moment she saw who sat behind the wheel, she knew who it was — Delicia Wright, Jonathon's youngest sister. She'd met her more than a few times before.

"Harmony!" she called out, waving.

They stopped and waited. The vehicle stopped beside them and the woman leaned towards them over the seats.

"Hello, Lis," she said. "How are you?"

"I'm okay." She flashed a smile at Lana as well. "I don't believe we've met. I'm Lis."

"Lana."

"Pleasure." She gave a short nod. "Sorry to bother you both, but I thought I'd offer up my assistance if you needed it. Well, mine and Archer's."

"And you knew I had moved out?"

She chuckled. "In our family, you learn things are never really secret." A shrug. "Most things. Anyway, Archer and I are more than willing to help you move some things, if you're getting anything and you don't want to wait for delivery." She reached into the bag on the passenger seat and dug for a card, which she then held out. "Here's my card with all my numbers. I'm free all day, so let me know."

Harmony took the card and said, "Thank you."

"Not a problem. Great to meet you, Lana." A wave and she was driving off.

"That is one crazy family," Lana commented.

"It's definitely a lot different than what I'm used to." They continued walking back to her new place. Out of habit, she walked up the stairs and at her door Lana laughed as Harmony opened it. "What's so funny?"

"You do know this place has a working elevator, right?"

She huffed with false indignation. "I was working off breakfast."

"And I thought the Wrights were crazy." She nudged her with a shoulder.

They spent the day getting some things and she called Delicia over. With the four of them, it went smoothly. She and Lana went out to dinner with Archer and Delicia afterwards, as a thank you for all the help. Lana took her grocery shopping on her way back and helped her carry all of that up as well, before she went back to her home.

After putting her food away, Harmony crashed on her new bed that Archer had brought up for her. She fell asleep with the photo of her and her grandmother tucked in beside her. The next day she began to put her things in even more order. She'd just made herself some lunch when the phone rang.

"Hello?"

"*Goreijou.*"

Daughter. Her breath hitched and she automatically stood straighter. It was her mother. "*Hahaoya,*" Harmony replied.

A moment of silence and she cringed from the disappointment she knew would be on her mother's face.

"Your brother told us you moved." She continued to speak in Japanese. In fact, she'd not heard her mother speak English unless absolutely necessary. "Why did you not mention it to us?"

"It was kind of not an intentional move, mother," she replied, also speaking Japanese. "My apartment burnt down and I had to find a new place. I stayed with...a friend until I got the money owed to me by the company and actually just moved in this weekend. I was going to call once I got settled."

The sound of disbelief made her shift uncomfortably. All this time and she still felt like a little child being disciplined with nothing more than a single sound.

"You are all right?"

"Yes. I wasn't in when it happened."

"Are you sure?" She couldn't miss the concern this time and it brought tears to her eyes.

She nodded until she realised her mother couldn't see that and responded. "Just sad that I lost everything." She wiped her tears and took a deep breath. "How is Father?"

"He misses you."

"I miss him too."

"We are coming to the States next month and would like to see you."

"I'd like that. Where are you going?"

"Your father has business in California."

"I could meet you out there. I just have to give a bit of notice at work so I can take the time off."

"I'll let you know as soon as it is finalised."

"It'll be wonderful to see you both again."

"Yes. We don't see enough of our only daughter."

She hung her head at the reprimand but didn't argue. She'd cut most ties after the accident.

"I will let you go and will talk to you soon."

"Goodbye, Mother."

"Goodbye, Harmony." A short pause. "We love you." Then she was gone with a click.

"Love you too, Mother." She spoke to the air as she hung up her receiver. Her belly was filled with uncertainty at seeing them again. Nerves had her rubbing her scar.

The doorbell rang and she walked to the door, still lost in thought about her parents. Pulling it open, her breath left her in a rush at the view waiting for her. Jonathon Wright stood there in one of his all too expensive silk suits.

"Hello," she murmured, stepping back to allow him entrance.

"I've missed you." He strode towards her, purpose all over his expression. He grabbed her upper arms and drew her flush to him.

"It's not even been a full day," she replied with a smile, brushing their lips together.

"It feels longer."

"Are you hungry?" she asked. His words had made her feel warm and gooey inside and helped banish the stress of the call from her mother. "I could fix us something."

His eyes burned as he stared at her. "I'm hungry all right."

"I mean for food."

He sighed and nodded. "I could eat. Looks like you got some things delivered. I'm glad."

"Yes. Lis and Archer helped Lana and I yesterday."

"Did they? They didn't say anything to me."

She moved away from him to the small but functional kitchen. "Were they supposed to?"

"Well, no. I suppose not."

She didn't respond, just let him think about it as he walked around. She made them sandwiches and while she placed them on plates, he came back in and carried them to the table.

"Are you sure you don't want a bigger place?"

Harmony blew out a breath and lowered the sandwich she'd been about to bite into. "Why is it so important to you for me to have a huge place?"

He blinked and took a drink. "It's not."

"Bull. Every time I've turned around you've been telling me I should get a larger place. Even before the other one burnt down, you continually looked at it like it was less because it wasn't as big or as fancy as yours."

Her emotions were a bit frazzled and this had kind of pushed her over the edge. She shoved to her feet and glared down at him.

"I didn't mean—"

"Don't lie to me," she snapped. "You may claim to be all about one thing but you can't tell me appearances and status stuff don't mean a lot to you. I have to have a car—heaven forbid I utilise public transportation. Just like what must I be thinking to not want a three-storey huge-ass home with a fancy manicured lawn! You live in the desert, for Christ's sake. Why do you need to waste so much damn water to keep your lawn like that? Live on a golf course if that's what you want. Pretentious—that's what it is. I like my apartment. I like feeling cosy where I live."

She wiped angrily at the tears that had formed at the sides of her eyes. "I've lived like you. I had the prestige and all that, and you know what? I wouldn't trade what I have any day for what you do. It's a prison. One I'll never live in again." She took a shuddering breath. "Get out."

"Harmony."

"Get. Out!"

He stood up, food forgotten on his plate. "I don't understand. Talk to me."

"Why? It all boils down to the same thing. I need a bigger place. I need to spend more money to make *you* happy about my living conditions."

"That's not what—"

"Get. Out!"

He seemed indecisive for a few moments before he gave her a sullen nod and walked to the door. As he slipped out, he paused and stared back at her. She turned her back on him, unmoving until she heard the door click. Then the tears fell unimpeded down her cheeks.

Chapter Eight

Jonathon stared sightlessly out of his office window. His mind played a continual loop of Harmony and her kicking him out. Was that truly how she felt? He'd thought she'd liked his place.

Okay, yes, so he had thought she should have something bigger, as well as a car. And he'd told her so repeatedly. She did have some good points, though. Especially about the yard. What disturbed him the most was how she'd said she'd never give up what she had for what he did. Did that mean she wouldn't live in his place when he asked her to marry him?

Whoa! Where the hell had that thought come from? Marriage? To Harmony? Well, it sure as hell wouldn't be to anyone but her. Still he shook his head and ran a hand down his face. It didn't matter—he wanted her to wear his ring, carry his last name as well as his child.

Good luck having that happen. She wouldn't even take his calls lately. It had been two weeks since she'd kicked him out of her place. She hadn't even been home when he'd gone to see her. Nor had she been teaching when he'd gone there.

So much for my theory on 'she can't hide from me in McKingley'. She'd damn near vanished.

Rising to his feet, he pressed the button to reach his assistant. "Elisa?"

"Yes, sir?"

"Cancel and reschedule the rest of my day."

"Right away, sir."

He knew he'd surprised her. He wasn't a man who skipped and ran. Hell, he was one who usually took on extra work. However, his productivity, which had increased after Harmony had moved in, had decreased over the past two weeks. Moreover, he'd got much surlier.

He grabbed his suit coat, draping it over his arm, as well as his briefcase and headed for the door. With a brief nod to Elisa, he hastened down to his coupé. Tossing his things on the seat beside him, he smiled as he recalled his sister using it and what had happened after. Then he pushed her to the back of his mind and got on his way.

At his destination, he pulled up and parked. Looking up at the apartment complex, he loosened his tie before getting out and heading to the door, locking his car with a push of a button.

He'd been here once before and knew where he was going. Still, his belly clenched a bit as he progressed. This was his last shot, really. If she wasn't here, he didn't know where else to go.

He took the elevator to the third floor and stepped out into the quiet hall. Tan carpet lined the floor and he moved with soundless steps to the apartment he wanted. After another deep breath, he reached out to press the doorbell.

A few moments passed before it swung open and he found himself staring into a pair of black eyes. Lana Kanseah stood there, watching him with a blank expression.

"Yes?"

"Where is she?" As he blurted out his question he was well aware of how gruff he sounded. He didn't care—he didn't have either time or patience to eventually work his way up to asking.

"If she'd wanted to tell you where she was, she would have."

Damn, and he'd thought he was cold in the courtroom. Her voice would have given a polar bear frostbite.

"Lana, come on." He leaned against her wall and stared at her. "I don't know where else to go."

She was obviously unmoved by his plea for she barely blinked. Inspecting her nails, she shifted her weight. "You're a lawyer so you know what it is when someone tells a person something and that person can't share it."

"Like attorney-client privilege."

The smile she gave him told him that was exactly what she meant. She wasn't going to tell him anything.

"Is she okay?" Yes, he may have sounded like he was begging, but at this point he didn't care.

Her phone rang and she walked off, door remaining open, to answer it. He didn't move. Her conversation wasn't anything he could understand and soon she hung up. Peering over her shoulder at him, she placed another call.

"Hey, hon. He's here and wants to know where you are. Do you want to talk to him or should I slam the door in his face?"

His heart rate escalated at the thought of hearing her voice again. It had never been so hard for him to stay still before. Normally he was the cool cat but this time, he just wanted to run into her apartment and jerk that phone away. She mumbled, still watching him.

"Okay. I'll let him know." She pulled the phone from her ear and his heart sank. Then she held it out to him. "She wants to talk to you."

He began walking towards her only to stop and ask, "May I come in?"

"Sure. Shut the door behind you."

He did and made his way to her side where he relieved her of the phone.

"Harmony?" he said, almost not believing it was true.

"Hi, Jonathon."

Relief swamped him. "I was so worried about you. Where are you?"

"No need to be worried. I'm fine. I'm in California — my parents are in the country."

He frowned at the stress in her voice. "What can I do to help?"

Her laugh wasn't at all humorous. She muttered something he assumed was Japanese before switching back to English.

"You've done enough."

"Bullshit!" he ground out only to take a deep breath when Lana arched a black brow at him. "Stop hiding from us, Harmony. This isn't fair."

"Isn't fair?" she echoed. "Fine. You want to know where I am? Get a pen and I'll give you the address."

He did and soon he jotted down in California where she was staying. There was so much to say to her and yet it wasn't anything to be done via the telephone, so he kept it inside.

"I'll be there soon," he promised.

"Let me talk to Lana."

He ran his tongue over his lips and nodded. Lana had her hand out expectantly and he reluctantly gave the phone to her. "Thanks." He spun on his heel and left her place—he had things to do and a plane to catch.

* * * *

His plane had departed at seven that night and he reclined in his first class seat, a drink in hand, as they streaked towards California. He'd called his assistant and told her he would be gone, then he'd handed off some of his most important cases that couldn't wait until his return. Normally he would have put the law first, but not this time. Deep down, he knew if he didn't go after her he would lose her forever. And that wasn't something he was willing to do.

After landing, he retrieved his rental and drove to the hotel where he had a room on the same floor as Harmony. It had been on the tip of his tongue to ask for the penthouse suite, but he'd remembered her final words to him.

Right before she had kicked his ass out of her place.

He blew out a pent-up breath. After signing in, he went to his room and unpacked. Once that was done, he freshened up a bit and went to the room she'd told him she was in and knocked on the door.

It opened and he found himself staring directly at the woman he'd come to see. And yet, she was totally different. She wore a black, long-sleeved, knee-length wraparound dress. It moulded to her in ways he wanted to. The V-neck showed off hints of her cleavage. It was not casual but not over the top formal either, although it leaned more towards formal.

"Hello, Harmony."

God, he couldn't get enough of her. Her hair was held up by a comb of some sort that had a flower design on it. With it drawn back like that, she looked more severe than he remembered.

"Jonathon." She gave a slight bow and stepped back to allow him in.

Christ, his hands itched to touch her. Kiss her. The moment he had stepped past the entryway and she'd shut the door, he reached for her, his heart splintering when she shook her head and stepped out of his grasp.

"Are you still mad at me?"

"No. I... I just have to get going. I have dinner to go to with my parents."

"Where are they?"

"They were at Papa's business thing. They'll be here in about fifteen minutes. I'm supposed to meet them downstairs so we can go to the restaurant."

"Fifteen minutes?"

She nodded, looking entirely too delectable and enticing as she stood there, her hands clasped before her.

"Not quite enough time, but it's a start."

She blinked, her confusion apparent. "Not enough time for what?"

He loosened the knot of his tie. "For me to give you a proper hello. I'll just have to make do with the time we do have."

He saw the moment understanding set in, for she shook her head and began to back farther away from him. "No, Jonathon. I have to meet my parents."

His tie fell to the floor and he unbuttoned his shirt, pulling it from his slacks. "You still will."

There was no disguising the raw hunger in her gaze and it spurred him on. The shirt went next and he undid his belt.

She shook her head. "I can't." Her tongue sneaked out and licked her lips, his groan slid free.

"Why?"

She reached out to him only to drop her hand back to her side. "Meeting my parents."

"I'd love to."

Her eyes widened and her gaze flew to meet his. "What?"

This time he did touch her. Curled his fingers around her wrist and drew her flush to his bared chest. Dropping his chin so they could be staring at one another, he smiled.

"Meet your parents. I'd love to."

He could see her gearing up for a big argument so he stopped it the best way he knew how. He kissed her. Lord, he'd missed this woman. Rejuvenating energy poured through him as her taste reawakened his senses.

She hesitated for about two seconds. Then responded with the fiery passion he'd come to crave from her. She wound her arms around his neck and he lifted her. Like usual, she hooked her legs about his waist, pressing them even closer together. He loved how tightly she held him.

Cupping her ass, he continued to devour her mouth. Their tongues danced and stroked along one another, tastes mingling. With one hand, he freed himself and jerked off her panties before sliding into her with a single, smooth stroke.

Her gasp was as potent as the feel of her tight sheath around his cock. He spun them, so her back was against a wall and began to thrust up into her. Hard and fast, he took her. Her nails dug into his back as she rode him.

In and out. Back and forth. She kept up with him, moving in the perfect tandem he knew and hungered after from her. He could admit it—she meant more to him than a random fuck. This woman made him see the future he had always wanted. But not with anyone other than her.

Her muscles clenched and legs tightened as her internal muscles gripped him harder, milking him. He couldn't hold out anymore and flicked her clit with two fingers. Her back bowed and her breasts were thrust forward as she came all over his shaft with a scream into his mouth. The feel of her coming on his uncovered cock was all it took. He drove home three more times before he unloaded deep within her core, bathing her channel with his seed.

Only once her shaking had stopped did he break the kiss they'd shared. Her eyes were hazy and glazed with passion, lips swollen and yet slightly turned up at the corners in pleasure.

"Hi," he murmured.

"Hi yourself."

"I missed you."

She glanced down to where they remained joined and grinned. "I see that."

Jonathon carried her to the bathroom where he cleaned them both up. He watched in silence as she threw away her torn panties and put on another pair before checking her reflection in the mirror.

"You're beautiful."

She gave him a soft smile in the mirror but didn't respond, just continued to fix the small bit of makeup she wore.

"I want to meet your parents."

Her small body stiffened again, and not for a good reason this time. "To what end?"

"Because I'm dating their daughter. And I want to meet the people important to you."

She uncapped her lip gloss and applied a light layer. "Dating?"

He crossed his arms. "What the hell do you call what we've been doing?"

"I thought after I moved out…" She trailed off with a shrug.

He narrowed his eyes. "You thought what? We would just end it? Go our separate ways? Because of the disagreement?"

"Disagreement? Is that what you call it? You constantly shoving down my throat how I should be living?"

"I said I was sorry."

"Not to me you didn't. And if you were truly sorry, it wouldn't happen over and over again."

He frowned, frustrated. "So you're mad at me because I don't want you living in a small place?"

She spun to face him. "No. I'm mad because you don't think I know what I want. How I want to live." A slash of her hand through the air. "Or what makes me happy."

"Didn't you like living at my place?"

"Sure. You have a very nice condo. But it's not me, Jonathon. Like I told you before, I've done the gilded cage. I don't want that. I don't need huge, expansive places. My little apartment had more warmth and feel to it, for me, than your whole place."

"You could decorate it."

"Why? I don't live there anymore. I am getting my place how I want it." She moved closer to him and touched his arm. "I'm sorry, Jonathon. I don't fit into your world. Look at how you live, your friend Deyon lives. Your older brothers. Hell, even your oldest sister. All of them have huge places. Arissa and Lis have smaller ones, but still. And your parents." She shook her head. "It's just not me. Not anymore." Harmony stole a glance at the delicate watch on her wrist. "I have to go. It was great seeing you."

Jonathon stood there in disbelief as she turned and walked out of her hotel room, closing the door silently behind her. *Not belong in his world?* He'd never cursed his family name or the money he had until just now. Then he jerked open the door and went after her. He couldn't let it go like this. Hell no. Not on his life. And that's exactly what she was to him, his entire life.

Harmony rode the elevator down alone. Her heart hurt from what had just transpired between herself and Jonathon. It hadn't been easy at all telling him those things, but she'd had to be honest with herself. And with him.

The doors slid open and she walked out, shoving Jonathon and that issue to the back of her mind for the time being. Right now, she had to focus on the dinner with her parents. Smoothing her hands down her sides, she took a deep breath and continued on to where they were supposed to meet.

Sure enough, her parents were there, early like usual. At least she wasn't late. She pasted a smile on her face and walked up to them.

"Ready?" her mother asked.

"Yes, ma'am."

She watched her father rise from the chair and shrug into his suit coat. Then he helped her mother up. Both of them paused and stared at something behind her. The feeling in the pit of her stomach and the way the hair on the back of her neck stood up told her in more ways than one whom it was that approached.

"Hello, Harmony," Jonathon said. "I saw you earlier and wasn't sure I wasn't mistaken as to who it was. Then I saw you walk in here and I knew."

She turned and met his gaze. Determination shone in it. *Damn Wrights. Always so sure of themselves and taking what they wanted.*

"Jonathon. Good to see you."

Before turning back to her parents, she shot him a glare, which she knew didn't faze him in the least. Still, it felt good.

"Who are you?" her father asked, his accent thick.

"I'm sorry, sir," Jonathon stated in his smooth lawyer way. "Forgive my lack of manners, I was so pleased to see her again. I'm Jonathon Wright."

She wanted to sink beneath the floor. However, her father was nothing if not a consummate businessman. He held out his hand.

"Katashi Oshiro. This is my wife, Diandra."

Jonathon bowed over her mother's hand and brushed a kiss on the back of it. "Lovely to meet you, ma'am."

"How do you know my daughter?" Her father posed the question.

"We live in the same town and have become friends." He gave her a smile. "I was happily surprised to see her out here."

"You live in McKingley?"

"Yes, sir. I have my whole life."

Her mother glanced between them both. "Would you like to join us for dinner, Mr Wright?"

"I'd love to. Only if you call me Jonathon, however."

She saw it on her father's face that he wanted to refuse. However, her mother rarely didn't get things her way. So she swallowed back her stress at the knowledge that he would be joining them for dinner.

Jonathon escorted her mother and left her with her father. They walked side by side, not talking, which was the complete opposite of Jonathon and her mother. He held her by the arm and was engaging her in conversation.

"How did you meet this man?" her father queried in Japanese.

"I met him one night at the auction I was at and then we ran into each other again at the college." She answered in the same language.

"He is going to school?"

"No, he was there teaching law, stepping in for a friend."

"A lawyer?"

"Yes."

Her father gave a noncommittal grunt and she licked her lips. They walked to the restaurant and she was grateful they didn't all have to be in a vehicle together. Her head hurt and she wanted nothing more than to head back to her room and sleep. Well, there was *something* else she'd be fine doing. That brief interlude in her hotel room had only fanned the flames in her, it hadn't dampened them.

Dinner wasn't all bad. Jonathon kept the conversation going by asking her parents all kinds of questions. And he had no problem answering theirs either, which she knew got points in his favour from her father. Just when she thought it would be okay and had taken a relieved breath to enjoy her dessert, she discovered she never should have assumed it would end any other way.

"When are you coming back to Japan?"

"I don't believe I am, Father."

"You need to. I have set up a concert for you."

Her heart seized, the spoon in her hand clattering to the bowl. "There will be no more concerts."

She could feel Jonathon's gaze on her but she steadfastly refused to meet his eyes. She didn't want to see the question in them.

"You are healed. After all our sacrifices, you can't just give up."

Tears pricked and she gulped, trying to hold onto her tears. "I am not 'healed', Father. It hurts to play. I can't withstand the rigours of a full concert. And *we* didn't have sacrifices, *I* did. Me! I was the one who wasn't allowed to play with the other children. I had to stay home and practise, or go to get tutored by your professional who loved to yell at me. I had to be perfect all the time—heaven forbid I messed up and embarrassed the Oshiro name."

Her mother's gasp almost stopped her but it couldn't. Not quite. The floodgates had opened.

"My first concert, do you remember what you said to me? There were no congratulations, nothing like that. You told me what I'd messed up then walked away. That was it. Do you know what that is like for a child? For a little girl who only wanted her father's approval?" She stared at her mother. "And you, never standing up for me when I wanted to do something else. Telling me how lucky I was to live in all those fancy hotel rooms as I travelled doing concerts. The money I got from endorsement deals, which you both took. I don't have the money."

"Then I had the accident and you make me feel like that is also my fault. Like I asked to be shoved through that window. The first thing you ask then is when do I think I'll be able to play again?" The tears escaped. "I can't do this anymore. I know, I know — you're disappointed in me because I'm a failure. Well, let me top it off for you. You really want to know how I know Jonathon? Because we were dating and sleeping together."

Yes, those gasps she'd expected. Shoving to her feet, she ran from the establishment and up the street to her hotel. Once she had made it into her room, she collapsed on the bed in a torrent of tears. Would she never learn? Would she always be a disappointment to her parents? Eventually the tears became too much and she sank into oblivion.

When she woke, she had a moment of panic. Strong arms were around her. The next second, before the scream could escape, she inhaled and knew exactly who it was. Jonathon was in bed with her. She'd know his scent and his touch anywhere.

They spooned in her bed and she could feel the strong cadence of his heart, calming her. He nuzzled her behind the ear and pressed a light kiss to the shell of her ear.

"I know you're awake, Harmony."

"How'd you get in here?"

"I have my ways."

Of that she had no doubt. "I don't have it in me to do this right now, Jonathon."

"Too bad."

She stiffened. "What?"

"That's your go-to phrase for everything and I'm tired of it. You need to face it, face me, face us."

She didn't want to face anything. *Nope, no thank you.* She wanted to go back to sleep and forget the entire day.

"Tell me about your accident."

Her fingertips itched to touch her scar but she refrained. One, because she didn't want to move and two, because it wouldn't help anything.

"What's to know? It happened."

"Why are you so set on being difficult, Harmony?"

"Why are you so damn set on figuring everything out for me?" she countered angrily.

He stiffened before rolling her towards him and holding her gaze. "Okay, we'll handle this first. I'm sorry. For all the times I pushed too hard about your living conditions or place. I'm sorry for wanting to treat you like a princess and put you in a castle of your own."

"Don't try to get me to feel guilty, Jonathon. You're ashamed of me living in a smaller place."

A tic appeared in his jaw. "We both know you looked me up. Do you really think that I give a damn about that?"

She sat up and he followed. Shoving a hand through her hair that had come free, she finally just jerked out the comb and let it all fall loose.

"Yes."

He blinked a few times and she knew he'd not expected that answer. "How can you say that?"

"You're questioning my opinion now?"

"Yes, I guess I am."

"On paper, all of your family is impressive and yes, you all do a lot of good for others. None of that matters about your personal feelings on those you may be dating."

He ran a hand over his mouth and sighed heavily. "We'll agree to disagree on that. Regardless, I am sorry I made you feel that way. Okay?"

"Fine."

He held her gaze a bit before nodding. "Now. About this?" He touched her scarred arm and hand that remained hidden beneath the sleeve of her dress.

"My scar."

Chapter Nine

"Yes, your scar. More specifically, your accident."

Jonathon stared at the woman he sat across from on the bed. The protectiveness that had surfaced when her father had started in on her had been expected. The fury that had accompanied it as she'd shot back at her parents hadn't been.

Each tear she shed was like a dagger to his chest. The torment in her voice had made him want to cringe and hold her. Tight. Protect her even more. And get her away from her parents. Having the family he did, he wasn't used to being treated as she'd obviously been her entire life.

Win or lose, his parents had always been supportive of their children. There was not a single time he could remember either of them walking up to him after something and telling him what he'd done wrong. Sure, in sports he could always go to his dad and ask him for pointers, but he would never have said anything like that to him at the game.

To not know the joys of going to school and having friends was something he couldn't fathom. When she'd told him she'd already done the living in fancy places, he honestly hadn't given it much thought, past that she was upset and ranting. But now… It was an entirely different situation. No wonder she'd resented it so much, his insistence over the house and pushing her for a larger place, as well as Deyon's amount of purchased clothing. As she'd pointed out, stuff she'd had to pay back because she wasn't about to take anything from him like that.

So yes, he'd screwed this up majorly. And wanted to fix it all, but first he had to get her to open up to him.

"Harmony?"

Her body jolted and he knew she'd been lost in a memory. From the look on her face, it hadn't been a pleasant one either.

"Tell me."

She blew out a breath and cleared her throat. "It was after a concert. There was a thing after it, you know, a food and drink kind of thing. Anyway, I was one of the youngest ones there and was keeping mostly to myself. My chaperone was off drinking."

"Where were your parents?"

"Home." A shrug. "Not sure. They rarely travelled with me. Paid another to watch me. I only had a chaperone to make sure I didn't get into trouble, and I'd always had one. Age didn't matter to my parents— they had their plans for me." She sniffed. "Anyway. There was a younger man who also played piano. Riku. Handsome and very talented. We were talking by a large window, looking at the fountain beyond it, when the girl who wanted to be his girlfriend came up and yelled at me for talking to him."

Jonathon got a nasty feeling in the pit of his stomach. He had a really bad feeling he knew where this was going.

"After some name calling, Riku tried to tell her she needed to calm down and it only upset her more. After all, if he was protecting me, then we must have been sleeping together."

She stopped and rubbed her arm. When she looked back up at him, her eyes shone with tears. "She shoved me. Hard. I threw my arm in front of my face, which is why it got so much damage. The rest is self-explanatory."

He felt like such a heel. Reaching over to her, he dragged her onto his lap. "Harmony," he began.

"Don't, Jonathon. I just... I can't."

"Your parents?"

"Are who they are. I know deep down they love me. Mom says it on occasion, but I also know how disappointed they are in me. I'd been groomed from a young age to play and I can't anymore. Not how I need to in order to do concerts. I can handle the short bits at school and I can play on occasion for Lana and her drama class. I don't like crowds anymore when I play, because I think they can tell I'm not playing as well as I should."

He shook his head. "Baby, you play better than many on their best day. You can't let that stop you."

"You don't know that, Jonathon."

He cupped her face and placed gentle kisses along her jaw. "I know a lot of things, Harmony Oshiro."

"This isn't talking," she sputtered around sharp breaths.

"Oh, but it is. I like this kind of talking the best."

A knock came on the door, interrupting them. Her entire body went ramrod straight before she relaxed. He watched her climb off him and slip from the bed, winding her hair up and using the same comb from earlier to secure it on her head. He stood up and straightened the bed before sitting on a chair. Tensions were high enough between her and her parents, and he had no wish to add to them.

He watched her talk to them in Japanese. Even from across the room he could see her tension increase. With an easy push, he got to his feet and made his way to stand behind her, offering strength and support.

"This is private," her father said in English.

"Harmony?"

She spoke to her parents again before they scowled at him then left. The door remained open and she looked up at him. "You need to go."

"What?"

"You wanted to talk, Jonathon. We talked. You know about my scar."

"We've not talked about us."

"There is no us."

Hearing those words did not feel good in any way, shape or form. He scowled at her. "Yes there is. Dating. Sleeping together. You. Me."

"We went over this already."

He chuckled but there was no humour in it. "Do you really think I would let it go so easily? I'm an attorney, Harmony. Arguing is nought but foreplay to me, especially with you. So you're gonna have to do much more than that to get me gone. You don't want me out of your life. You're scared. I get it. We can work through it."

Lightning flared in her gaze and she shoved his chest and knocked him through the door to the hall. "You arrogant bastard! I... You... Argh!"

Bam! The door slammed in his face. He blinked at it a few times before knocking. Nothing. He waited but she never opened it. Reluctantly, he left and went to his room down the hall from hers. He tried several times to call her room and in the morning, he called down to have some room service delivered to her room. They could eat and talk this out.

"I'm sorry, sir, but there is no one in that room. The guest has checked out."

Hanging up, he swore a litany his mom would not have liked to hear. Getting the first flight he could, he placed a call while waiting for the boarding call.

"Hello?"

"Lis? It's Jonathon."

"I know, I have caller ID. What's up?"

"I need to talk to you and Arissa. Can you meet me at the place we used to hide when we tried to skip school?"

"Everything okay?"

"No. Not yet. But it will be. I'll be home in a few hours."

"Okay, we'll be there."

Thankfully, she didn't ask any more questions because honestly he didn't have any answers right now. That call done, he placed another to Elisa.

"Mr Wright," she said on the first ring.

"Elisa. I need your help on something."

"My help? Sure you don't want one of your paralegals?"

"Nope. You're the one, Elisa. Will you do something for me?"

"I'm at your disposal."

"Thank you." He told her what he wanted and ended the call.

Once on the plane, he rested his head back and breathed easier. Only a minor setback. Soon he would be able to have a face to face with her. He may have to tie her up so she couldn't leave, but one way or another they would find the underlying cause of this.

* * * *

Harmony sat at the piano in the large hall. It had been a week since she'd got back from California. She'd not seen any sign of Jonathon and while she knew it was her decision, she still missed him. It was for the best. Or so she continued to tell herself.

One hand idly played as she mulled over the past few months. Fall had come in force to New Mexico and she loved it.

"Hey."

She looked up to see Lana walking towards the stage. "Hey, yourself."

"What are you still doing here?"

"Tinkering."

Lana sat beside her on the bench. "Thinking up another piece?"

"Yes." She nudged her friend. "What are you doing here?"

"I came to find you. You weren't answering your phone. And I figured I knew where to find you."

"I shut it off. Tired of avoiding my parents' calls."

"I'm so sorry you had to go through that with them."

She lifted one shoulder. "Not your fault, but thank you anyway."

"You know I'm here for you, right, Harmony?"

"I know. You hungry?"

"Always."

She stood and allowed her hand to linger lovingly over the sleek instrument. "For?"

"Oysters."

Harmony shuddered. "That is just nasty."

"Okay, fine. Where should we go?"

"Let's just walk and see where we end up. Pick a place that looks interesting."

"Ohh, an adventure. I'm all in."

They drove downtown and parked before getting out. Up and down streets, they walked and window-shopped. Eventually they entered a small, out of the way place. The interior was darker and only had a few tables.

"I don't remember this place, do you?" she asked Lana.

"Nope. Smells good, though."

And it did. Rich, pungent aromas surrounded them and tantalised her taste buds. A small woman with darker skin and thick black hair walked up.

"Welcome. Allow me to take you to a seat."

They followed her and soon had drinks before them while they waited for their food.

"So, are you staying here or going back?" Lana asked, blunt as always.

"Haven't made up my mind yet. I talked to my brother who says Mama isn't doing that well since she got back from here. I just... Maybe I'll go for a visit. I just can't..."

"I know, sweetie. No need to explain it to me."

"Thanks."

"You do, however, need to explain this thing with Jonathon Wright."

"What's to explain? I broke it off."

"Why? Sex no good?"

She rolled her eyes. "No. The sex was fine... That's not the point here, Lana. We're just from two very different places."

"Ahh. Right, right. You both come from caring for one another. I see how that is so different."

"Not what I meant. You saw how he lives."

"So what? You're condemning him because he has money. Weren't you accusing him of doing the same to you because compared to him you didn't have any? I'm no genius or anything, but that don't seem fair." She took a drink. "Rich or not, poor or not, you can't be mad at him for something then turn around and do that to him."

Harmony didn't say a word. She couldn't. Hell, she'd not even thought about it that way. Nevertheless, Lana was absolutely correct. She'd done just what she'd accused him of doing. And had refused to listen to him.

"I'm such an idiot."

"No you're not, Harmony. You're a woman who's scared of the feelings she has for this man. Which isn't hard to believe. Love isn't something you're well acquainted with. Not out in the open and sharing it with the world."

"How can I face him, Lana? Knowing now what I've done."

"The great thing about being human is knowing we will make mistakes. Go apologise to him. Now if you tell me he is an ass and he hit you, then I say to hell with him and we can bury his ragged ass out in the desert somewhere. But for him to just want you in a nice place… That's something which can be worked out."

"You're the best friend anyone could ever have."

"And shameless enough to use that to exploit you as well," she retorted with a wicked grin.

They ate and talked. All the while, Harmony knew she had to get to Jonathon and apologise for her actions. She still didn't want him to push his lifestyle onto her but she did feel the need to set it right.

Back in the car, she frowned when she realised Lana wasn't heading back to her house.

"Where are we going?"

"I'm dropping you off at his house."

"He may not be home."

"Then you can wait."

Lana said it so matter-of-factly she laughed. With a kiss to her friend's cheek, she slipped from the car and made her way up the walk to his door. She peered over her shoulder to see Lana giving her a thumbs-up before driving away.

Reaching out a hand, she licked her lips then pressed the doorbell. No answer. She pressed it again. Same thing. Great, now she had to take the bus home. Spinning around, she walked back to the street.

"Harmony?"

She froze and glanced back to the door. Jonathon stood there, framed by the doorway. He wore a loose shirt and jeans.

Part of her wanted to run and hide. She made herself return to stand before him. "I'm sorry to bother you, I just had something to say."

His expression was guarded but he gestured her inside. She entered, careful not to touch him, and kept her hands in her pockets.

"What can I do for you?"

Cripes—he sounded all kinds of formal. "I came to apologise."

"For?"

"For being mad at you for one thing and then doing it myself."

"What are you talking about?"

"Judging you because of the money you make and how I said it makes you not like how I live. How my lack of it was embarrassing to you. It wasn't only you. It was me. I was doing the same thing. Mad at you for having so much money."

He didn't speak, just stared at her, his arms crossed and blocking the door.

"That's what you came to tell me?"

She nodded. "I just wanted you to know I'm sorry I had been doing that."

"And us?"

"I'd like to be friends."

"Friends."

"Or not."

He shifted his weight, feet shoulder width apart. Damn, she wanted him. Reining in her desire, she focused on what she'd come here for. To apologise. Moreover, she'd done so.

"Excuse me, I'll just go."

"No."

The firmness in his voice brought her head back up. "What?"

"No. You don't get to keep doing this to me, Harmony. I love you."

Her body went numb for a minute and her legs wobbled. "W...wh... What did you just say?"

"You heard me just fine, but I'll tell you again. I love you. I. Love. You. I am going to tell you this every single day for the rest of our lives."

"You love me?"

"I love you." He spoke it with such conviction.

"But... But..."

"I know you don't like fancy, Harmony. That's fine. I had planned to have a family in this house one day but if you don't like it, we'll find one together. One that will feel like a home to you."

"A home?"

"Yes. I don't want to just be friends. I want you, Harmony Yuna Oshiro—the location doesn't matter to me. I'll follow you to Japan if you want to move back closer to your family. So long as you agree to be my wife, nothing else matters."

"W...wife?" Good Lord, she couldn't wrap her head around any of this.

"Yes. Will you marry me?" He dropped to one knee as he posed the question.

She heard Lana's voice in her head telling her she deserved to be happy. And when she thought about what made her happy, it was this man right here before her. *On his knees, for crying out loud.*

"Yes." The word sounded more like a croak than anything, but he got the gist.

He pulled her in close and kissed her. "I love you."

Tears flowed over and she just held on, unable to think much right now. He carried her upstairs and made love to her on his bed. It was slow and tender and perfect.

Afterwards, they lay, limbs intertwined upon the bedding.

"I have something for you," he said, dragging a finger up and down her spine.

"I don't need anything."

"Indulge me." He rolled from the bed, tossed her his shirt, and drew on his pants.

She pulled his shirt on over her head and followed him to a room on the second floor. He pushed open the door and guided her in past him. Resting on a table in the middle was a sight that made her cry all over again.

The entire collection of vases was gathered there. Obviously not the set she'd had, being as it had burnt in the fire, but a complete one nonetheless.

"Oh, Jonathon." Staring at them through the tears, she made her way and touched one. "This isn't your mom's set, is it?"

He chuckled behind her. "No. This one is all yours. I know nothing can replace the ones your grandmother gave you but I know how much the set meant to you."

She faced him. "When? How?"

"I have been collecting them for you for a while now. I just had to find the final two. They came in this week."

"So you..." She trailed off.

"Wasn't about to let you go."

It didn't freak her out. She didn't want him to let her go. "Ever?"

"Ever."

He pulled her close and brushed their lips together. "I love you, Harmony."

"I love you too, Jonathon."

"I've waited to hear those words from you. Don't ever stop telling me."

She didn't plan on it. The road may have some bumps in it along the way but as far as she was concerned, it would be so worth it.

He crept his hands under her shirt and began to lift it. She shivered at the feel of his touch. Why she had spent so much time avoiding this, she hadn't a clue. She wouldn't be avoiding it any longer. She had him and she wasn't about to lose him again.

"I want to make love to my fiancée."

She smiled as he nibbled down her neck towards her breasts. Sounded like a good plan to her. He lowered them to the floor and took her on another trip to the stars. Pure harmony was how she would describe the feeling of being with Jonathon Wright. Moreover, it was one she wanted to keep forever.

About the Authors

McKenna Jeffries

McKenna Jeffries has loved the written word from time she picked up her first book. Soon she was creating tales of love and family.

Although McKenna used to make up stories she never thought to put them on paper until…she realised the stories would keep filling her head until they were written. Since then she's been writing and sharing her books.

There is always some new story floating around her head. An itchy feeling in her fingers fills her until she can get a piece of paper to write it down.

She writes because it's a love affair. Writing is in her blood and she enjoys taking readers on a journey.

Aliyah Burke

Aliyah Burke is an avid reader and is never far from pen and paper (or the computer). She is married to a career military man, and they have a German Shepherd, two Borzois, and a DSH cat. Her days are spent sharing her time between work, writing, and dog training.

McKenna Jeffries and Aliyah Burke love to hear from readers. You can find their contact information, website details and author profile pages at http://www.totallybound.com.

Totally Bound Publishing

www.ingramcontent.com/pod-product-compliance
Lightning Source LLC
Chambersburg PA
CBHW021517240626
47154CB00002B/669

* 9 7 8 1 7 8 1 8 4 6 4 9 0 *